D0392987

"I'll make you a deal," Aiden murmured into Sadie's ear.

He held her tightly against him as he steered her in another circle on the dance floor. "I'll make love to you. And I'm talking about the kind of long, slow, agonizing, so-good-it-hurts love."

She shuddered in his arms. He nipped and suckled her earlobe, whispering, "I'll make love to you until your toes are permanently curled."

A small sound escaped her throat. One he'd bet she didn't mean to let loose.

"Until you're too weak to move," he continued, tonguing her ear.

Sadie's fingers fisted the front of his shirt, wrinkling it all to hell. He couldn't care less. Nothing thrilled him more than the sound of the sharp intake of air between her teeth. Proof that her control was shattering into a million little pieces at his feet.

"But I have stipulations."

ACCLAIM FOR
TEMPTING THE BILLIONAIRE

"A smashing debut! Charming, sexy, and brimming with wit—you'll be adding Jessica Lemmon to your bookshelves for years to come!"
—Heidi Betts, *USA Today* bestselling author

"Lemmon's characters are believable and flawed. Her writing is engaging and witty. If I had been reading this book out in public, everyone would have seen the *huge* grin on my face. I had so much fun reading this and adore it immensely."
—LiteraryEtc.wordpress.com

"If you are interested in a loveable romance about two troubled souls who overcome the odds to find their own happily ever after, I would certainly recommend that you give *Tempting the Billionaire* a try. It was definitely a great Valentine's Day read, for sure!"
—ChrissyMcBookNerd.blogspot.com

"The awesome cover opened to even more awesome things inside. It was realistic! Funny! Charming! Sweet!"
—AbigailMumford.com

HARD
to
HANDLE

HARD
to
HANDLE

JESSICA LEMMON

FOREVER

NEW YORK   BOSTON

This book is a work of fiction. Names, characters, places, and incidents are the product of the author's imagination or are used fictitiously. Any resemblance to actual events, locales, or persons, living or dead, is coincidental.

Copyright © 2013 by Jessica Lemmon
Excerpt from *Tempting the Billionaire* copyright © 2013 by Jessica Lemmon
All rights reserved. In accordance with the U.S. Copyright Act of 1976, the scanning, uploading, and electronic sharing of any part of this book without the permission of the publisher constitutes unlawful piracy and theft of the author's intellectual property. If you would like to use material from the book (other than for review purposes), prior written permission must be obtained by contacting the publisher at permissions@hbgusa.com. Thank you for your support of the author's rights.

Forever
Hachette Book Group
237 Park Avenue
New York, NY 10017

www.HachetteBookGroup.com

Printed in the United States of America

Originally published as an ebook

First mass-market edition: March 2014
10 9 8 7 6 5 4 3 2 1

OPM

Forever is an imprint of Grand Central Publishing.
The Forever name and logo are trademarks of Hachette Book Group, Inc.

The Hachette Speakers Bureau provides a wide range of authors for speaking events. To find out more, go to www.hachettespeakersbureau.com or call (866) 376-6591.

The publisher is not responsible for websites (or their content) that are not owned by the publisher.

For my brother, Nick, who shares Aiden's unbreakable spirit.

"Life is a beautiful struggle."

ACKNOWLEDGMENTS

First and foremost, my humble thanks to God for giving me the amazing opportunity to write and create. I love this gig! Thank you to my husband, John, who puts up with deadlines (and lack of food in the house during deadlines) like a champ. Thanks to "cheer-readers" Niki Hughes, Amy Wade, Amber Dunlevy, and Jennifer Hill, who can't wait to read my next book no matter what stage it's in.

Fellow writers on Twitter and beyond (too many of you to name!) for encouraging me when I was in the freak-out stage. Nicole Resciniti, my agent and friend, for fact-checking motorcycle stuff (all mistakes are mine) and for loving my work. You make me smile.

Lauren Plude, my editor and other half, for loving Aiden with a purity that rivaled my own. (Invite me to the Plude/Downey wedding, will you?) Everyone at Grand Central Publishing/Forever for your hand in polishing this book, especially the editors who make me look like I know the difference between *blond* and *blonde*.

Thanks to everyone at Reliable Construction, where I worked while creating this book. It's the little things that meant the most. To Dave and Richard for your constant encouragement, to Tammy for teaching me to recycle paper and use the back for note-taking (you have no idea how much of this book is jotted on half sheets of paper!). And to Chuck Bern...I'm not saying you're Axle Zoller, but he certainly has your mustache.

Unlike Shane's story, Aiden's didn't flow out in a smooth ribbon of inspiration. As open and awesome as Aiden is, you wouldn't think he would've been such a hard nut to crack! Eventually, though, I *found* him. In the midst of my writing and rewriting and tweaking, finally, he appeared. Thanks to all the readers who let me know you couldn't wait for Aiden's book. You inspired and challenged me to be true to who Aiden is, and give you the best story I could write. I pray I succeeded...and hope Aiden is worth the wait!

CHAPTER ONE

*A*iden Downey spun his beer by its neck, the now-warm contents sloshing against the sides of the bottle. He'd been watching Sadie from his chair at the back of the reception tent for the better part of thirty minutes, unable to shake the guilt swamping him.

Shane and Crickitt, God bless them, had been so careful when they asked Aiden and Sadie to be the only two members of the wedding party. But if there was one thing he and Sadie could agree on, it was doing right by their friends. They'd put aside their differences for the big day and had managed to be cordial, though not sociable, until the start of the reception.

That's when Aiden had bumbled his way through a long-overdue apology. While he'd never apologize for prioritizing his mother during her fight with cancer, he realized too late it was a mistake to allow his ex-wife back into his life. He meant well when he decided to keep the divorce quiet, but Aiden should have told his mother before she died. Now she'd never know the truth, never get to meet Sadie. A regret he'd have to live with.

Sadie's buoyant giggle, a fake one if Aiden had to guess, lifted onto the air. He turned to see her toss her head back, blonde curls cascading down her bare back as she gripped Crickitt's younger brother's arm. Garrett, who had been Krazy-Glued to Sadie's side the entire reception, grinned down at her, clearly smitten. Aiden dragged his gaze from her mane of soft golden waves to her dress, a pink confection hugging her every amazing, petite curve. He couldn't blame the kid for staring at her intently. Sadie was beautiful.

"Rough," he heard Shane say as he pulled out the chair next to him and sat, beer bottle in hand.

His cousin looked relaxed with his white tuxedo shirt unbuttoned and the sleeves cuffed at the elbows. He'd taken off the tie he'd worn earlier, a sight that almost made Aiden laugh. Before Shane met Crickitt, Aiden would've bet Shane slept wearing a tie. Crickitt had vanquished Shane's inner workaholic and in return, Shane had stepped up to become the man Crickitt needed.

Aiden had had a similar opportunity with Sadie. It was a test he'd failed spectacularly. "She has a right to be mad," he said, tilting his beer bottle again.

"You were in a difficult situation," Shane said magnanimously.

Maybe so, but after his mother succumbed to the cancer riddling her body, after he'd grieved and moaned and helped his father plan the funeral, Aiden had seen things more clearly. Remembering the way he'd shut Sadie out of his life, rejected her in the worst possible way, stung like alcohol to a fresh cut. He should have brought her in, no matter how bad the circumstances. His mother would have accepted her.

His mother would have loved her.

"If I could go back, I'd tell Mom the truth." He swallowed thickly. "She deserved the truth."

"Don't do that, man." Shane clapped him on the shoulder. "You did what you believed was best. It was never going to be an easy situation."

True, but he'd taken an already hard situation and complicated the hell out of it. At his mother's diagnosis, Aiden went into Responsibility Mode. With his sister in Tennessee, a brother in Chicago, his other brother in Columbus, and his father simultaneously grieving and working, everything had fallen on Aiden.

When his mother said she wanted to move to Oregon to seek alternative treatments, Aiden rearranged his entire life and helped her do just that. Later, his siblings had argued with him that they would have helped if they'd known about any of it. Aiden had known in his gut there wasn't enough time to pull everyone together for a pow-wow.

"I appreciate you being here," Shane said.

Aiden snapped out of his reverie. "Oh man, I'm sorry. I'm being a jerk on your big day." He straightened in his chair, ashamed to have let melancholy overshadow his happiness for Shane and Crickitt.

Speaking of, here she came, poured into a slim white wedding dress, fabric flowers sewn into the flowing train. She grinned at Shane, her face full of love, her blue eyes shining. When she flicked a look over to Aiden, he promptly slapped a smile onto his face.

"You look amazing, C," he told her.

Crickitt's grin widened. "Thank you."

"And this reception"—he blew out a breath for effect—"the lights"—he gestured to the hundreds of strands draped inside the tent—"the flowers, the band." The three-piece band included a formerly famous singer a decade past his heyday, but the guy still had it.

Crickitt rested a hand on her husband's shoulder. "Shane insisted on all this. I wanted something simple. When he suggested getting married in a tent in Tennessee...I didn't expect *this*." She waved a hand around the interior of the tent: the shining wooden dance floor, the thick swaths of mosquito netting covering every entrance, the tall, narrow air conditioners positioned at each corner to keep the guests cool and comfortable during the warm June evening.

She smiled down at Shane. "But it is pretty great."

"*You're* pretty great," Shane said, tugging her into his lap and kissing her bare shoulder. The wedding photographer swooped in, capturing the picture for posterity, a good one by the looks of it.

Aiden picked the moment to excuse himself for a refill. Or maybe two.

* * *

Sadie caught movement out of the corner of her eye and swept her attention away from Crickitt's attentive brother to see Aiden tracking his way across the tent in that easygoing lope of his.

She'd never seen him in a suit until she preceded Crickitt down the aisle. He didn't wear the tie he'd worn earlier, picked to match her bridesmaid's dress. She knew the intricate design by heart. She'd traced the tiny pink and silver paisley design, all the while trying not to allow the sorrow in his voice to crack through her defenses. He'd not only broken her heart last summer with a phone call, he'd broken her will, demolished her sense of true north. She couldn't forgive him—or herself—for allowing it to happen.

She'd cut the conversation short tonight, recalling the promise she'd made to never show her vulnerability to this man again, and stalked away from him as fast as her sparkly pink heels would carry her.

Garrett turned his attention to someone else standing in their little circle, and Sadie took the opportunity to watch Aiden. Tailored black pants hugged his impressive thighs and led up to a tucked white shirt, open at the collar and showing enough of his tanned neck to be distracting.

I made a mistake last summer, Sadie. One I'll regret always.

A pang of guilt stabbed her. She hadn't expected the flood of emotion that crashed into her when she saw him for the first time in nearly a year. She'd planned to tell him she was sorry he lost his mother. And she was. She may have never met the woman, but she saw her once. And she saw the connection between mother and son as clearly as she saw Aiden now.

Sadie kept up with Aiden's mother's illness via updates from Crickitt. The decision not to go to the funeral went without saying, but Sadie hadn't been able to stop herself from sending an anonymous bouquet to the funeral home. Losing a parent was one of the worst things in the world, she knew.

Sadie straightened her spine, wiggled her heel into the

floor, and reminded herself *again* not to dwell on her own heartbreak. Her best friend's wedding wasn't the place to dig up the past. Even so, she'd spent most of the day desperately trying to tamp down one emotion after the other. Thank goodness girls were supposed to cry at weddings.

Which is why she'd been avoiding him. Aiden had a knack for seeing right through her. That was the clincher. He *knew* her. Picked·her apart with those clairvoyant sea green eyes of his, and left her defenseless. And being called out by Aiden Downey was at the tippy-top of her "To Don't" list.

Aiden pulled a hand through his thick hair, the length of it landing between his shoulder blades. Sadie recalled the texture of it as if she'd run her fingers through it yesterday. She hated that.

Damn muscle memory.

Crickitt's mother, Chandra, approached the bar and gave Aiden a plump hug. Aiden smiled down at her, but Sadie saw the sadness behind it, and for a split second, it made her heart hurt. She'd gotten good at reading him, too. Knowing that reminded her of just how close she'd been to losing her heart to him...until a phone call annihilated everything between them.

Whether it was the invisible cord of awareness strung between them or coincidence, Sadie wasn't sure, but Aiden chose that moment to look in her direction. His smile faltered, the dimple on his left cheek fading before he flicked his eyes away.

Sadie used to love the way he shook her up. From across a room. With nothing more than a look. But now her heart raced for a far different reason. One she refused to name. She frowned down at her empty champagne flute. She was going to need more alcohol if she hoped to toughen her hide. This exposed vulnerability simply wasn't going to cut it.

"Refill?" Garrett asked, gesturing to her empty glass.

"Yes," she said, grateful for his doting. She handed it over. "Keep 'em coming."

* * *

Aiden bid the last lingering guests farewell, watching as a sophisticated older couple by the name of Townsend walked out to the driveway.

Shane and Crickitt August had made their exit hours ago, amidst cheers and handfuls of heart-shaped biodegradable confetti. Since he was staying at Shane and Crickitt's cabin for the weekend, Aiden was left in charge of supervising the caterer, breaking down the tent, and clearing away the remains of the celebration.

"Do you need me to get you to a hotel, Sadie?"

Aiden turned in the direction of the slightly exasperated voice to find Garrett gesturing with his hands. Sadie was the picture of stubbornness, her arms folded over her ample breasts, her bottom lip jutting out. Aiden allowed himself a small, private smile.

"You're in no condition to drive," Garrett said. He reached out to palm her arm and Sadie expertly swung out of reach.

Aiden felt kind of bad for the kid. Twenty-two-year-old Garrett Day was far too inexperienced to handle a woman of Sadie's magnitude on his best day, and even then...

"There a problem?" Aiden approached with his hands

in his pockets, trying to broadcast that he didn't care if Garrett was trying to take Sadie with him when he left. He supposed he *shouldn't* care. Aiden had no interest in getting into a pissing match with him, but if Garrett tried to take Sadie when she didn't want to go, he'd have hell to pay. C's little brother or not.

Garrett gave Aiden an assessing glance before answering. "Just making sure Sadie has a ride tonight."

"I don't need a ride. I'm staying here," she practically spat.

Aiden rocked back on his heels. She was staying at the cabin? Hell's bells. What were Crickitt and Shane up to?

"I'll make sure she gets inside okay," Aiden said.

"I'll get *myself* inside, thank you very much." Sadie tipped her head and propped her hands on her nipped waist. Aiden knew he shouldn't allow his eyes to chase the line of her slender neck to the bodice of her dress. And he shouldn't linger at the point where her breasts met in shadowed cleavage, but he did anyway. Good thing he was watching her. A moment later, she took a step toward the cabin and wobbled in her dangerously tall heels.

Both men rushed forward to steady her. Aiden got there first. A victory. He gripped her waist and Sadie's hand came up to clutch the front of his shirt. He desperately tried to ignore the warmth spreading across his chest, the feel of her against him. Even though the circumstances were all wrong, the timing completely off, there was no denying this gorgeous woman belonged in his arms. Sadie didn't let go, and Aiden didn't think he could unless someone physically pried his hands off her.

He turned his attention to Garrett. "You can head out. I have her." Aiden held his eye. Dared him to argue. Garrett frowned, and for a second Aiden thought he might, but then Crickitt's mother, queen of impeccable timing, intruded.

"Garrett, we have the car. Is Sadie...Oh! Aiden, perfect." She sent him an approving smile. "Do you need my help?"

"No, Mrs. D, I'll make sure she's all right."

She made a *tsking* sound. "Poor dear had an entire magnum of champagne."

Garret didn't look as if he wanted to leave but did anyway, walking his mother out of the tent. Maybe he'd come to the conclusion Sadie was more than he could handle after all.

Aiden guided Sadie to the house as she teetered on those pink stilts she called shoes. He had fond memories of her shoes. Fond because the added inches brought her within kissable reach. His heart gave an echoing ache. "You should take those off," he said, stopping short of offering to carry her. He'd lifted her in his arms once before. One year ago. Felt more like a dozen.

"I'm fine," she said, tipping again. Her argument was garbled but genuine.

"I assume your things are already in your room?" He tucked her against him as they stepped inside the cabin, then shut the door behind them. He also assumed their matchmaking friends had put them both upstairs. Since there were only two bedrooms on this floor, and since he was staying in the master on the right, he assumed Sadie's was to the left.

She mumbled something and he moved to settle her into the recliner.

"No," she protested, locking her arms around his neck.

"I have to get out of this stupid dress." She gazed up at him, her brown eyes slightly glassy.

Aiden swallowed thickly, taking in all that blonde hair falling in waves around her heart-shaped face. She always was beautiful. And those lips. She licked her bottom one and he was half-tempted to lean in for a taste.

She's drunk, you idiot.

She started toward his room and he caught her hips and steered her away. "Not in there."

She spun on him, narrowing her eyes. "Why not?"

Lie. But he couldn't lie to Sadie. He never could. Even when it would have benefitted him the most. "Because my stuff's in there," he mumbled.

She blinked at him and he readied for a fight. It didn't come. "Fine. I'm too tired to argue. And I have to get this off." She moved one hand to the bodice of her dress and wiggled it back and forth, sending her breasts jiggling inside the fitted top.

Aiden stared. Actually *stared*. Like when he'd found his older brother's stash of *Playboy*s for the first time. No one filled out their clothes like Sadie.

She cleared her throat and he jerked his eyes north. "Help me?"

Crap.

He was being tested, here, in the cruelest way. She was asking him to undress her? Exposing herself to him, and Aiden to her naked body? He couldn't do it while sporting a woody or she'd cut him off at the knees. Drunk or not.

Aiden mentally tied a noose around his mojo. And pulled. "Sure thing."

He followed her into the room and she dropped on the

bed, falling back with an *oomph!* She toed at her shoes until they hit the floor. Aiden retrieved them, dangerous-looking spikes covered with winking rhinestones. How women walked in these things, he'd never know. Sadie told him once that because of her diminutive size she preferred the tallest shoes. He'd concurred at the time. Without them, Sadie only came to the middle of his chest. He was in favor of any contraption if it meant bringing her lips closer to his.

And now he was thinking of kissing her. Again.

He shook his head to wipe away the memories of the intense kisses they'd shared in the past: the sound of her truncated breaths against his ear, the feel of her fingernails spearing into his hair. He tracked back to the bed, jaw set, brain focused squarely on the Stay Puft Marshmallow Man. He pulled back the covers intending to bury the tempting vision of her breasts bursting from the top of her dress, but she rolled onto her side before he could.

"Unzip," Sadie demanded, her manicured nails fumbling at the back of her dress. When he hesitated, Sadie shot him a displeased look over her shoulder, crinkling her heavily made-up eyes at him.

Even sexier when she's angry, he thought with a groan.

Aiden reached for the zipper, ignoring his impulse to go slowly, listen to every snick as he examined all of her smooth, porcelain flesh beneath the bridesmaid's dress. It'd been too long since he'd been allowed to touch this woman. Too. Effing. Long. The zipper parted to reveal what appeared to be a sleeveless white straitjacket with about a hundred hooks.

"Now this." She did a backward point.

Aiden paused. The thing looked as penetrable as Fort Knox. "Can't you sleep in it?"

"Just do it. Nothing you haven't seen before." She turned her head at an awkward angle so she could look at him. A little pleat formed on her brow as if she was reconsidering. "I mean, not me, but other girls." She flopped her head onto the pillow with a *whump*.

Thanks for the reminder, Aiden thought tersely.

He and Sadie hadn't had a chance to get that far. Okay, that wasn't true. They'd had plenty of chances. Each time they saw each other, the dates had lasted at least six or seven hours. Or overnight. They couldn't seem to escape each other, or stop talking, or stop *touching*. She'd seen him stripped down to his briefs, and he'd seen her bare legs poking out from under one of his T-shirts, but they'd always stopped short of going further. Both of them had been hurt before and neither of them was anxious to repeat their painful pasts.

So, yes, Sadie was right. He hadn't technically *seen* her naked, but he had felt enough of her bare flesh under his palms to give his imagination a hell of a show.

He scooted the bedside lamp closer to investigate the contraption she'd bound herself in. He could dismantle a car; surely he could handle this. Turns out he had to make the thing tighter before the hooks would release. Each time, Sadie grunted, until he got halfway down her back and she blew out a *whooshing* breath. He made quick work of the rest.

"Thank God." She sat up, one hand covering the sagging top of her gown, withdrew the corset, and dropped it unceremoniously to the floor. "I owe you, Downey. Now help me out of this dress and go away."

He swallowed thickly, recognizing the painful famil-iarity of the moment. The night she was on his couch and slipped her bra out from underneath her tank top. He'd clutched her to him, and she'd panted against his neck as her nipples abraded his bare chest. It was then she'd hesi-tated. Wordlessly, but he'd felt the slightest bit of tension creep into her shoulders. He backed off, but didn't let her go, tucking her into bed against him and sleeping next to her through the night.

That was his Sadie. Minx on the outside, lamb on the inside. Seeing this side of her again, being reminded of what they'd had—what he'd thrown away...

Man. It hurt.

"I'm too tipsy to do it myself," she growled. Despite her efforts to keep it out, vulnerability leaked into her voice. Aiden's weakness was her trust in him; her show-ing who she really was. He gripped her elbows and helped her to her feet, stopping short of crushing her lips with his and admitting he was wrong a hundred ways from Sun-day.

He steadied her elbows as she wiggled out of the dress with a perfunctory "No looking." He obeyed, keeping his eyes focused out the bedroom window. But with the bedside lamp on, he couldn't see out the window, only himself reflected in the pane, and Sadie's thong panties as she stepped out of the dress. He shut his eyes and re-minded his johnson to remain *at ease*.

"Aiden."

"Yes."

"I need you to get my pajamas for me."

"Okay."

"No peeking while I crawl into bed."

This was the side of Sadie people *didn't* see. Her modest side. Everyone assumed they knew her—with her litany of first dates and explosive personality, Sadie was mistaken as confident and outgoing. Which she was, both of those things. She was also modest, careful. Fragile. And despite the increasing pressure in his pants, Aiden vowed to honor her request.

"Okay," he muttered.

"Promise," she commanded, brushing against his arm as she turned. Something very soft grazed his skin and he tried to convince himself it wasn't what he thought it was.

"Promise," he said through clenched teeth.

When he heard the wisp of sheets he opened his eyes. Sadie wore the comforter over her breasts and pointed with one arm. "The big suitcase," she said around a yawn.

The big suitcase also had a big lock. The key, he assumed, was in her purse. He approached The Purse, which was about the size of a small country, and stopped short. Going through a woman's purse was a lot like sticking a hand in the garbage disposal. While he was pretty sure he'd be able to get what he needed out of it, there was the risk of losing a digit while rooting around in there.

He glanced back at Sadie, who had lain back and shut her eyes. Her breathing was already steady and deep. Making a snap decision, he walked to his room and dug a T-shirt out of his duffel bag. When he returned, he wondered if it was even worth it to wake her. But then he thought of her waking in only her panties—a thought that had him swallowing a lump of lust—and worried she might think something had happened tonight. He regarded the gray shirt in his hand. Not that she'd be thrilled about waking in one of his tees. Again.

Was that night on auto-repeat?

Ignoring the overwhelming sense of déjà vu, he stretched the neck and slipped the shirt over her sprayed hair, feeding first one arm into a sleeve followed by the other. Now the tricky part. Looking up at the ceiling, he palmed her back and pulled her toward him. But as he started to tug the shirt down, Sadie's arms clamped around his neck, her breasts smashing against his cardboard dress shirt.

A sound emitted from his throat he was pretty sure was a growl.

"I loved you," Sadie said, her eyes wide and earnest. "And you blew it." That said, she tugged the shirt to her waist, flopped onto one side, and pulled the covers over her head.

Aiden's shoulders slumped, heavy from the weight of her admission. She loved him. Or at least she used to. He'd had his suspicions but had never known. Would it have changed how he ended things between them? Would he have confessed the same?

Of course he would've.

And you blew it.

He had. Completely effing stepped in it.

And now it was too late. Sadie probably never would have told him what she just had if she hadn't been marinating in champagne tonight. As much as he'd love to deny hearing her say it, there was part of him glad to know the truth. The masochistic part of him, apparently. He'd earned the pain fair and square, but Sadie...Sadie had come out the other side. She was okay now, or would be after a couple of Advil in the morning. Her journey with him in it had reached an end. Now he was a by-stander and couldn't allow himself to be anything more. Asking her to take another chance on him was wrong. Maybe more wrong than the way he'd ended things with her last year.

After several seconds, he finally stood from the edge of the bed, as heavy as if he'd strapped a pair of anvils onto his back. At the door, he hesitated over the switch, watching her take a few deep breaths. One night, a long, long time ago, he'd been right next to her, feeling as hopeful about their future as he felt devastated now.

If only time were reversible. If only he knew then what he knew now.

If only.

Most useless two words ever.

* * *

Stupid champagne.

Sadie downed the last sip of her coffee and dragged her suitcase to the car. She hauled it ungracefully into her trunk and vowed to call Crickitt and give her what-for for pulling the Aiden-and-Sadie-slumber-party bit.

Only she couldn't. Because Crickitt and Shane were on their honeymoon having the blissful, married time of their lives. She stalked back into the house, doing a once-over to make sure she hadn't left anything behind. That's when she spotted Aiden's T-shirt.

When she'd woken up wearing it, she'd tossed it aside and run around packing with the one single goal: get the hell out of the cabin before he woke up and offered breakfast. The morning was already beginning to smack of the morning they'd spent together a year ago—a morning she wouldn't dare repeat.

She held the soft cotton between her fingers, recalling the night he'd tenderly dressed her and curled up next to her to sleep. That morning she'd woken to his shirtless back, traced the length of the scar with her fingers, and come to the terrifying realization that if he'd died in that motorcycle accident before she met him, she'd have missed out on knowing Aiden Downey.

Yeah. Well. He's fine, she reminded herself. *And so are you.*

Yippee-skippy. Everyone was fine.

She tromped to the room he'd slept in. Empty. Turned out Aiden was an early riser nowadays. She threw the wadded-up shirt onto the rumpled bedding, shutting out the memory of what the length of his seminude body looked like taking up half a bed.

Time to go.

Outside, she shut the trunk and reached for the driver's side door handle. Aiden's motorcycle, Sheila, stood on the driveway, her orange glittery paint job sparkling in the sun. She shook her head. Just seeing it there reminded her that Aiden had wrecked once before. *Damn death machine. Why did he ride it all the way down here? Wasn't there a safer mode of transportation for a six-hour trip?*

She reminded herself she didn't care. *Couldn't* care. Not after what had gone down between them. Not after the phone call that tore her heart out, left her weeping and curled into the fetal position.

But then you got up.

Hell yeah, she did.

Aiden appeared from the woods wearing a white shirt with the sleeves cut off. She could see the entire length of his torso as he jogged to her and a flash of something...a tattoo? *Doesn't matter.* His steps slowed, and he palmed his side, puffing and watching her as if he was afraid to come any closer.

That's when the memory of what she'd said to him last night hit her like a freight train. She'd looked into his ethereal green eyes and confessed she loved him. Wow. Stupid.

By the hurt-slash-reproachful look on his face, it was the moment he was recalling now, too. He started walking toward her, but before he got any closer, Sadie clambered into the car, started it, and drove down the lane. She stopped short of turning onto the steep mountain road and allowed herself a final glance back. In the rearview mirror, she saw Aiden pace over to his bike, run a hand through his long hair, and then, noticing her hesitation, raise a hand and wave good-bye.

Sadie didn't wave back, turning down the tree-lined road and driving as fast as she dared. Good-bye between her and Aiden had happened a long time ago.

And that was something else she wasn't willing to repeat.

CHAPTER TWO

$\mathcal{S}$adie stepped out of her car and smiled up at the too-warm August sun. It'd been a month and a half since Shane and Crickitt's wedding. Since one of the worst hangovers of her life. Since she'd woken the next morning in one of Aiden Downey's T-shirts.

Her epic dose of melancholy could be laid squarely at Crickitt's feet. Indirectly, of course. Any woman as happy as Sadie's best friend hadn't meant to create a virtual vortex of happiness that sucked everyone in around her. With that kind of joy flooding the air, Sadie had only been able to feel two things: thrilled beyond compare for Crickitt and Shane, and anguished over her own failed relationship with the man she thought she'd loved.

That wiped the smile right off her face.

Sadie pushed the memory back into a drawer and filed it under *L* for "Leave it Alone." The same place she'd filed the day Trey called to confess he couldn't marry her because he was in love with her sister. Funny how memories from that drawer unfiled and spread themselves out for her at the worst possible times.

Not today.

That's right. *NOT* today. Aiden could wreak havoc on her subconscious another time. But today, she needed her A game when she walked into Axle's.

The custom motorcycle shop stood before her, her own personal Mount Doom. One of five stores in Ohio, Axle's in Osborn was the first store, the highest-grossing store, and the store where the man himself continued to work.

She'd tracked the company's sales and orders for years, but Axle Zoller's second-in-command, Harry Truman, insisted on sticking with List for their motorcycle parts and supplies. She often wondered if he did it just to spite her. She'd worked hard to schmooze Harry, but made the mistake of addressing him as "Mr. President." Turned out the man had no sense of humor. Seemed a silly reason to pay more for lower-quality products, but no matter. Harry Truman had recently been impeached.

With *President* Harry Truman out of the picture, Sadie knew she had to swoop in before Axle replaced him. She was confident she could charm Axle into signing with Midwest Motorcycle Supplies.

Sadie peered into the side mirror of her car and checked her reflection. Her blonde hair hung in loose waves from where she'd slept on it wet, and her freckles were out in droves thanks to a weekend visit to the pool. Deep magenta lipstick accented her wide mouth, and a thick layer of black mascara coated her lashes. She adjusted her wardrobe, a black pencil skirt paired with a Harley-Davidson polo shirt.

She strode to the shop, her heels almost sinking into

the soft black asphalt baking in the ninety-eight-degree day. Her thoughts returned to her goal, sending her adrenal glands into silly spins. No one at MMS had knocked Perry Bradford off his number one pedestal since he started six years ago. Landing Axle's would shove her over his numbers by thousands of dollars.

Do or die time.

Inside the store, chilly air wafted the smell of fresh leather into her nostrils. Various splashy signage and displays showcased List parts and swag, along with the unmistakable orange and black of Harley-Davidson.

Axle spotted her from his position behind the special order counter, signaling he'd be with her in a minute. She waved back, heading to a particularly impressive shelf stocked with List's bold black and white boxes. Of course the major brands were all represented: Harley, Suzuki, Kawasaki. Sadie didn't dream that MMS parts would take the place of the big guys. What she wanted was the chunk of pie belonging to the off brands. MMS and List were both respected brands, but beneath their glossy exterior, Sadie knew List's parts were substandard.

Axle's deep baritone echoed across the store a few minutes later. "Come on back, Sadie."

Determination lengthening her stride, Sadie stood tall and proud in her studded black heels, lifting her to almost five foot six. Axle angled down a long corridor and led her to a cramped office, where shelves sagged under the weight of hardcover books on everything from bike repair to *Catcher in the Rye*.

He hulked over his desk, long gray braid trailing down his back, tree-trunk legs testing the task chair's weight limit. He was also a former boxer, which one would guess given the way his massive chest nearly burst the seams of his shirt.

Smoothing his thick, walrus-like moustache, Axle folded meaty hands in front of him on the desk and addressed Sadie with a quick lift of his eyebrows.

Sadie smiled, her confidence soaring. Axle liked her. She'd cultivated a careful professional relationship with him for the past three years, just waiting for the day Truman left. Axle endured her persistence, never once asking her to leave him alone. A good sign.

"Let me stop you there." Axle's flat gray eyes gave no hint as to what he was about to say. "You're going to pitch this to my new second-in-command." He gave her a gruff smile...or at least she thought he did. His moustache twitched on one side. "I'll go get him."

"But—" was all Sadie got out before Axle was out of his office. He moved fast for a big guy. She adjusted her skirt and mentally reviewed her sales pitch. The one she'd be giving to a newcomer. Whom she knew nothing about.

She'd need to be professional, of course. And not as familiar as she would have been with Axle. If the guy was a recent college graduate or CEO type, she'd have a lot of glossing over to do to explain her less-than-professional attire. She grimaced down at the silver studs on her feet. Why hadn't she worn sensible pumps?

Taking a breath, she considered the more likely scenario: that Axle had hired someone like himself. Someone with a penchant for hogs, an admiration for irreverent T-shirt sayings, and a strong head for business. Axle wasn't stupid. Far from it. She'd learned his IQ hovered around genius level though she couldn't dredge up the figure. Sadie's talent with numbers extended only to the ones with dollar signs before them.

She leaned and peeked through the doorway and down the hall, and caught a glimpse of an arm behind Axle, who came toward her like a tank in Tiananmen Square, his big body obscuring the rest of the man behind him.

No matter who the new guy was, Sadie had just one chance to impress him, not insult him, and get a sample of his penmanship on the bottom line. Sadie straightened in the out-of-date, stained guest chair. Sure she could be prickly, smart-mouthed, and sarcastic. But she also could be charming. And she knew her stuff. She could handle whoever came through that door.

Then Axle entered, his new second-in-command at his side, and Sadie felt the blood drain from her face.

Anyone except for Aiden Downey.

As big as Axle was, Aiden dominated her vision. His muscular legs in a pair of soft worn denim frayed over black motorcycle boots, broad shoulders and firm chest covered by a black collared shirt with the word *Axle's* embroidered over his right pectoral. And his face. The jaw she had kissed, had raked her fingernails against; the same jaw that had scraped the softest part of her neck when he kissed her, was covered with enough scruff to make her feel the phantom scratch of it on her skin now. And then there was his hair...long, thick strands she used to spear her fingers into—

Oh God.

She blinked, sure she must be imagining things, and swallowed the gasp working its way up her throat. Somehow she had to keep from appearing alarmed while her stomach took a dive to her toes. The dark blond ponytail he normally wore low on his neck was...*gone*. The strands that used to hang loose and brush his cheekbones, *shorn*. His hair had been such a part of him, so...*Aiden*. And that she'd loved touching it, feeling it brush against her face when he kissed her, had surprised no one more than Sadie.

Kind of like the next four words out of her mouth.

* * *

"You cut your hair."

Aiden's smile broadened as he took in the sight of Sadie Howard perched on the guest chair, eyes wide, jaw dropped.

Of all the motorcycle shops in the world...

He palmed his neck, still getting accustomed to the recent change. "Yeah. I did."

It probably should have occurred to him he might run into Sadie eventually, given they worked in the same, often overlapping field. But then, he'd been busy rebuilding his life—*reclaiming* his life after he finally decided what to do with it—so he hadn't given running into Sadie much thought.

He'd made it a point to put the plucky blonde out of his mind since the wedding. He spent the week following the wedding holed up at Shane's Tennessee cabin. Despite jogs in the woods, swims at the lake, and one ill-fated attempt at whittling, Aiden had nearly gone mad with boredom. That's when he decided to make a life plan. Decide what, once and for all, he wanted to do with his career. With his future. Focusing on the future quieted the thoughts banging around in his head about his failed marriage, the loss of his mother, the career he'd tanked.

Six weeks ago, he'd been plagued with guilt, but he'd since spent many mornings in silent reflection, examining his life and accepting where he'd arrived. His conclusion? He'd made plenty of mistakes but refused to haul them around like burdening weights.

Little by little, the guilt swimming in his gut evaporated. Anger flashed in Sadie's dark eyes. Perhaps she didn't share his renewed view on life. "Good to see you again," Aiden said, offering his hand to see if she'd take it.

"You two know each other?" Axle asked, flicking a look between them.

"Sort of," Sadie grumbled, standing. Tossing her head, she regarded Aiden's outstretched hand before giving it a brief, rough shake.

Aiden couldn't repress the smile that inched its way across his face. Sadie's flow of fair curls, lush pink lips, and pert little body had nothing on the razor-sharp wit and flair of confidence hard to find in the opposite sex.

And since Sadie embodied characteristics the exact opposite of his laid back, ambivalent, careless ex-wife, it shouldn't come as a surprise how appealing he found Sadie. Her barbed comments and the way she sliced him in half with one look was a red cape to his inner bull.

And she'd caught him on a day he wanted to run.

"We used to date," Aiden blurted. Sadie's eyes and mouth popped open simultaneously.

Axle remained silent, never one to wear his emotions on his bulging biceps. He turned to Sadie. "Aiden is in charge of the retail portion of Axle's," he said evenly.

"Sorry to do a bait and switch on you, but he knows what he's doing. I trust he'll make the right decision."

Sadie wanted to argue. Aiden could see it. She closed her mouth, opened it again, then finally snapped it shut with a click of her pearly teeth.

Axle wished them luck and stalked out of the room. Even though it wasn't necessary, Aiden closed the office door. Rubbing his hands together, he turned to Sadie, who greeted him with narrowed eyes and crossed forearms. "I understand you have a contract for—"

"'We used to date'?" she snapped.

"Yeah." He grinned. "I know."

Sadie huffed. "Why did you say that?"

"Because it's the truth."

"It's an unnecessary bit of information."

"He wondered how we knew each other. I was just—"

"What are you doing here?" Sadie interrupted.

"I work here." Aiden eased into Axle's chair and leaned back. He briefly considered propping his boots on the desk but opted not to. Sadie's rage was barely harnessed as it was.

Sadie slanted a glare at him, reminding him of the night he met her in the club. "I know you work here. I mean, why did Axle hire you? What experience do you have in retail?"

"First off, this is a motorcycle shop, not the mall." Aiden hoisted one finger. "And second, I have been underneath a car or bike since I could hold a socket wrench. Plus, my dad knows Axle."

"Ha!" Sadie stood, pointing an accusatory finger at him like a late-night-TV lawyer. "I knew it."

Aiden couldn't keep his eyes from skating down the

snug black skirt clinging to her thighs. He licked dry lips. *Good Lord.* Sadie, though petite, had curves that turned both women's and men's heads. Her narrow shoulders gave way to a swell of ample breasts before diving inward to her slender waist, and out again to allow for rounded hips.

Snapping his attention to the coffee mug on the edge of a desk, Aiden rummaged for an ink pen. Not because he needed one, but because he needed a safe place to rest his eyes.

"Three years," Sadie said, pacing the narrow space between the guest chair and desk.

Aiden tried to drag his eyes off her perfect butt. And failed. Luckily, when she turned, he was able to meet her eye.

"I have been massaging this account for three years." She leaned over the desk, the soft scent of her swirling around him. "I am *this close* to securing the number one sales position at Midwest. And Axle has handed my future to you. *You!* Someone he hired because..." She waved a hand. "Because...he and your dad were old war buddies!"

"War buddies? How old do you think my dad is? He and Axle used to work at the factory together." The factory where his dad still worked. The factory where Aiden would *end up working* if he didn't make this job at Axle's work.

Aiden had branched out once before—into the volatile field of real estate development. Even if he and his former buddy Daniel had survived the bubble that eventually bankrupted the company, Aiden had no idea his business partner would stoop to the depths of sleeping with Aiden's then-wife. A hole in a wall, a few choice words to Danny, and a motorcycle wreck later, and here Aiden was, attempting to make it on his own again.

What Sadie didn't know—what no one knew—was that Axle Zoller was selling out and retiring. And that left five stores available for purchase. If Aiden could wrangle the funds to buy him out, and not lose his ass in the process, that's exactly what he planned to do.

Sadie flopped into her seat again, face pink, lips downturned. She tossed a high-gloss black folder with a red stripe down one edge in front of him. "Just sign it and we can both get on with our day."

Aiden flipped the cover open and started to read.

"What are you doing?"

He looked up. "Reading your proposal."

Her nostrils flared. "Do not ruin this for me, Aiden Downey. I've worked too hard to land this contract."

Aiden kept his expression neutral. "Something in here you're afraid I'll find? Price gouging? Remanufactured parts instead of new? Zero buyback policy?"

"What?" Sadie barked. "No, of course not."

Aiden released the folder and leaned back in Axle's chair, hands laced over his stomach. Sadie's chest heaved. Such a temper on that girl. "Well, how am I supposed to know what it says if I don't read it?"

Sadie pressed her lips together. She could have defended herself with a *You know me*, or *You can trust me*. She could have made an emotional plea of *How can you say something like that after all we've been through?* But she did neither. She'd never expect someone to give her something she hadn't earned. And she'd sooner die than have Aiden feel sorry for her.

Settling into the guest chair, she crossed her legs and brushed something from her skirt. "Take your time," she said, refusing to look at him. "I'll wait."

Aiden skimmed the cover letter, then flipped to the price list, and finally, to the contract. In reality, he'd stopped reading with comprehension a few pages ago. But he drew out their time together, not ready to be apart from her just yet, and because Sadie was gorgeous when her hackles were up.

The few dates he and Sadie had been on last summer, Aiden had been lucky enough to see her iron curtain drop. Seeing the woman behind it left him speechless, as if he was witnessing something rare and precious. Sadie may have an exterior made of Naugahyde, but inside, she was pudding.

He closed the folder and found Sadie watching him, waggling one dangerous-looking stiletto back and forth. "Well?"

He almost blurted, *Let's talk about it over drinks*, but bit his tongue. Then again...why not? They knew each other, had things in common. His cousin and her best friend were husband and wife. Not to mention Sadie looked like a woman who could use a drink. Plus, it'd be fun to mess with her. Just a little. Just one more time.

Aiden closed the cover on the proposal. "I'll sign it." Sadie's shoulders dropped an inch. He told himself to stop there, not to say another word. But in the end he couldn't help but add, "Under one condition."

Sadie tensed.

Aiden smiled. "Go out on a date with me."

* * *

Of all the—!

If Aiden thought he could—!

"Argh!" Sadie stomped into the hall, peeking into each room along the way, looking for Axle, her heels clacking in distressed rhythm.

"Sadie," Aiden said again. He was right behind her. She ignored him. What was he thinking? That he'd take all of her hard work, years of effort, wad them up, and toss them in her face? Aiden may not take the job his daddy got him seriously, but Sadie was different. She took pride in going after her goals, in getting what she wanted. And what she wanted was Axle Zoller's parts contract.

Angling toward the showroom, she spotted Axle standing over a vintage Harley-Davidson, talking to a customer. Sadie walked faster.

"Sadie!" Aiden whispered this time, as loudly as he could without drawing attention. A few people turned in their direction and Sadie shot them a nothing-to-see-here smile. Just as she was about to tap Axle's shoulder, a hand clapped onto her arm and whirled her around.

Aiden held his palms up in an *I surrender* pose. "I was kidding, Sadie." He was still whispering. "I swear."

"Kidding?" Sadie gave him a derisive smile. "I see. You think my career is a joke."

"I don't think that." Aiden's eyes went from her to Axle. "So, what, you're going to tell on me?"

She glanced over at Axle, then back at Aiden. "I think he should know that you're trying to coerce—"

"Everything okay?" Axle rumbled, his tone a warning.

Aiden crossed his arms. Smiled smugly. Yeah. She was going to tell on him. She turned to smile at Axle.

Salt and pepper eyebrows were drawn over gray eyes, the corners of his moustache accentuating an unseen frown.

His face was so foreboding, Sadie actually backed up a step. She bumped into Aiden, who caught her by the waist, stopping her short of stepping on his feet. Ignoring the heat seeping through the cotton of her shirt, Sadie muttered, "Knucklehead."

"Hey—"

"The bike, not you," she grumbled to Aiden, moving away from him.

Axle's expression eased. "Yes, ma'am. 1940 EL 1000 Knucklehead, to be precise."

Sadie smiled up at him. "I know my hogs." She also knew a good diversion tactic when she saw one. Get a man talking about what he loved, and he'd forget he was ever upset. And while she was at it...

"By the way..." Sadie placed a hand on Aiden's arm then nearly forgot what she was going to say. His skin was warm, muscle thicker than she remembered. She removed her hand. "Um. Everything's a go. Aiden is one shrewd deal maker." Aiden clenched his jaw and she gave him a sweet smile. "Midwest is officially your new parts supplier."

"Great," Axle said, not sounding as if he meant it. He sent a glance at the customer to his right. "Is that all?"

"Yes." Sadie could take a hint. "I'm just...very excited."

"Yippee," Axle said flatly.

* * *

Sadie's good mood faded the moment she set foot inside her cubicle at work. Perry Bradford hovered over her in-box, rifling through her papers. "Excuse me."

"Excuse you?" Perry turned, his tie swinging with the motion. "All right. You're excused." He continued digging.

Sadie pushed past him, dumping her bag onto the desk. She'd used the last of her fury on Aiden and couldn't call up enough to unleash on her moron coworker. "Can I help you?"

Perry abandoned his search, leaning on her desk and crossing his arms over his chest. "How should I answer that?"

Sadie sucked in a cleansing breath. Perry was a consummate flirt, but harmless, and under pain of death she may even admit he was kind of cute. He was also a hustler and a ruthless salesman. Perry had been number one in sales at MMS every year. Every. Single. Year.

Sadie couldn't believe it when she'd come close to beating him last quarter. She'd kicked her productivity into high gear since then. Now, *no thanks to Aiden*, she'd secured the account that bumped her to the lead.

"I signed Hawgs." A smug smile stretched across Perry's face. "You know Hawgs, right? Little garage south of Arbor Lane? Specializes in—"

"I know it," she cut him off. "You know I know it; I tried to sign them myself."

He winked at her, his cocksureness a bad mix with her own. Perry's features were almost boyish, a quality that would keep him charming for years to come.

"I was looking for your proposal for the file. You know, the one they turned down." He gave her an exaggerated pout.

"I guess I'll have to dry my tears on this," she said, producing Axle's contract Aiden had signed under duress.

Perry frowned at the paper before snatching it from her hands. He muttered a curse. "You got them."

"I did."

"All five stores?"

"All five stores," she repeated.

Perry pushed away from her desk and blinked as if absorbing the news. A second later, he nodded slowly, figuring it out. Unless he pulled some serious strings, or if Sadie didn't work another day for the next month, the promotion and accolades typically befalling Perry would be hers.

"We'll see, Sadie." He turned his back on her, repeating as he stalked away, "We'll see."

Rather than gloat, she kept her comments to herself. What, really, was there to say? She'd worked hard and arrived at her goal with time to spare. She was getting what she wanted. What she deserved.

So why didn't she feel like celebrating?

*C*HAPTER THREE

*M*ike Downey flipped a burger on the grill, waving hello with the spatula as Aiden rounded the backyard. "Hey, son, how was work?"

"Good."

"Axle's a good guy."

"How 'bout you?"

"Good," Mike said noncommittally. "Well, 'good' might be overstating it. Marty pitched a fit today."

Aiden's biceps tensed. Marty Kincaid was a loud-mouthed prick giving everyone headaches when Aiden worked there briefly last year. Not that he'd expected the guy to change.

"You hungry?" Mike asked, flipping another burger.

"Yeah," Aiden called over his shoulder as he stepped into the garage and dug a beer bottle out of the fridge. He twisted the cap and stood next to his father at the grill.

If Aiden thought too hard about the fact he was thirty-one and living at home, he might very well burst into tears. Last year Aiden had lost his business, then a chunk of money to his lecherous ex-wife and her pit bull lawyer, and then came the news about his mother.

The family had taken the news—that the doctor had given her three months left to live—hard. Kathy Downey had made her mind up after five years of battling cancer: she wasn't going to get chemo. She'd found The Holistic Care Center in Oregon. The live-in healing resort had everything: acupuncture, meditation, herbal supplements, even a "thought doctor" who Aiden suspected was a quack. Aiden didn't hesitate to move out there in his father's stead, while Mike stayed in Ohio and worked all the overtime he could to afford the facility. When Dad's money ran out, Aiden put his house and his prized collection of motorcycles up for sale.

Dad didn't know until it was too late. Aiden knew his old man would sooner join a burlesque show in Vegas than ask his children for money, which is why Aiden had kept it from him.

Yet none of it had mattered.

Not the "healing mountains" of Oregon, the spring water, or the prayer—more than Aiden had ever prayed in his life. They'd lost her anyway. When Landon, his millionaire ad exec brother, found out Aiden had used his own money, he tried to send him a check. Aiden wouldn't accept it. Even Shane's insistence to contribute was met with stern refusal.

If Aiden had learned anything during those weeks at the care center with his mother, it was that they were each on their own path. At some point, there was only the option of going it alone. Mom's path was to fight and fail.

And Aiden's was to give up everything to fund her ability to do just that.

Aiden rubbed his right side, where the tattoo he'd gotten to remember her sat etched into his skin, and shut his eyes against bad memories.

"Hey." Mike shoved his shoulder and Aiden opened his eyes. "Don't do that." He turned back to the grill. "Life turns out this way sometimes. It's not your fault your momma was sick."

Was sick.

Mike never said *died*, or *passed on*, or *is in a better place*. Not that Aiden expected him to be morose and pensive like Landon, or loud and angry like Evan. Losing Mom had reduced Aiden into a sobbing puddle of tears. He'd failed her, and no matter how many times he reminded himself that things happen for a reason, there was a certain percentage of the blame he wasn't willing to unshoulder.

But the way his father handled his mother's passing... it didn't seem natural. Aiden had never once seen the man cry—not when Mom took her last breath, not at the funeral, not after. Mike's solution was to move on. When someone asked how he was, he'd offer a bit of fortune cookie wisdom or share a platitude about God's timing. And while it could very well be true, it wasn't easy to hear.

Aiden was grateful to have Shane. Sure he was family, but he was also Aiden's best friend, and Aiden looked up to him as much as he did his father. What Shane had gone through—his father blaming him for his mother's death—was something Aiden knew his own father would never do. But it didn't make it any easier to look him in the eye whenever Mike lamented the weeks he'd lost not being at his wife's side.

"I'm going to go to the cemetery tomorrow," Aiden said.

Mike grunted, sliding the burgers onto four waiting buns.

Aiden accepted his plate and dragged up the courage to ask, "Would you like to go with me?"

Predictably, Mike shook his head. "No, no. Nothing but bones in a cemetery."

He bet Dad hadn't been to the cemetery since the funeral. Even then, he'd refused to take the chair in front of the casket, instead hovering at the rear of the crowd that had gathered. Mike had been the first to head for his car after the pastor finished speaking. Aiden stayed longer than he should have, watching as they lowered her body into the cold earth.

"Thinking of a ride later. Interested?"

Taking their bikes out was one way they'd bonded since Mom was gone. Aiden didn't feel like riding tonight, but wouldn't refuse his father's request. Even if Dad's idea of bonding was sharing an hour on the road without speaking.

"Yeah. I'm in."

Mike smiled, the scar running the length of one cheek puckering slightly. "Good boy."

* * *

At the entrance of Axle's, Sadie tugged the hem of her shirt and pulled her shoulders back. She could do this. She had to do this.

The contract Aiden signed two days ago may have been a smidge overzealous. She blamed three years of pining for Axle's stores for her campaign-esque promises. She'd given them MMS's lowest rates, slashing her commission in half in the process, and promised to personally oversee the transition at this, their largest, busiest store, from their former parts supplier to Midwest. And while she was throwing in the cart with the horses, why not toss in the driver and cobblestone road, too? That was her only explanation for offering to buy back any of MMS's competitor's parts that didn't sell over the next month. Of course, she'd assumed she'd be dealing with Axle and that she could charm a few of those extras into oblivion.

Sadie yawned. She'd spent half the night reading and rereading the contract for loopholes. No such luck. That Ericka in Legal was thorough. When Sadie woke this morning, however, she'd had a different attitude. Even if she could weasel her way out of the contract, or if she could convince Aiden to sign a new one, there was no way she would. The moment he found out he had something she wanted, he'd lord it over her, watching gleefully as she disassembled displays and hustled to sell out of her competitor's parts. She wouldn't have guessed Aiden was that kind of person until he attempted to trade a date for his signature on the contract. The thought made her frown.

She caught her reflection frowning back at her and plastered a smile on her face better suited to a beauty pageant contestant. Sadie Howard didn't roll over. Sadie Howard didn't lose. And even if she did lose, she thought as she knocked on the glass door, she wasn't about to *look* like a loser.

She took in her surroundings while she waited to be let in. Axle's sat on a highly manicured portion of downtown Osborn, cheery rows of potted flowers sitting on the brick-lined sidewalks, black light poles with waving city flags interspersed in between.

She liked this town. She liked her job, oddly enough. It had surprised everyone when she'd snuggled in at a motorcycle parts supplier after attaining her marketing degree. Probably because her father had lost his life on a bike, and Sadie refused to ride. But Sadie was good at sales and, aside from Perry being a thorn in her side, really did enjoy her coworkers. Being around people who loved motorcycles made her feel closer to her dad. She didn't remember much about him, but his love for the open road was no secret. If only he'd have loved helmets as much.

She heard the lock disengage on the door and turned to find Aiden peering at her. He gave her a crooked smile, encouraging his dimple to appear. His shorn hair caught her by surprise again, so much shorter than she was used to seeing, though the front still fell in disarray over his forehead.

So he's cute. So what?

Aiden pushed the door open and leaned with one arm drawn across the handle, forcing Sadie to brush by him when she entered. "Miss Howard."

"Mr. Downey," she clipped. She strode into the store in a pair of patent leather pumps perfectly suited to the red scarf around her neck and matching short-sleeved blouse. The four-inch heels, she hoped, were doing wonders for her backside, which she'd squeezed into a pair of tight vinyl pants.

Out of her peripheral vision, she watched Aiden's eyes graze her outfit. It was immature, but she couldn't help but feel smug.

Yes, sir, get a look at what you've been missing.

"Get lost on the way to a sock hop?"

Or not.

Sadie spun and pierced Aiden with a glare, her high ponytail nearly slapping her in the face with the movement. "I have work to do."

Aiden shrugged. "Whatever you say, Sandra Dee."

Ignoring the temptation to stick her tongue out at him, Sadie gathered her bag and walked to the other side of the store, where she'd be stocking Midwest's complete line of motorcycle parts.

Sadie pulled out a pen and her notebook and sketched a rudimentary map of the store's layout. The space was long and narrow, one entire end lined with windows facing the parking lot. In the window sat a remarkable vintage bike she knew belonged to Axle. When Axle had told her the bike was his creation, she'd marveled that he'd built it with his own huge mitts. The man was far more dexterous than she would have guessed.

Unfortunately, the bike wasn't meeting its potential as top model. A shelf sat next to it, stocked with an uninspiring array of bumper stickers, T-shirts, and coffee mugs in random, busy colors while a mannequin in a "Biking is my Life" shirt stood guard. He'd lost an arm—which didn't bode well for bike sales—and a creative profanity had been scrawled on his remaining limb.

She added the display to her list, jotting down to bring in some Midwest Motorcycle Supplies signage and retire the mannequin. This particular Axle's shop was unique from its sister shops dotted around Ohio. Many customers who came here not only loved motorcycles but also took pride in doing their own repairs and upgrades.

Rows of MMS parts lined in the window around Axle's custom-built cherry Harley would have the locals drooling like one of Pavlov's canines before they ever entered the store.

She trekked over to the parts aisles, wincing as she took in the staggered, mismatched rows. Some parts were unboxed, others marked with Post-its (really?) instead of price tags, while several others weren't marked at all.

Since she'd promised to sell the old inventory or buy it back out of her pocket—not her brightest move—she'd have to get these parts sellable and gradually replace them with the Midwest brand. If she was stuck with them, she may be able to put them up for sale on eBay, but it wasn't like she wanted to lug all of this stuff home with her.

Scratching another note onto her pad, she sneaked a peek at Aiden at the front door. He signed for a box, making a joke to the delivery guy she couldn't hear, his smile wide and bright, his posture relaxed.

That's what had towed her in all those months ago— forget his rare-colored eyes, sexy body, and easy smile. She'd been taken with the whole package. The whole *Aiden*. She hadn't been able to resist.

Allowing the door to swing shut, he knelt and lifted the box. Sadie couldn't keep from appreciating the way the muscles in his arms shifted and straightened as he adjusted to the weight. And, evil vixen her brain was, a memory presented itself. One of being held in his arms while he caressed her lips with his, while he kneaded her thighs just below her miniskirt with one slightly roughened hand.

"Need something?"

Sadie started, realizing she was leaning against the endcap, head tilted, staring directly at Aiden. Straightening, she turned her attention to her notebook and pretended to write on it. "Just, uh, planning."

"Is that so?" He dropped the box and sauntered in her direction.

"Yes." Her voice was thin, her heartbeat rapidly increasing as Aiden approached with the agility of a lithe jungle cat.

His attention flickered to her lips. "What are you planning?"

She swallowed, unable to think of what to say while he was standing over her looking at her like…like…she didn't even know. "Um…"

"Well, if you need anything else…" Aiden pulled a stray strand of her hair away from her lipstick and smoothed it behind her ear, brushing her cheek with the back of his hand as he did. "Be sure to let me know."

His lips quirked and she studied the short, pale patch of hair beneath his lower lip, unable to remember why she wasn't allowed to kiss this bronzed Adonis.

But when he pulled his hand away, the words from their final phone call echoed in her ears. When he told her his mother was dying, and he was moving with her to the facility in Oregon. His family hadn't known he was divorced, so it wasn't like he could have introduced Sadie to them. And it wasn't like she could have gone with him.

She wondered if she would have. Maybe.

No matter. Sadie hadn't fit into his life then. She didn't

fit now. Aiden, no matter how attractive, no matter what her body insisted she do to him, had chosen to end things with her last year. And just because he regretted it now didn't mean Sadie had waited around for his epiphany.

She learned her lesson. Once from Trey. Once from Aiden. And twice was enough.

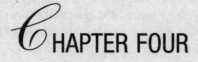

CHAPTER FOUR

*A*iden literally counted his steps to the counter, wondering the entire way if Sadie still watched him. He told himself to keep his distance today, but then he caught her checking him out and couldn't resist seeing how close he could get before she swatted at him like an irritated cat.

Closer than he thought.

And he could swear she'd stared at his mouth as he stared at hers. Under the pretense of moving a hair stuck to her glossed lips, he'd brushed his hand along her cheek, but he'd wanted to do more. So much more. Lean in and kiss her like he had last year, if for no other reason than to remind himself what it felt like to be wanted.

Aiden dug a box cutter out of the drawer next to the cash register, risking a look at the rear of the store. Sadie knelt on the floor, studying several sheets of paper lined up in a row. *Those pants.* Was she trying to give him a heart attack? The shiny black material barely qualified as material at all, hugging her curves like they'd been spray-painted on.

Blowing out a breath, Aiden sliced through the tape. A large bag filled with colorful key chains was on top, directions and several numbered pieces for the five-foot-tall display beneath. Tossing aside the directions—they'd do more harm than good anyway—Aiden began assembling the display.

At first his mind was consumed by the task of getting all four sides to sit on the swiveling bottom portion. But once the skeleton was built, it was only a matter of snapping a hundred tiny pegs into the holes, and soon his thoughts wandered to the blonde at the back of the store.

Sadie was gorgeous in red. When he caught sight of her outside this morning, she stole his breath. Her smooth blonde ponytail and tall heels were the stuff of men's fantasies. And yet, the sexiest thing she wore was the delicate red scarf tied around her neck. There was something about the skin hidden beneath the shock of sheer fabric that tempted him to undo the knot and slide it aside, rasping her neck with his mouth.

Hiding behind the display, he adjusted his too-tight jeans and pushed the thought out of his head. Turned on by a neckerchief. Quite a feat considering she should have a permit to wear those pants.

One thing was for sure, Aiden was going to have to rein in his roving hormones if they'd be working together for the next month. And, according to the proposal and contract he'd signed, it'd be at least that long. Sadie would be organizing shelving, reducing prices of other parts stocked in the warehouse, and buying any she didn't sell out of her pocket. He wasn't the least bit surprised she'd taken on the initiative personally. Sadie was no stranger to taking charge.

Like that night at his house when she'd tugged the tie out of his hair and breathed into his ear. That was all it'd taken for him to dive into her mouth and lay her flat beneath him.

Ah, hell. He readjusted himself again, this time hiding behind the cash register before Sadie caught him fantasizing like an eighth-grade boy who couldn't control his hormones.

Sadie stood on her tiptoes to measure a shelf overhead, the movement inching her shirt up and revealing a slice of pale, flat stomach. Maybe he could talk Axle into making her wear a uniform. But picturing her in a black Axle's polo and jeans didn't quell the lust bubbling in his stomach.

He crammed another peg into the display. Somehow, he'd have to find a way to get things done with the petite object of his infatuation hanging around.

Which begged the question, why was he infatuated? Sadie should be the last woman on earth stirring him up. On a good day, Sadie all but hated him. And he couldn't blame her. He knew how it felt when Harmony had chosen another man over him. He'd done a version of the same thing to Sadie. Granted, he didn't go back to Harmony, but he'd invited her back into his life. And despite his noble reasoning—to protect his mother from what she didn't know—it was the wrong call.

Though they'd only shared a few dates, he'd shared something real and precious with Sadie. He may have met her in a club, may have followed her home that night, but that was where the forgone conclusion ended. Nothing after the moment he'd entered her tiny apartment kitchen had been expected.

Sadie had stood behind her refrigerator door, blocking her body from his, and offered him a drink. He took one look into her dark, troubled eyes and saw his own pain reflected there.

"Who'd he leave you for?" he'd asked.

She blinked, not expecting the question. "What?"

"The guy who caused you to make a one-date-only rule for the rest of us. Who'd he leave you for?"

That pointed question set the tone for the rest of the night. They spent the evening sitting on the floor of her apartment, backs against the sofa and adjacent chair, and shared every ugly thing from their pasts like they were one-upping each other.

He'd seen her again after that, had brought her to his place and slept next to her without sleeping *with* her. To this day, Sadie marked the deepest, most emotional relationship of his life.

Leaving her behind was one of the hardest—and dumbest—things he'd ever done.

After Aiden went to Oregon, he thought of Sadie several times. How she would have handled his mother's illness with grace. How she would've stuck by him, been a strong support while he bobbed in a sea of uncertainty.

Again he lamented keeping the truth from his mother. If only he'd told her sooner that Harmony had left him—that he'd been divorced and unemployed for months, that he'd met the woman of his dreams.

Aiden had been trying to put his mother first, protect

her from the stress of knowing how badly he'd screwed up his life. Worrying would cause stress. Stress would make her battle more difficult. And Aiden had been trying to give her the best chance possible to beat the disease determined to rob her of her life.

In the end it hadn't mattered. Harmony vanished into the ether. Mom lost the battle. And Aiden burned the bridge he and Sadie used to stand upon and view their future.

He'd begun to see his self-sacrifices weren't actually helping the people he cared about, but were, without a doubt, crippling him. There was a lesson in there. About doing what was best for him for a change. Maybe the right thing for him had been the right path all along. Who the hell knew?

He crammed a peg into the hole. It snapped in half. "Shit." He looked up and noticed Sadie standing on the other side of the counter. "Sorry."

She waved him off. "Don't waste your manners on me."

He stood, tossing the broken plastic into the trash can. "I've been trying not to swear," he said, not sure why he was admitting part of his journey toward self-improvement.

"I've been dieting," Sadie said, picking up on the angle of his thoughts. She got him. She always had.

Aiden took in her lush curves, unable to see a single area in need of improvement. Every dip and bend was just as it should be. He started to say something to that effect but decided against it. "Why are you dieting?"

Sadie frowned back at him. "Because."

"How well do you know Axle?" Aiden asked, shifting to the other subject loitering in his brain.

Sadie shrugged, folding her arms on the countertop between them. "I don't know. Why?"

Because the deal he and Axle had discussed—the one that included a hefty down payment and the sale of all five stores to Aiden—wasn't going to come to pass exactly the way Aiden had planned. Axle told him originally he was planning to retire in three years. Yesterday, he'd casually mentioned he was going to be out of there "by Christmas" and suggested Aiden get his ducks in a row.

Problem was, not only did Aiden *not* have his ducks in a row, he was short about fifty thousand "ducks," since the timeline had been significantly shortened. Aiden had to be creative, come up with a plan to pitch to his oversized boss that would both pacify Axle and allow Aiden to get what he wanted under his terms.

A hundred fresh ideas kept him up late last night and woke him early this morning. But before Aiden approached Axle with any of them, it'd be nice to know if Axle would be open to negotiation. The man was as movable as Mount Rushmore. But Sadie knew him. Maybe she could offer some insight.

"I need to talk to him about something," Aiden said. "But you can't tell him I told you."

Sadie's eyes widened, interest swimming in their cinnamon-colored depths. "It's, like, a secret?"

Aiden shrugged. "He didn't *say* it was a secret. But he only told a few people."

"And you trust me with this information."

"Can't I?" Aiden knew the answer. Or hoped he did. Whenever he thought about how Harmony had taken his trust and repeatedly fed it into the garbage disposal, he wondered if he was being naïve. But he knew Sadie. He *trusted* Sadie. Still. Even after all that had gone down between them.

Sadie fiddled with a pen on the counter, avoiding his eye. Aiden waited. Her feelings may not be on her face, but he could read them in the stiffness in her shoulders and her lack of a snappy comeback. "You know you can," she said quietly.

Because she'd never betray me.

The thought was like a sock to the gut. He knew she'd never use his secrets against him, never throw them in his face. Even after he'd stated unequivocally things were over between them, Sadie hadn't gone out of her way to harm him. She'd simply . . . gotten out of the way. Allowed herself to be brushed aside.

He'd been such a jerk. "I'm sorry about . . . everything," he said, flattening his hands on the counter. Inept, but he didn't know what else to say. He expected her to rebuff him like she had at the wedding.

She placed cool fingertips on his hand. "I'm sorry your mom died. I'm sorry I didn't come to the funeral."

Raw sincerity flooded her eyes. *There she is.* Sadie without her shell. She was vulnerable, exposed, and the most beautiful thing Aiden had ever seen. He turned his hand over and gave her fingers a gentle squeeze. His heart squeezed right along with them.

Nothing had prepared him for the tightness in his chest at seeing her like this, or how just holding her hand in his comforted some deep, dark place inside him.

"Morning, kids." The front door swung open and Axle barged in like, well, a barge.

Sadie pulled her hand out of Aiden's, breaking the spell.

"Donuts," Axle announced in his foghorn voice.

"Good morning, Axle." She offered a sweet smile, her newly painted façade firmly back in place.

Axle dropped a white box in the center of the counter and flipped open the lid. "And coffee," he said, setting the cardboard drink carrier next to it.

"I'm dieting," Sadie said, eyeing the pastries.

"You're drooling," Aiden teased.

She glared at him.

Axle handed her a napkin. "You don't need to diet."

Sadie pulled her steely glare from Aiden and beamed up at their boss. "Thank you, Axle." Then she dug out a glazed donut, grabbed her coffee and notebook, and returned to her task.

"You handled that better than me," Aiden said after she'd gone.

Axle chewed, powdered sugar dotting his thick moustache like a blanket of fresh snow. He shook his head at Aiden in a show of disappointment. "Duh."

* * *

It'd been two days since Aiden asked for her advice.

Since then, Sadie had been itching for more details on the mysterious Axle situation, but she didn't want to seem overeager. Every time she thought Aiden was going to talk about it, he didn't. She was beginning to wonder if he decided he didn't trust her after all, which hurt...and kind of ticked her off.

Sadie was not only trustworthy with private information, she was good at giving advice. According to Crickitt, anyway. Crickitt told Sadie the reason she always sought her out was because Sadie had an honest, no-nonsense answer. Maybe Aiden didn't want her no-nonsense honesty. Maybe, as Trey had often reminded her, Aiden appreciated a woman with a more flattering disposition.

Someone like her sister.

Sadie huffed to herself as she inspected another motorcycle part from a rival company. She considered its condition and resale value before marking it with a brightly colored 50-percent-off sticker.

Well, if Trey liked his women prissy, he'd chosen the right girl. Sadie's half sister, Celeste, was a daddy's girl—*Celeste's* daddy, anyway. Wendell DeWalt was Sadie's stepfather. Celeste and Sadie may have shared a mother, but they were as different as diamonds and cubic zirconium. And Celeste knew her jewels.

Trey's infatuation with her higher-class, polite sister may have been why Sadie sharpened her edge to a razor-thin point in the first place. Becoming more like her sister would only prove Trey right, that Sadie needed some softening.

After he left her, she started serial dating—er, serial *first* dating, anyway. Each and every first date proved the man sitting across from her as flawed as Trey, and likely to let her down as hard. Until Aiden. He'd changed everything. At first, she thought for the better.

Boy was she wrong.

She marked another few pieces of inventory for clearance and put them back on the shelf. In search of more bargain-basement products, she headed for the warehouse, stopping short when she spotted Aiden. And a woman.

Sadie froze, her eyes skating down the other woman's thin but muscular frame, and back up to the short dark hair barely brushing the tattoo on the back of her neck. She was in good shape, probably a runner like Aiden. Sadie pretended to straighten the shelf next to her as she watched them.

The woman held up a black and pink T-shirt and posed for him. Aiden nodded his approval. Was he attracted to her? Was this the type of woman he wanted? And why did seeing them talk to each other make Sadie's skin crawl?

They chatted all the way to the cash register, where Aiden rang up her purchase and handed over the receipt. The woman didn't leave immediately, lingering at the counter, *flirting*. Sadie knew flirting when she saw it, and the way the woman tilted her head and rolled her shoulders back to push her chest out was definitely flirting. She had a small chest. At least Sadie had her in the boob department.

When the woman got to the door, Sadie felt her shoulders relax some. *Good. Keep walking, honey.* Until she returned to the counter and Aiden held out a pen. She took it, jotting something down on the back of her receipt and handing it to him.

Sadie's jaw went tight. And a little tighter when Aiden smiled, exposing the dimple low on one cheek. Dammit, that was *Sadie's* dimple.

Before she could rationalize her way out of it, Sadie was marching full steam ahead toward the counter—to do what, she had no idea. Scold Aiden for talking to a woman?

The woman left, and as the door swung shut, Aiden called after her, "Thanks, Sonya."

The sound of his voice stopped Sadie short. When the red spots cleared from her vision, she noticed Aiden watching her expectantly. Her eyes darted to the sheet of paper on the counter—yep, there was a phone number on there—to the pen in his hand. She snatched it from him and forced a tight smile. "Can I borrow this?"

Without waiting for an answer, Sadie pointed her frustrated, jealous, and clearly insane self in the direction of the warehouse and didn't look back.

* * *

Aiden narrowed his eyes at Sadie's retreating back before allowing a ghost of a smile to sneak onto his face. If he wasn't mistaken, Sadie did not like that *Mrs.* Sonya Rollins had slipped Aiden her husband's phone number a moment ago. How else was he supposed to alert the couple when their special-ordered leather saddlebags came in?

Sadie had practically been foaming at the mouth as she crossed the room. Aiden half expected her to snatch the receipt and tear it into a million pieces. This was the woman who'd fed her wedding invitations through a shredder, after all. If she could obliterate expensive card stock without a second thought, the thin sheet of thermal paper in his hand didn't stand a chance.

And what did she need his pen for, anyway? His eyes went to the full cup of ink pens on the corner of the counter. She hadn't grabbed one of those.

Yeah. Something was up.

For the last few days, Aiden had watched her work. She came in when the store opened, or just before, and stayed for two or three hours to arrange, and help sell, the parts she'd dug out of the warehouse. Aiden helped, referring customers to the clearance display and explaining they were making room for new inventory.

In the case of parts the clearance rack didn't hold, Sadie had equipped Aiden with a Midwest brand price sheet with their most popular items on it. Yesterday when she'd overheard Aiden say a certain Midwest part would need to be shipped, Sadie had run out to her car and dug the part out of her trunk.

She was driven, no doubt about it.

Aiden smiled at the empty doorway leading to the warehouse where she'd disappeared in a blur of blonde, pen-wielding beauty. Sadie was about to become number one in sales thanks to the Axle's contract. In pursuit of the goal, she wasn't about to let any detail fall by the way.

His admiration for her work ethic stirred something familiar within him. His own drive. His goals. Aiden had finally, *finally* taken a step toward getting what he wanted when he'd accepted the job at Axle's. Not that he wouldn't do what he'd done for his mother a hundred times over, but this was his chance. A new chapter of his life. A brand new day.

Or it would be, as soon as he nutted up and talked to Axle. He needed to quit putting it off, lay out his pitch, and see what his gruff employer thought of it.

Aiden had a break coming up, and no plans other than finding a sandwich shop where he could fill his empty void of a stomach. He could invite Sadie to come with him, get what he knew would be her blatantly honest opinion of the business deal he was considering.

A plan. Simply having one made him feel as if

he was halfway to victory. Aiden abandoned the sales floor and walked to Axle's office. He poked his head through the open door to find Axle sitting at his computer, pecking away at a snail's pace with the tips of his sausage-like fingers. "I'm going to take a break soon. Cover me?"

Axle turned, the chair beneath him creaking in disagreement. Over a pair of his wife's flowered pink reading glasses—Axle lost a pair of reading glasses a week, at least—he gave Aiden a solemn stare. "Okay," he said, his tone revealing nothing.

Aiden headed down the hallway away from Axle's office, shaking his head as he wondered at his burly boss. Any inside information on how to scale the granite wall that was Axle Zoller would be appreciated. The man was about as readable as a braille instruction manual for complicated electronics.

In the warehouse, Sadie was standing on a stepladder straining for a box just out of reach of her slight height.

"Need a hand?" he asked.

"Oh!" He'd startled her, and Sadie grasped the shelf for support to keep from falling. Over her head, the large box swayed and began to tip.

Aiden rushed for her, and before he'd worked out how to do it, pulled Sadie off the stepladder and folded her into him, protecting her with his body.

And then time stopped.

Her scent wrapped around him, tickling his nostrils and reminding him of the times he'd held her and kissed the sense right out of her. Her silken blonde hair wound softly around his fingertips where his palm cupped the back of her head. The press of her breasts against his chest, the way his arm locked around her lower back, made him want to pull her close and never let her go.

Then, in a cascade of clanks and clatters, the box overhead toppled and delivered an array of parts to the warehouse's concrete floor. And one heavy piece in particular drilled into Aiden's shoulder.

He let out a sound between a growl and a grunt as the sharp edge hit his shoulder, but he didn't let Sadie go until he was sure it was done raining metal. Only then did he allow her to pull away. She did, slowly, turning those brown eyes up at him as one hand fisted the side of his shirt.

Those petal soft lips parted and all Aiden could think about was tasting her...until her eyebrows slammed down and she barked, "What the hell are you doing?"

"What the hell am *I* doing?" Aiden asked as she backed away from him. "What the hell are *you* doing?"

Her eyebrows shot up. "I'm working."

"Looks more like you're trying to get yourself killed." He didn't mean to raise his voice, but she was yelling at him. She should be thanking him.

Aiden palmed his right shoulder and winced. Now that the adrenaline had ebbed, his shoulder was beginning to throb.

Sadie reached out a hand. "Are you okay?"

"Fine," he said. "Probably just a scratch." The pain wasn't intense. After the bike wreck, *intense* took on a whole new meaning. Nothing before or since had hurt worse than his back after he'd played chicken with a tree...and lost.

He pulled his hand away to find red liquid on the tips of his fingers.

"Aiden!" Sadie clasped his wrist. "You're bleeding!"

Pshaw. Merely a flesh wound. "I'm fine."

Sadie's frown deepened and she latched onto his wrist, dragging him with her as she sidestepped various mufflers, oil filters, and dash panels scattered across the floor. "Where is a first aid kit?" Her grip was tight for a little thing. She was squeezing his forearm so hard he wasn't sure if he wanted her to give him first aid.

"I'm fine." He stopped walking and she sent him a glare over her shoulder. "Bathroom," he said, giving in and gesturing to the right.

Sadie led him in and opened the mirrored medicine cabinet, rooting around until she found bandages. "Sit," she commanded, pushing him onto the toilet seat. She wet a pile of paper towels and turned back to him, plucking the edge of his shirt. "Off."

"You're bossy, do you know that?"

"Take your shirt off, Aiden."

What he wouldn't give for her to be purring that into his ear instead of barking it at him like a drill sergeant. No, actually, that worked, too. He hid his smile as he tugged the neck of his shirt and pulled it over his head.

Sadie dabbed at the cut, her ministrations gentle. "I had it," she said, her voice soft. "You just scared me."

"You did not," Aiden said, winding his shirt in his hands. She swiped again and he sucked air through his teeth, frowning over his shoulder at her.

She gave him a tight smile. "Sorry."

Aiden turned back around. "Next time you need something back here, ask for my help."

She switched from a wet paper towel to dry. "You were busy," she bit out.

Aiden kept his head down so she couldn't see the curve of his lips. So he hadn't imagined her reaction. Her *over*reaction. How interesting.

He heard the tear of paper, saw the movement out of the corner of his eye, and waited for her to lay the bandage over his cut and give it a pound with one fist. Instead, she laid it on his shoulder and used gentle pressure to secure it at the edges.

He turned his head slightly, weighing his next words. "Sonya's married. That was her *husband's* phone number she gave me so I could call him about a special order."

"I don't know what you're talking about," she said.

"Sadie..." But her fingers moving away from the bandage drawing a long, slow line down his back made him forget what he was going to say. She was following the trail of his scar, he guessed. Most of it was numb from the nerve damage, but then, she knew that already.

She'd touched him like this before, the morning he'd woken next to her. The morning he left to pick up breakfast to keep himself from begging her to make love to him. He didn't think he'd ever wanted someone as badly as he wanted Sadie.

He still wanted her.

Her fingertips veered to his side, probably tracing one of the thorny branches of the tattoo wrapping around to his back.

"When did you get this?" she asked quietly.

"A couple of months ago."

Her fingers continued down his ribs. "Can I see it?" She sounded pained to ask.

"Sure."

He stood and lifted his arm, giving her a view of the ink running the length of his flank. After Mom died, the subject of his first tat was a no-brainer. A red rose bursting from a tangle of thorny vines. The thorns signified hardship, the red rose his mother.

Sadie traced the flower, and Aiden swallowed hard. He missed her touch. His fist closed around the shirt in his hand as he gritted his teeth.

She stroked his skin, having no idea she was turning him inside out. "Your mom's roses."

God, how this woman got him. "Yeah," he said, swallowing around a lump in his throat. "A heart with the word *MOM* in it seemed a little cliché."

He heard her blow air from her nose, an attempt at a laugh that didn't quite make it.

She laid her palm flat over the rose and the warmth expanded from his belly to his chest where it wrapped around his heart. He lowered his arm, trapping her hand against him. The expression on her face, a mixture of sorrow and longing, nearly dropped him like a sack of grain.

He closed the distance between them, bringing up a hand to cup her chin as he thumbed her bottom lip. He had so many things to say. Like how sorry he was, how he'd do anything to take back the day he'd lost her for good. How he wanted her with an intensity time and space hadn't been able to lessen.

And God knew how he'd tried to stop.

"You should put on a clean shirt," she whispered, not speaking the words he read so easily in her eyes.

"You should kiss me," he murmured.

Her eyes sank closed as her hand gripped him tighter. Aiden kept hold of her face, lowering his head to her glossed lips. The sweet scent of strawberry rolled off her mouth, and he wondered if her waiting tongue tasted as sweet...

"Everything okay back here?" a voice bellowed through the warehouse.

Sadie's eyes snapped open.

Aiden stood over her, debating whether or not to kiss her even though Axle's head would appear in the doorway in a second.

She pulled away from him before he could and busied herself by cleaning up the paper towels and washing her hands.

Axle poked his head in, his face an Easter Island statue. He took in Sadie's flushed cheeks and Aiden's state of undress and his eyes widened a fraction. "Lose your shirt?"

"Nope, he's got it right here," Sadie lifted Aiden's hand holding his soiled shirt and pressed it over his bare chest. He could still see the heat in her eyes. Heat he'd put there.

Aiden glanced at Axle. *He couldn't have given me five more seconds?* Sadie licked her bottom lip. The lip Aiden had nearly had between his teeth a moment ago. *Okay, ten more seconds.*

Sadie stepped away from him. "We had a minor accident. I had to patch him up," she told Axle, her voice forcibly casual. Aiden considered dropping a kiss onto her lips just to see what she'd do, but Axle's surly presence was sort of ruining the mood.

Aiden walked for the door and Axle backed out of the doorway to let him by. "Thanks for the first aid," he said to Sadie.

"Thanks for saving me," she said, her lips twitching into a smile. "I had it."

Instead of arguing, he decided not to let an opportunity as ripe as this one pass them by. "I never gave you an answer," he said.

Her eyebrows pinched over her nose in the cutest look of confusion.

"I'd love to go to lunch with you." He grinned at her as he backed away from the bathroom. "I'm going to change."

CHAPTER FIVE

Sadie pressed her tongue against the back of her teeth to keep from responding.

She wasn't about to argue in front of Axle. Aiden had used her own trick against her, roping her into lunch. Sadie was torn between being upset and impressed. She probably deserved it after the way she'd forced Aiden into signing the contract.

Axle either hadn't noticed or didn't care. Sadie didn't know how. The small bathroom where he'd discovered his manager and parts supplier standing way too close to each other, one of them missing their shirt, snapped with sexual energy.

Sadie paced through the warehouse to the overturned box and scattered parts. Axle lowered to his haunches to help her clean up, but Sadie waved him off. "I got it, really."

With a scowl that said he'd rather help her than not, he stood. "Sure?"

"I'm sure." She smiled. Axle may not look the gentlemanly type, but he was. "I need to arrange them in a certain order," she lied. What she needed was a moment alone. Some time to calm the jittery shake radiating through her limbs.

With one last glare at the mess at her feet, Axle stalked off.

Sadie turned the box over and started piling parts into it. When she'd instructed Aiden to take his shirt off, she knew what to expect. Golden flesh, fair hair covering his pecs and leading down to firm abs, a scar bisecting his otherwise perfect back.

The scar was less angry now. The red had faded to pink, the edges white. Until she traced it with her fingers, Sadie had been sure that like the scar on his back, she was healing, too. That she'd grown numb where Aiden was concerned.

Nothing could be further from the truth.

From the moment he embraced her to keep a fifty-pound box from emptying onto her head, to the way he looked into her eyes and demanded she kiss him, Sadie had been nowhere near numb.

And spotting that point of black-blue ink peeking out from his side, realizing what it represented...the pain of losing Aiden washed over her as fresh as if it'd happened a minute ago instead of a year ago.

The tattoo. Thorns and vines crisscrossed down his side, from the top of his ribs, and disappeared into the waistline of his pants. Thorns signifying pain. Struggle. Loss. Then the bright spot of color, the red of his mother's roses, a symbol of her beautiful if brief life. And Aiden's gorgeous body a worthy canvas for the artwork.

She couldn't keep from touching him. As if she could ease the pain the thorny expanse represented with her palm. Her hand on his skin invited the heat of his gaze on her lips and the look in his eyes brought reality crashing down around her.

He still cared about her.

She didn't know how that made her feel. Hopeful, maybe? And fearful. Definitely some of both.

Being in his arms again, feeling his thumb brush her lip, reminded Sadie that once upon a time, she'd had it good. For a few isolated days last summer, she'd had more understanding, undeniable attraction, and connection than she would have dared to pray for.

Enough.

Sadie dropped the last oil filter into the box and stood, dusting her hands on the back of her pants. Last year didn't matter. *Now* mattered. And right now, Aiden was her coworker—albeit her very attractive, tattooed coworker—who had goaded her into lunch.

If Sadie was smart, and she was, she'd redirect her thoughts before sitting with him for an hour. The last thing she needed was for Aiden to see the ripples of attraction she felt when she was near him.

Part of her wanted to psychoanalyze the way she'd clutched on to Aiden, had shut her eyes, had so willingly waited for his lips on hers. Or maybe she just wanted to imagine they hadn't been interrupted. That he had kissed her. That she'd kissed him back, right there in a cramped warehouse bathroom, her hands on his bare skin, the feel of his hot mouth turning her inside out...

But that wouldn't be smart.

Giving her hectic thoughts one final shove out of her

head, she walked down the hall in search of Aiden to remind him he was buying.

And he'd better not cheap out.

* * *

Sadie pushed her partially eaten salad aside, and Aiden
plucked a piece of chicken off the top and ate it. As he
chewed, he considered that he hadn't asked and Sadie
hadn't argued. She'd been pretty agreeable all around,
considering he'd conned her into going to lunch in the
first place.

"Think you're pretty clever, don't you?" she'd asked
him as they found an unoccupied table in the gourmet
deli. She'd tried to sound scathed, but he'd seen the flicker
of appreciation in her eye. He'd played her own game
against her and Sadie, on some level, liked it.

"You've kept me in suspense long enough." Sadie took
a long swallow of her iced tea. "When are you going to
tell me this big secret involving Axle Zoller?" she asked,
wiggling her fingers for effect.

Aiden hadn't brought it up over the last few days because, until today, his thoughts had ebbed and flowed like
the tide. One minute, he was ready to go all in, the next
he couldn't imagine Axle's shops working out any better
than his previous endeavor into real estate development.
He and failure were on a first-name basis.

He had the fleeting idea to keep his head down and
work for someone else for the rest of his life. It was a lot
less risky than taking on the largest motorcycle shops in
the Midwest. Then he'd think back to the six agonizing
months he'd worked side by side with Dad at the factory

after Mom passed, and changed his tune. That place ate souls for dinner, and the drudgery had nearly killed him. Dad didn't mind it. Hell if Aiden understood how.

"You have to promise not to tell anyone," Aiden said, hoping sharing with Sadie wouldn't return to bite him in the ass. This was a delicate balance he was trying to strike, here. "I mean it."

"Yes! Yes, already, spill it." Sadie frowned and a frustrated, adorable wrinkle appeared between her eyebrows.

He nearly smiled.

"When I stayed with my mom in Oregon last year, I wasn't exactly honest with my dad about how much her treatment cost."

Empathy colored Sadie's eyes at the mention of his mother, but she didn't interrupt.

"I made an arrangement with a guy at the center to send the bills, and direct all billing questions, to me. When Dad's money ran out earlier than we anticipated, I made up the difference."

He took a drink of his soda. Contributing his money had been a no-brainer. Mom had been at the facility two months by then, was looking better than ever, and, Aiden thought, had a good shot at a full recovery.

Didn't work out that way.

"I put my house on the market," he continued. "But that was more a long-term plan than anything, so I arranged to sell my vintage motorcycle collection to Axle." Aiden inhaled and blew out a breath. Axle had kept his secret. Aiden had Fed-Exed his garage key to Axle and told him to take all of them but Sheila. The money from the bikes went to his mother's stay, and when she took a turn for the worse, the remainder went to making her as comfortable as possible when he brought her home to die.

"At least Mom got to spend her final days at home... with us." He paused to clear his throat, wadding the napkin in his fist to keep his emotions at bay. Losing her had nearly killed him.

Sadie's hand covered his, reminding him she was here. Another show of support. He swore he felt the echoing heat on his ribs where she'd touched him earlier. He started again, only to trail off. "After she..."

Sadie nodded, giving him permission not to say the words, giving him an out. He took it. Even though he felt a little like his father doing it. "After...I went to work with Dad. I didn't know what to do with myself and I couldn't leave him alone. He was so...okay with everything. Never saw him cry or mourn.

"In the god-awful monotony of factory work"—he slid her a dry glance—"I had a lot of time to think about what I really wanted, what I wanted to do with the rest of my life. And one day, it hit me. What made me happiest? The answer was easy: my motorcycles."

And you, he thought but didn't say.

Sadie moved her hand back to her lap.

"Axle had mentioned his retirement plan when I arranged the sale of the bikes. So a few months back, I called him up and asked if he'd like to train me in-house and sell Axle's to me. He liked the idea."

"You're going to be the new Axle?" Sadie asked.

"Well, I'd be the new owner. To be the new Axle, I'd have to gain a hundred pounds of muscle and grow my hair long again, wouldn't I?"

At the mention of his lost locks, Sadie's eyes flared

with desire. Or maybe he was projecting. Aiden had fond memories of her hands threaded in his hair while he kissed her into submission. Of the sound of her soft mewls, the feel of her pliant lips... He shifted in his seat and searched his addled brain for where he'd left off.

"Are you buying all five stores?" Sadie asked, thankfully steering him back onto topic.

"That was the plan. Until his three-year retirement was bumped forward to three months."

"Three months!"

Aiden dropped the napkin on his empty plate. "Yeah. I'm a little shy on the down payment, and loans aren't looking good, since I have no house." He sent her a sideways smile. "And you thought I couldn't get any sexier than the divorced, jobless thirty-year-old you met last year. Now I live with my dad." He nodded, teasing to lighten the mood. "I'm a chick magnet."

A small smile played on Sadie's face, but she didn't laugh. Aiden didn't feel like laughing, either. At one point, he'd had more money than he knew what to do with. Enough to buy Harmony a booth at The Brink so she could spend all summer pretending to make a living weaving hemp into bracelets. Enough to build a bike collection he could be proud of. Enough to dump a huge portion of that money into the hotel and casino right before Daniel and Harmony had the affair.

Aiden had walked away from all of it. Had given Harmony everything she wanted in the divorce with barely a fight. Had walked away from the business he'd cofounded, the business that eventually buckled under the soon-to-be frigid economical climate.

The urge to get everything back didn't just revolve

around his motorcycles. Sure, he wanted them, but he
wanted more what they represented.

Passion.

At some point, before Aiden went into business for
the money and married Harmony for...God knew what
reason, Aiden was passionate about his life. Losing his
wife, his business, his mother, and Sadie...had sucked
the passion, *the life*, right out of him. Until the day he
was stamping holes into flat metal pieces at a rate of a zil-
lion a minute at the factory. His mother's final words to
him, before she'd grown too weak to speak, hit him like a
sledgehammer to the temple.

*You're like me, Aiden. You have this unwavering opti-
mism. Never lose that.*

Unwavering optimism. He had to sift through a mountain of refuse to remember what he'd been like before.
What better way to honor his mom, to keep that part of
her alive, than to find what he loved and make a living doing it?

"I have a plan," Aiden said, his purpose renewed. "I
just need to pitch it to Axle. If he turns me down, he'll
sell to the highest bidder...and I can assure you, it won't
be me."

Sadie's face went visibly pale. "But the Midwest
contract..." She blinked, winced. "That was selfish."

Aiden couldn't help chuckling. "We signed you for a
year, Sadie. You'll be okay for a while."

She didn't smile. "Yes, but I have a five-year plan
for Axle's. Whoever takes over might not like Midwest,
might not like me," she added, her eyebrows bowing in
worry.

"Impossible," he muttered, meaning it. He couldn't

figure for the life of him why her weenie of an ex-fiancé had chosen her sister over Sadie. He'd choose her Lava-soap abrasiveness any damn day of the week.

She ignored his compliment, eyes widening. "What if you're not there...What if Axle's gets bought out by some corporate giant who already has a national contract with another supplier? Probably 'Something' Unlimited. Motorcycles Unlimited." Her lip curled.

Aiden put a hand on Sadie's wrist to halt her tirade on the woes of corporate restructuring. "All the more reason for you to help me convince him I'm the right buyer."

She looked at his hand covering hers, then back at him, her expression hardening. "Okay." She folded her hands together on the table and the sharp glint returned to her brown eyes. "Tell me your plan and I'll tell you if it's crap or not."

* * *

"Going to see your boyfriend today?" Perry chimed in as Sadie knelt to retrieve a granola bar from the break room vending machine.

Clenching her teeth into a forced smile, Sadie stood and faced him. "Which one?"

"Touché. I'm talking about Axle. You have to be doing *something* to have landed that five-store deal. He turned you down for three years straight," Perry said, suffering no shyness when it came to reminding her how she'd struggled.

Sadie closed her fist around her breakfast, the foil wrapper crinkling. "My persistence paid off, I guess," she said as she headed for the door.

"Or maybe it's because you used to date the new guy."

Sadie halted midstep. She shouldn't turn around. Shouldn't give merit to Perry's jabbering. But neither could she let him spread rumors and tarnish her reputation. She forced a placid expression and faced him. "What are you talking about?"

"Word gets around," Perry said, not bothering to answer her. He didn't say *like you*, but his smarmy smile implied it.

"Well . . . he had nothing to do with it."

"Yeah, you're probably right," Perry said with an exaggerated shrug. "He dumped you, right? Probably doesn't take you into consideration at all."

When Sadie pulled in and parked in Axle's lot, she was still seething from her run-in with Perry. Normally Perry was flirtatious just this side of annoying, but ever since she'd landed Axle's stores, he'd been downright mean. He'd hit her below the belt this morning, and without a twinkle of levity in his eye. He'd meant to throw her off, make her stumble. She recalled the smirk on his face.

Bastard.

She stomped to the front door. It was unlocked, but the store didn't open for another fifteen minutes. *Good.* She could use a few minutes to pull herself together. Her anger was burning off and if she wasn't careful, would turn into tears. She may as well have eaten an estrogen sandwich this morning for how emotionally off-kilter she felt.

This, she could not allow.

She took a few deep breaths, sealing her emotions behind a brick wall of confidence. She could do this, could ignore the shake working its way down her arms to her fingers and causing her pen to rattle. Or so she thought. It was hard to write legibly when her body shook like she'd mainlined a triple espresso.

Giving up her note-taking, she propped her elbows on a shelf. She was grateful the store lights were off, and sucked in a clarifying breath. She visualized her anger ebbing, but it didn't recede. It persisted, simmering just under the surface. How had Perry found out about Aiden? They didn't know each other. She hadn't shared her heartbreak with anyone at work. Unless...

She had several phone conversations with Crickitt last year, especially after Aiden left for Oregon. Many of them were made from the faux privacy of her open-air cubicle. Anyone could have heard. Perry could have easily eavesdropped and mentally logged the conversations for later... to throw her off when she was getting ahead.

"Bastard," Sadie growled as the overhead lights winked on.

"Hope you're not talking about me," Aiden said, strolling down the aisle in her direction.

Sadie faced him. He looked as warm and welcome and familiar as Perry did standoffish, undesirable, and douchey. She shook her head. "Not you."

Aiden assessed her before offering her the mug in his hand. "You look like you need this more than I do."

"Only if there's whiskey in it."

"Like I said."

She couldn't help it, she smiled. And at Aiden's insistence, she accepted the mug and took a sip. No whiskey, but it did have some sort of flavored creamer in it. "Thank you for this," she said.

"You're welcome." He put his hands in his pockets.

Boy, could the man fill out a pair of jeans. "Who's giving you trouble?" She dragged her eyes from his muscular thighs to his face. "I'll beat him up for you. Unless it's Axle, then you're on your own."

"Just some jerk I work with." Her smile remained. She couldn't call up her anger at Perry. Whatever fury saturating her bloodstream earlier had evaporated, fleeing with Aiden's arrival. He watched her with those sparkling green eyes of his, half his mouth quirked into a sideways smile. There had always been something about him that calmed her, eased her from the ledge of emotions she sometimes teetered on.

The night she met him at the club, she'd attempted to be mean. He didn't let her. Simply took her hand and dragged her onto the floor, matching her step for step to "The Electric Slide." She didn't know what was more ridiculous: the stupid line dance or that the worst song ever recorded was linked to one of her most cherished memories. The thought made her pause, caused her smile to drop.

Aiden didn't notice. He'd already started toward the back of the store. "Gonna get more coffee," he called over his shoulder, reaching up to tap the doorway over his head as he walked under it. "Since somebody is drinking mine."

* * *

Giving Sadie his coffee hadn't completely erased the devastation she'd hauled into the shop with her this morning. Not that he'd expected miracles, but he made really, *really* good coffee. She'd snapped out of her bad mood for an hour or so, but after, there'd been a constant frown marring her features.

Watching her dash back and forth to the warehouse, take things off of the display tables only to put them back on, and switch out the mannequin's clothing in the front window three times (that he'd seen) was wearing *him* out. Normally she'd have left by now, to run more sales calls or go back to her office and finish out the day.

Not today, though. Today, she was avoiding something. If he had to guess, the office, and her insulting coworker.

Just some jerk I work with.

Aiden could meander on over to Midwest Motorcycle Supplies and find said *jerk she worked with*. He could have a talk with him. Or hit him. Whichever came first.

An hour before Axle's closed, Aiden spotted Sadie at the window, fretting over what geometric shape to stack the Midwest boxes on the table. She darted past him and went outside, scowling through the window at her display. Unhappy, she came back in and started dismantling the pile. Again.

With a shake of his head, Aiden returned to the chore he'd been avoiding all week. Stocking key chains wasn't exactly the pinnacle of stimulation, but it was a necessary part of running the store. He knelt and opened the box and pulled out several bags filled with assorted plastic key fobs. Each had a funny saying on it, but he'd since stopped reading them with comprehension, losing track of time in the task of filling the pegs on the shelf he'd assembled.

"'You look like I need a drink.'"

Aiden looked up to find Sadie standing at the counter,

a key chain dangling from her finger. "Is this supposed to be funny?" she asked, waving the square of plastic.

Aiden stood and unhooked the key chain from her finger. "Well, not when you read it like that." He returned it to the display and handed her another. "I do like this one, though."

"'I pray God's not too picky,'" Sadie read. Her glossed lips tilted, but more in a show of indecision than amusement. She spun the rack before pulling another off the peg and holding it up for him to see.

Mirror, mirror on the wall, make him rich and make him tall.

"Well, I'm tall." He took it from her and returned it to its peg. "But Shane's the rich one." Aiden leaned in a little closer and watched Sadie's eyes darken despite her attempt not to react to his nearness. "Sorry, he's married."

A smile tickled the corner of her mouth but rather than comment, she pulled another key chain and handed it to him.

Aiden raised an eyebrow at her. "'Never miss a good chance to shut up'?" It was a small laugh, one she recovered from quickly, but he was making progress. He turned the stile, choosing his comeback carefully. "Ah," he said when he landed on it. He slid it across the counter in front of her.

She leaned over it and read, "'Remember this face; you'll see it in your dreams.'"

He mirrored her posture. "So true," he murmured softly.

Her smile faded and her cheeks went pink.

He held her gaze. "What's his name?"

Her eyelashes fluttered as she regrouped. "Who?"

"The jerk at Midwest I need to have a chat with."

"Perry," she said, wrinkling her nose. "He thinks I sleep with my clients."

Aiden narrowed his eyes. "And by *chat* I mean *force feed a knuckle sandwich*."

"Easy, tiger." She put her hand on his arm and Aiden felt a tiny bead of sweat prickle his upper lip. If she did sleep with her clients, he'd be first in line...and pummel anyone else who dared get in line behind him.

Sadie bit her lip. "Can I ask you something?"

His eyebrows shot to his hairline, his mind still on Sadie sleeping with him. He licked his lips. "Sure," he croaked, inappropriate ideas popping in his head like a string of firecrackers.

"Do you think I muscled you into signing the Midwest contract?"

"Yes," Aiden answered.

Sadie winced.

Aiden caught her hand when she started to walk away from him. "I'm glad you did. It's fair. And the work you're doing is beyond what anyone else would have offered."

"Perry wouldn't have had to swindle you. He would have bought you an expensive gift and taken you out for drinks," she grumbled.

"You can take me out for a drink," Aiden said, suddenly wanting that more than anything.

Sadie didn't bite, pulling her hand free. "Ha-ha. You know what I mean. He would have wined and dined you. Wooed you. I offered to clean out your warehouse."

Aiden's thoughts were stuck on the wining and dining part. Or, more accurately, the one dinner date he'd taken

Sadie on last year. The date had continued through morning. After breakfast, he'd sneaked her to the back of his parents' property and led her up to his childhood tree house. Since his parents had no idea he was divorced, he had to settle for introducing Sadie to his mother from afar. Sadie had leaned against him, golden sunlight filtering through her hair, and watched his mother prune her prized rosebushes. Neither of them spoke. Neither of them had to.

It was a memory he'd never, ever forget. Sadie may not have met his mother, but she'd seen her. He considered how special that was, how anyone he dated in the future wouldn't have the same opportunity. Sharing those precious minutes with Sadie made her uniquely qualified to understand what he'd been through. Some of the tension knotting his chest loosened.

The way it always did when she was around.

He opened his mouth to ask her out to dinner. Out for a drink. Out, hell, anywhere for a few stolen minutes, but Sadie backed away from him before he could.

"I should get out of here," she announced. "Lots to do." She muttered something about finishing the display window later.

Her loud farewell was such a departure from his thoughts, Aiden simply watched as she gathered her things and walked out the door.

CHAPTER SIX

*S*adie sat at her desk, fingers nested in her hair, and stared at the invitation on the screen. Rick Hammond's Summer's Passing party happened every year. She'd attended *every year* for the last four years.

How had she forgotten?

Now she stared at the colorful website and debated which of the responses to click. There was a YES, a MAYBE, and a clever NO, I'M LAME. She considered clicking the latter. That would be the most honest response. She *was* lame.

Perry's words needled her all over again. She *had* dated a client. Granted, she didn't date Rick to secure an account, and she certainly hadn't *slept* with him. Last December, Rick had asked her to go with him to a fancy hotel party and ring in the New Year. Sadie should have told him no.

She didn't.

After Aiden had gone to Oregon, after she'd cut all

communication off from the man, Sadie had given herself twenty-four hours to recover and move on with her life. Problem was, her emotions hadn't heeded her timetable.

Reminders of Aiden cropped up everywhere, when she least expected it. For months to come. And without him, she felt empty and sad. Putting on a front was brutal and, during the holidays, nearly impossible.

Seeing people at their happiest, watching Celeste and Trey snuggle by the Christmas tree, made Sadie want to hang herself with tinsel. Add the idea of spending New Year's Eve alone, spending *every* New Year's Eve alone since she'd banished herself to the kingdom of eternal singledom for her remaining years, and it wasn't any wonder why she'd accepted Rick's invitation.

She figured she could get out of the house, have some free drinks, and pretend to like the kiss at midnight. And she did. Pretend, that is. When Rick asked her out again a few weeks later, she told herself she was okay with the idea of dinner and a movie with a man she wasn't attracted to. Look where attraction had gotten her with Aiden: riddled with holes and leaking emotion like a worn garden hose.

Rick, on the other hand, was safe. Predictable. There was no passion, but he could hold a conversation, and they had motorcycle supplies in common...

Wow. That was a really sad justification, Sadie thought, reaching for her coffee mug and taking a sip.

Almost as sad as the day she realized she'd let their casual dating go too far. Rick had extended an invitation for her to join him on an out-of-town weekend trip. When he mentioned the shared room at the Bed and Breakfast, Sadie knew she had to end it. Right there in his car, her eyes fixed on her black Michael Kors platform heels, she let him down as gently as she could. He didn't like it, but he didn't argue. Maybe he'd known all along she was holding back.

She hovered the mouse over the MAYBE response and chastised herself for being indecisive. If she replied MAYBE, or NO for that matter, it would look like she was avoiding the party because of the awkward breakup all those months ago. Which, of course, she was.

Rock, meet hard place.

Rather than debate any longer, she clicked YES and typed out a response before she could overthink it.

It read: *Wouldn't miss it!*

She added a smiley face. It mocked her. She backspaced, deleting the closed parenthesis, dash, and colon, and clicked SUBMIT before she changed her mind.

There. Done.

She shut her computer down and gathered her things, nearly bowling over Perry on her way out. Of course she'd run into Perry on her way out. This was the way her life was working out lately. She wanted to shake her fist at the ceiling, but with her luck, a fluorescent light fixture would come loose and crash onto her head.

"Do you live here?" She was still seething from earlier and hated how her sharp tone gave her away.

Perry smiled. The bastard. "Can't wait for Rick's party. You planning on"—he winked and clucked his tongue—"renewing that account?" He elbowed her. "If you know what I mean."

Unwilling to show that he was getting to her, Sadie pulled her shoulders back and skated a derisive look down his average frame. "Why, planning on fighting me for him? I don't know if he's into cocky brownnosers, but you could certainly give it a shot."

Perry flinched, struck speechless. *Hallelujah.*

She brushed by him and walked to her car. She ought to introduce Aiden to Perry; that'd get him off her case for a while.

Her lips curved.

That wasn't a bad idea...

* * *

Aiden finished scrawling a note for Axle and taped it to the cash register. A knock sounded at the front door, and even though they were closed, he half expected to see a customer standing there. It wasn't uncommon for one of Axle's buddies to swing by after close to shoot the shit. It was the kind of business Axle had built—more of a hangout than just a retail space.

Imagine Aiden's surprise when he found a petite blonde dressed in jeans and a pink hoodie peering through the glass. Damn, she looked good in pink—like a cupcake with too much frosting. Guaranteed to make his teeth ache.

"Sadie. Didn't expect to see you today." He opened the door, catching the first honest-to-goodness whiff of autumn. Soon the air would be mild, smell of browned leaves, and be best complemented by bonfires, haunted hayrides, and mugs of warm cider.

He couldn't wait.

Sadie breezed past him, interrupting his fall fantasies with the soft fragrance rolling off her hair. He didn't know what it was, but it always turned his head and shifted his thoughts to a time when he'd had her in his arms. A predictable, answering ache speared his heart.

"I...left something..." She trailed off and vanished behind a shelf, emerging waving a paper in the air. "Kind of hard to put in the order on Monday without my order sheet."

"Not if you had telekinesis."

"True," she said. "But then I'd just use my ability to set buildings on fire from afar."

"A valid point."

She flashed him the briefest smile and he considered maybe Sadie did have the ability to set things on fire with her mind. The longer she looked at him, the warmer he got.

"Well, good night." Sadie rushed for the door and Aiden followed. She'd been running away from him a lot lately. She didn't walk out right away, however. She paused at the door, rolling and unrolling the paper in her hands before opening her mouth only to close it again.

Aiden could see she had something else on her mind; he waited for her to say more. Finally, she did.

"Are you...done here?"

Aiden glanced around at the store, to the dark show-room beyond. "Yeah. Just have to make sure everything is locked up."

"Oh." Sadie rolled the order form again.

"Did you need anything else?"

"Um. Not really. I mean, not...especially. I guess I'll see you Monday."

"Sure, see you Monday."

Aiden waited until she got into her car and reversed out of the lot before turning from the door. *Well, that was odd.*

He did a final walk-through. Mack always locked up the showroom, so Aiden's double-checking was hardly necessary, but he did it anyway. Soon, if everything worked out, this place would be his. And he didn't dare leave anything to chance.

With his mind on a late-night ride, cool breeze on his face, road speeding by beneath him, Aiden walked toward his bike parked at the corner of the lot. Sadie's car pulled in when he'd gotten halfway to Sheila, and stopped beside him. The driver's window slid down, revealing Sadie chewing her lip and looking as indecisive as she had a moment ago.

"You're back," Aiden said. She offered him a tight smile. "Forget something?" Funny how she'd left minutes ago and he was already glad to see her again.

She'd turned him into a damn golden retriever.

"Yes," she said, followed by... nothing.

He raised his eyebrows and lowered his chin, prompting her to speak. She didn't. Only turned her head and stared in the opposite direction down the road. "Okay," he said. "Have fun doing... whatever it is you're doing."

He turned his back on her and counted to three, unable to keep the smile from spreading his lips when she spoke. *Right on cue.*

"Do you think I could talk you into going to a party?"

* * *

"You're inviting me to a party?" Aiden looked confused.

That made two of them.

This was why she hadn't asked him yet. She couldn't decide if she should play the angle of him setting Perry straight, or mention she needed him to run interference in case Rick asked her out again. Maybe she should admit the underlying truth. That she kind of, sort of wanted to hang out with him. Aiden was fun. And good in uncomfortable situations. She could hide behind him tonight while he charmed everyone within earshot.

"Every year a client of mine has a Summer's Passing party," she started.

"'Summer's Passing'? I like that."

"Yeah, me, too." Sadie found herself giving Aiden what might be perceived as a shy smile. Suddenly it was so important for him to say yes. Which put her at a disadvantage. She didn't like that but plowed forward anyway, her eyebrows pinched together in concentration. "There's a big bonfire and beer. I just need you for a few hours."

Aiden rested his palm on the edge of the open window. He had such nice hands. Strong, slightly rough. He was good with his hands.

"What was that last bit?"

She wrenched her gaze from his hand to his face, where she was greeted by those depthless sea green eyes. She managed to speak, albeit through a lump of lust. "Um...I need you...for a few hours?" She wasn't sure if that's what he was clarifying or not.

"You need me," he repeated, holding her gaze. The cool evening breeze sent his short hair over his forehead, and that irresistible dimple dented his cheek. Seeing it made her remember how she'd kissed it once, darted her tongue into the groove and back out again. Her heart fluttered. She did need him. In more ways than one.

"I guess I do." She forced the haze from her brain. It was only fair he knew the truth, knew what he was walking into. "The host, Rick, and I dated. Briefly," she added.

Aiden nodded but said nothing, his handsome face unreadable.

"I ended it. I don't even know why I let it get as far as I did." A flash of something lit Aiden's eyes. Anger? Hurt? She couldn't tell. "I mean, it didn't get *that far*, but I definitely went to more two-for-forty-dollars dinners than I wanted to. This is the first time I've seen him since I dumped him. And I can't *not* go, since he's my customer," she said, unable to stop rambling. "I guess I'm asking you to come with me because I need…"

"A buffer," Aiden finished.

She bit her lip. The definition of irony was asking Aiden to be a buffer when Aiden was the one she needed a buffer *for*. She nodded.

Hand still on her car, Aiden leaned his head through the open window. Sadie held her breath, watching his lips draw closer to hers. He stopped short of brushing her nose with his and she licked her bottom lip.

His voice was low when he spoke. "Why didn't you say so?"

Before she'd succeeded to pull air into her deflated lungs, Aiden was in the car, belt buckled. "I'll even let you drive," he said with a wink.

Sadie pulled onto the street, utterly distracted by the heat emanating off her passenger. Woodsy-smelling, toothpaste-commercial-worthy Aiden Downey. Right next to her. Her hands grew damp on the steering wheel. He was sitting too close, was too distracting. Operating the gas pedal and steering wheel simultaneously wasn't normally an issue she struggled with.

Maybe she *should* let him drive.

His bare arm brushed hers as he turned down the radio, sending goose bumps to the surface of her skin and her thoughts into dangerous territory. She jerked her arm, nearly veering into a cornfield.

"I was planning on taking the bike out," he said, sounding terribly calm. Being near her hadn't robbed him of his faculties. "It's the perfect night for doing something outside." He glanced her direction. "I'm glad you invited me."

Sadie flinched. She could picture him weaving along a dark ribbon of unlit road on his motorcycle. She refused to get on one. That hadn't changed since last year.

"I can't believe you still hate Sheila," he teased, picking up on her thoughts. Or maybe he noticed her absently rubbing her arm with her free hand.

"If she weren't *lethal*, I might give her a chance," Sadie mumbled.

"Maybe you should give her a chance anyway."

She spared him as long a glance as she could before returning her eyes to the road. His loaded statement seemed to be about more than her motorcycle phobia.

When Sadie knew she was getting close to Rick's house she pulled out her cell and studied the GPS on the screen. They passed a sign, then another, but Sadie couldn't read the street names despite her squinting, straining, and bending over the steering wheel.

"Keep hunching like that and I'll have to find you a bell tower to live in."

She sat up. "You're hilarious."

He grinned over at her, attractive even in the eerie blue lights emanating from the dashboard. Her pulse skittered. "Did you consider asking for my help?" he asked.

She hadn't. And it wasn't like she could forget she had a copilot. His presence clogged the very air she breathed. But asking for help hadn't occurred to her. Not once. Why was that? *Because I never ask for help* came the swift but sure answer.

Rather than examine the reasons behind her actions, she handed him the phone. "Here."

Aiden dropped it in the cup holder. "You have a ways to go."

"You know where we are?"

"Friend of mine used to live out here—Peachpine Road."

"Peachpine?" She wrinkled her nose. "Berrymaple? What kind of weird neighborhood is this?" His chuckle sent another wave of goose bumps over her arms. She liked talking to him. Even about nothing.

"All the lanes back here are a mash-up of fruit and tree names," he told her.

"Nuh-uh."

"Yes-huh. There's Grapewillow, Raisinfir, and Cantaloupe...uh, Dogwood."

His hesitation gave him away. "You made that last one up," she said, swatting him playfully. He caught her hand and didn't let it go.

"You got me," he said softly. A moment later, he pointed. "Berrymaple."

Sadie took her hand back. The slide of his fingers against hers made her want to sigh. She turned down the long lane, missing his touch already.

"Spooky," Aiden said, checking out their surroundings.

It was, a little. Tall trees shrouded the lane in darkness,

their fading leaves waving overhead and blocking out the stars. They parted to a massive field where silhouettes circled a huge bonfire burning in a clearing. Sadie angled her car into the grass and parked. Hers was one of few four-wheeled vehicles, the rest of the space littered with motorcycles.

"You didn't tell me it was a *biker* party. I would have brought Sheila."

"Yeah, well, I didn't think of it," she lied.

Aiden *tsked*. "She's gonna be mad when she hears about this."

"You have an unhealthy relationship with that bike," Sadie said, dropping her keys into the pocket of her hoodie.

"Yeah, I have a weakness for gorgeous ladies," Aiden quipped, adding a long-lashed wink. Sadie was glad the interior of the car was dark so he couldn't see her face grow warm. On Aiden, something as simple as a wink packed enough innuendo to bring the female population to their knees. And she was already showing her weakness for him tonight.

Sadie retrieved a six-pack of beer from the backseat and got out. Aiden took the beer and caught her hand with his free one.

She looked down at their linked arms, Aiden's tanned one resting against her fairer skin. "This okay?" he asked, his voice gentle.

She nodded and he gave her fingers a reassuring squeeze as they walked. At least it felt reassuring to her. Yes, he made her pulse jump-start, conjured up goose bumps, and heated her cheeks, but something about him also calmed her. Always had.

They breached the outer rim of the party, and a few people turned to watch them. She pictured what they must see: Sadie, with a tall, buff, dark-blond-haired guy. A guy holding her close to him, claiming her. She liked that much more than she should.

"Sadie!" someone behind her squealed.

"Jade, hi!" Sadie caught the tattooed twentysomething against her in a tight hug. Jade held on a little too tight—maybe for support. She smelled like a distillery.

"I meant to text you," Jade slurred. Every year they promised to catch up between Summer's Passing parties. It never happened. Sadie doubted they had much more in common than the yearly shindig.

"This year. We'll do it this year," Sadie assured her.

"For sure." She held up a water bottle filled with a brownish liquid and shook it. "I started way early." She seemed to notice Aiden and stuck her hand out, wobbling slightly in a pair of wedge sandals. "Hi. Jade."

"Aiden."

Jade held his hand longer than the social norm, then turned to Sadie and blurted, "He's superhot."

Aiden's deep chuckle near Sadie's ear caused the fine hairs on the back of her neck to stand on end.

Jade beamed up at him. "That wasn't a whisper, was it?"

He shook his head. "Afraid not."

Before Jade could embarrass herself further, another "Sadie!" interrupted them. Sadie turned to greet more once-a-year friends and introduce Aiden to everyone in as vague a manner as possible. *This is Aiden. He works at Axle's.* Almost everyone knew the place, and had good things to say about the store, and about Axle. Sadie watched in awe as Aiden answered questions patiently.

The man did not know a stranger. They had that in common. She hoped he ended up with Axle's. He deserved something good in his life. Her smile faded. So did she, for that matter. They both did.

"Sadie, hey."

She turned toward Rick's voice. He approached, a bottle of beer in each hand. "Brought you a Yuengling," he said, his smile hopeful. Too hopeful.

She heard Aiden finish up his conversation before slipping his hand into hers.

Rick blinked, out of surprise, at their linked fingers. He weighed the bottles in his hand. "I guess...I brought beers for both of you," he said, his smile tight.

"No, thanks, brought my own," Aiden said, pointing out the six-pack at his feet.

Sadie's heart hammered. "I'll have one," she said out of guilt. *Oh, the guilt.*

He nodded at Aiden. "I'm Rick."

"Aiden." He was taller than Rick, his thick hair making a mockery of Rick's thinning scalp. His *everything* made a mockery of their host. Aiden was a great-looking guy. She shut her eyes and reminded herself not to compare. Still, it was hard to accept that she was standing with the last two men she'd kissed.

There was no comparison. Aiden won that battle hands-down. At the thought of his hands, her mind wandered off. She caught it by the tail and dragged it back before it got too far.

"Aiden and I are..." She hadn't meant to start the introduction that way, and had no words to finish the sentence. What *were* they? Friends? Coworkers? She smiled thinly.

Aiden picked up the slack. And choked her with it. "Getting married."

He did not just tell Rick Hammond they were getting married. Only he did. She recovered on the outside, or at least she hoped she did. The false smile on her face felt as if it might crack and fall to her feet at any second.

"Well." Rick looked from Aiden to Sadie. "I guess congratulations," he said, trying to mask the hurt she could see on his face. "Sadie always told me she was never getting married."

Aiden squeezed her hand. Curiously, the part of Sadie that wanted to slap him had surrendered to the part of her enjoying the warmth of his palm. "She told me the same thing, didn't you, sweetheart?"

Sweetheart? That might be pushing it. Sadie gave Aiden a warning glare. He ignored it.

"How long did it take?" Aiden asked her. "Two, three weeks to wear you down?" Keeping their hands intertwined, Aiden wrapped her arm behind her back and pulled her to him. "She couldn't resist me."

He really did smell good, she thought as he brought her against the wall of his strong chest. Wait. She was supposed to be upset. Or something.

She inched away from him when Rick offered a generic "Guess when you know, you know." His smile was tight. Sadie remembered their handful of dates in January and February and felt another pang of guilt. Using someone to salve her wounds, when she knew he felt something for her, was reprehensible. Sadie should have broken it off early, or never gone out with him at all. Rick was a nice guy. A really nice guy. And she hated hurting him. But, nice or not, he hadn't made her pulse shake like a pair of maracas.

Not like Aiden.

Rick pointed out the food tables and tubs of ice where they could stow their beers and took his leave. Sadie blew out a breath, feeling like a dirty liar.

Aiden chuckled softly.

Sadie glared up at him. " 'Sweetheart'?"

"Yes, dear?" He beamed down at her.

"You shouldn't rub it in his face. What was all that about?" She pulled her hand out of his.

"I'm buffering." Aiden rubbed his hands together. "As requested."

"But married, Aiden? Really?"

Aiden's eyes narrowed. "He seemed pretty upset to hear about our engagement. I thought you said things weren't serious between you two."

She took in Aiden's stiff posture, the intense look on his face, the frown lines bracketing his mouth. Was he...jealous? Of Rick? And why did she feel a rush of exhilaration at the idea? "I—"

"There she is!"

Oh no.

Perry. He strode through the grass in loafers, sliding a hand down his ugly maroon tie. A tie and khakis. Always on the clock. Perry may have been good at sales, but he was crap at reading body language.

He ignored Aiden, a virtual wall of tension by her side, and said, "So. Did you 'close the deal' with Rick yet? If you know what I mean." He rolled his eyes, then seemed to notice Aiden. "Hey. Perry Bradford. I work at Midwest with Sadie. You in the business?"

Aiden stood, hands at his sides, and glared at Perry. "Aiden Downey, manager, Axle's," he announced, his voice as rigid as his body.

"Oh-ho!" Perry got in Sadie's face. "My God, you *do* get around."

She'd barely had time to get offended when Aiden reached past her and wound a fist around Perry's tie. They were the same height, but Aiden had the benefit of brawn and somehow still managed to look down at Perry. "Say it again," Aiden said as calmly as if discussing the weather. But he wasn't calm. His nostrils flared. A muscle in his jaw jumped.

Aiden looked mad.

And *hot*.

Perry attempted to pull away, sloshing beer onto his shoes in the process. He clasped on to Aiden's wrist, his teeth drawn back in a grimace. He forced a shaky smile. "Easy, buddy. She knows I'm joking."

Aiden tightened his hold and hauled Perry half an inch closer. "Yeah, but I don't." He released Perry a moment later. Perry stumbled, straightening his shirt with one jittery movement after the other. He stalked off, muttering something incomprehensible as he did. When he got far enough away, he threw the word *asshole* over his shoulder.

Sadie winced, worrying Aiden might tear after him and break his nose. Worrying more how she might like to see that play out. But Aiden's face had lost all rage, and he laughed lightly, his easy smile sliding across his lips as if it'd been just under the surface the whole time.

"There," he said. "That ought to help."

Sadie didn't think she'd ever had someone stand up for

her honor before. Stand up for her at all, actually. She rose to her tiptoes and grasped Aiden's neck and kissed him. Just a brief press of lips, and not nearly long enough for her taste. She lowered to her heels.

Aiden's lips were still pursed when she drew away. His hands landed on her hips. "What was that for?" he asked, his voice rough.

She couldn't look at him. Couldn't take the dark intensity in his eyes. But she looked anyway. "Thank you."

His infallible smile returned, the intensity in his eyes replaced with impishness. "What do I get if I punch him?"

An hour later they found a pair of empty lawn chairs. Sadie collapsed into one while Aiden went to grab her another beer. Jade flopped down into the chair next to her and leaned over the arm, nearly tipping it over.

Sadie held out a hand to help but Jade righted the chair with an awkward splay of one leg. "Hottie with a body is your fiancé?" Sadie guessed she was attempting a whisper. She didn't quite make it. Sadie sent an apologetic smile to a few people hovering nearby.

"Wow, word travels fast," Sadie said.

"Yeah." She glanced at the fire. The flames were no longer two stories high, making it safer to sit close. "Perry is trying to take Rick's account out from under you," Jade said with a sloppy wave. "But I heard Rick say he wasn't going to sign with that bag of dicks."

Sadie chuckled. "Did he, now?"

Jade let out a sharp laugh. "He may not have used that exact terminology."

Sadie felt Aiden before she heard him. A tingling on the back of her neck like static electricity. "Hi, Jade."

"Hi, hottie," Jade said with an exaggerated wink. "Have you two set a date yet?"

Aiden didn't hesitate. "Well, I would get married tomorrow, but Sadie wants a huge wedding. *Massive.* One that trumps the royals."

"No way, you should go to Jamaica." Jade shoved Sadie, bringing her back from blankly staring into the flames. She gave her an impatient smile. Thankfully, Jade said nothing more on the subject after that, excusing herself and clambering out of the chair. She nearly spilled out of her top in the process.

Aiden sat, eyes wide, looking shell-shocked. "Could have gone my whole life without seeing that," he joked. He handed over Sadie's beer and took a drink from his own.

Sadie didn't laugh.

"What's wrong?"

Nothing. Everything. "I don't want a huge wedding," she said.

"No?" Aiden shrugged with his mouth. "What'll it be, then? Courthouse? Vegas? Jamaica?"

She didn't feel like playing any longer. "I don't want a wedding at all."

"Well, don't I feel the fool."

"Stop joking about this, okay?" Sadie wasn't sure where that came from, but suddenly her patience was very thin. She guzzled down a few swallows of beer.

Aiden leaned in and forced her to acknowledge him. "I'm sorry if I took things too far. I didn't know."

And she was overreacting. "It's fine." She raked a hand through her hair.

After a moment, Aiden asked, "You really don't see yourself ever getting married?"

She thought of the wedding she'd planned. The caterer she'd booked. Invitations she'd ordered, then subsequently shredded into tiny pieces. The flowers she'd debated over. The chicken-or-steak option she'd been sure to include on the RSVP cards. It'd all been for naught. Wasted time, wasted hopes.

"Never," she said.

"That's too bad."

Sadie turned to see Aiden tip his beer to his lips. A wave of melancholy washed over her, almost like she regretted giving such a final answer on the subject. *So change the subject.* "What do you think about putting a second motorcycle in the display window?"

Aiden turned to her, a puzzled look on his face. "You really don't think I could talk you into marrying me?"

Sadie nearly choked on her beer. All the blood rushed from her face to her toes, making her brain temporarily seize. *No, of course not. Just say it. No way, Jose.* But she didn't. She just sat there, staring at him, eyes as round as a pair of Harley Daymaker headlamps.

"Yeah," Aiden sighed. "Rick probably didn't buy it, either." He spared her a glance. "Think I jumped the shark? Want me to tell him I lied? That I'm a client who has no friends, so you invited me out of pity?"

His careless smile was intact, but Sadie could see a dab of sadness in his eyes. She knew he'd lost his best friend when he found out Daniel slept with Aiden's then-wife. She wondered how many people he'd alienated in the process of walking away from his and Daniel's business. She wondered if she counted as his friend. If she wanted to...

She put a palm on his arm. "You have friends. You

made two or three friends within five minutes of being here. And I'm fairly sure Jade would have your babies if you asked nicely."

He sputtered, spitting beer on himself. He sent her a dimpled smile as he swiped the foam from his lip and nose, brushed stray droplets off his shirt. Sadie stared a little too long at his lips. They were slightly damp and causing an equal reaction in her nether regions.

She cleared her throat. "Whatever you do, don't confess we're not really engaged. Perry doesn't need another thing to tease me about. And Rick might get angry enough to cancel our contract."

She felt the weight of Aiden's stare and turned to find him frowning. "You're seriously worried about losing Rick's account."

Sadie wasn't sure if *worried* was the right word, but she was concerned. Who wanted to lose anything? Be it a client, a game of checkers, a fiancé… "If I do, I'll find another," she said, not feeling the conviction of her words.

"Sadie." Aiden took her hand. He'd touched her a lot tonight, and damned if she didn't like it. "You have to know people work with you because of who you are, not because of your dating potential."

She thought back to when she'd first encountered him at Axle's. Aiden had offered to sign the contract if she went out with him. "And when you tried to bribe me into dating you?" she asked.

She didn't know what answer she hoped for. While being bribed wasn't flattering in the least, the idea that he'd done it because he *wanted* to date her was. And, she realized now, even if she hadn't then, part of her wanted to date Aiden again. She'd enjoyed this evening with him.

Enjoyed the way he touched her, was touching her now, like it was the most easy, natural thing. Enjoyed the way she'd kissed him, also the most easy, natural thing. She wanted this, she decided abruptly. Even if it was temporary.

Aiden dropped her hand and gripped his beer bottle in both of his. "That was—I owe you an apology. I shouldn't have done that."

A more solid *no* could not have been uttered.

Disappointment settled on her shoulders, but she rolled them back, brushing it off, refusing to show it. She shouldn't long to be closer to this man. She shouldn't harbor any feelings for him. Not after everything he'd put her through, after everything she'd put herself through. But she wouldn't get angry or pout because he didn't say what she hoped he would.

"No, you don't," she said, meaning it. "If you apologized to me, I'd have to apologize to you. I got you to sign because I dared you to argue with me in front of Axle. Now you know my tricks," she said, picking at the label of her bottle. "Looks and bribery."

"Yeah right," Aiden said, his voice flat. "Which is why you come to this party every year. Just to keep Rick as a client, string him along?"

She frowned.

"If that were the case, you'd still be dating him. And what about Axle's? You do plenty of things that aren't outlined by your contract. Like the extra hours you spend rearranging the shelves, or when you help sell merchandise to customers. And what about the front window display? That's not something you do because you have to."

He'd noticed. He'd noticed the way she'd been pouring herself into Axle's, the work she'd done to ensure she left the store better than she found it. Her heart swelled the tiniest bit. She liked that Aiden noticed. And had pointed it out. It made her proud.

"And I know you're not hanging out all those extra hours just to be near me," he said.

That wasn't entirely true. Sadie opened her mouth to protest, but thought better of it and stayed quiet.

Aiden only winked at her. "Admit it." He leaned in and bumped her shoulder with his. "You care." He was close enough to kiss, his green eyes reflecting the firelight, his lips pursed slightly.

She *did* care. About her clients, about her friends. About Aiden. Maybe she'd never stopped caring. Eyes trained on his mouth, she found herself wanting to steal another kiss, but not the thank-you peck she'd stood on her tiptoes to give him earlier. A real one. With tongue and everything.

"And your customers know it," Aiden said. He sat back in his chair and robbed her of his scent, of his attention.

Sadie made a tiny sound of protest in her throat. She covered it by coughing. Then she sat back in her chair, finished her beer, and considered drinking about four more of them.

$\mathscr{C}$HAPTER SEVEN

$\mathscr{S}$adie said her farewells, endured a few more hearty congrats on her engagement—insert eye roll here—and walked with Aiden back to her car.

"I'll drive." He held out a hand for her keys.

"You played Flip Cup, too," she said of the drinking game they were talked into at the last minute.

"Yes, and I was disqualified after one round." Aiden lifted and dropped the front of his damp shirt. "I'm wearing more than I drank, trust me."

"I didn't have much more than you," she said, yawning. The beer may not have her stumbling for the car, but it had made her tired. Or maybe she was tired because it was after midnight. Truly sad. She relinquished the keys and buckled up. After a few lingering seconds, she noticed the car hadn't moved.

"Aiden?"

He was staring out the windshield. "I shouldn't have told everyone we were engaged." He turned his head but kept his grip on the steering wheel. "I'm sorry. It was immature. It was..." He shook his head instead of continuing. Sadie started to interrupt and tell him it didn't matter. She saw these people once a year. Next year when she arrived without Aiden in tow, she could easily pass it off like they'd broken up.

And why did that thought cause an echoing ache in the center of her chest?

"I was jealous," Aiden admitted.

Sadie blinked at him. "Why?"

"Why?" Aiden reversed over the bumpy ground and navigated onto the lane. He spared her a wry glance before turning onto the road. "Because you went out with that guy. And you *don't* hate him."

Sadie heard what he wasn't saying. "I don't hate you."

He remained quiet.

"I only went out with Rick for a few months..." She paused, understanding. She'd only gone out with Aiden for a few *days* and had fallen ass-over-teakettle in love with him. Suddenly she saw his concern. "Rick and me weren't anything like you and me," she murmured.

Never would she have shucked her bra and shirt in a steamy make-out session on the couch with Rick. And she never would have let Rick tuck her into his bed and hold her through the night. She wouldn't have let *anyone* do the things Aiden had done with her. Only Aiden.

There went that ache again. She rubbed her breastbone.

Streetlamps above cast his face in light then shadow as he drove. "I guess we were different," he said.

They didn't say anything more on the way home, and despite Sadie trying to distract herself by flipping through the radio stations, she still felt the tension snapping between them.

Tension echoing a memory of the night they met, the night she'd invited him home with her. The night they'd spilled their guts, told their unflattering tales of woe. Sometime in the wee hours, she'd walked him to the door. She'd wanted to kiss him, to touch him, all evening. Instead they'd sat, their backs against opposite pieces of furniture, and talked.

He'd stepped outside, and leaned on the door frame, watching her. "I know you only do first dates," he said. "But I don't think this counts, do you?"

Her heart had kicked into overdrive. She'd decided earlier to toss out the rule and make an exception where Aiden was concerned. To hear he wanted the same thing was...thrilling. Almost as thrilling as the idea of getting to kiss him.

She'd played it cool, crossing her arms over her breasts and lifting an eyebrow. "I think we might be able to throw it out. You know, over a technicality."

"Good," he said. Without warning he brushed her lips with his, and she'd heard the low groan of approval in his throat. When he pulled away, he tweaked her chin and smiled. "I'm not nearly through with you, Sadie Howard."

The car came to a stop and Sadie blinked back to present to find they had arrived at Axle's. She gave herself a mental shake and reminded her brain not to dwell. Thinking about the past was dangerous. Going there risked her safety, her ability to wall off her emotions. Besides, memories of the past hurt. The memory of Aiden declaring he wasn't through with her would only remind her of the day he called to tell her he was.

She'd spent a lot of time tonight thinking of Aiden, of all the good things they'd shared. If she wasn't careful, she could get nostalgic enough to wind up braless and in his bed again. Heat pooled between her legs at the memory of his hot hands around her waist, his erection pressing into her backside as they slept. Intimacy but no sex. Who knew what a turn-on that could be?

And we don't want to end up there again, she sternly reminded her inner Pussycat Doll.

Aiden turned off the engine and sent her a sideways glance. Sadie wondered what he'd been thinking about the entire time she'd sat here and thought about him.

The glint in his eye, the sexy curve of his lips, matched the expression on his face a year ago when he'd lingered in her doorway. Heart thudding heavily, she waited... waited and hoped and prayed he'd erase her mind with his tongue and the heat of his lips.

Aiden unbuckled his seat belt and leaned an elbow on the steering wheel, his bicep flexing in the pale moonlight. He locked her into place with his steady gaze. "I had a good time tonight."

She gauged the distance over the console, the position of their bodies, and undid her own seat belt before turning her body slightly toward his. "So did I."

Here it was. The dating dance. How many times had she been in this very position? Waiting for her date to dredge up the courage to lean in and kiss her, or trying to make her getaway before he did.

Though she didn't remember Aiden having to steel himself to approach her. And she certainly hadn't been planning on running. He had a way of busting through all her defenses before she realized she'd had a lapse in security.

He glanced at her mouth. "Thanks for inviting me."

Sadie nodded, licked her lips, and balled her fists together so tightly her fingernails bit into her palms. She wanted the kiss his eyes promised.

But instead of coming closer, Aiden leaned back, opened his door, and got out.

Got.

Out.

The driver's side door shut with a *whump!* wobbling the car and leaving Sadie alone and thoroughly *unkissed*. Fury simmered on her brow. Why she was angry, she had no idea, and before she wondered at her own indignation, she'd already climbed out and slammed her own door.

Aiden had crossed behind the car and approached, his hand out. His brows raised in surprise when he saw her standing there, seething. She forced her shoulders to relax.

"I was going to get your door for you." He studied her a little too intently, the quirk of his lips a little too bemused. "Something wrong?"

Other than a gross overreaction I can't explain? No, nothing at all.

What had she planned on doing anyway? Bursting out of the car and demanding he kiss her before he left to go home? "I need to get something else." She gestured to Axle's. "Inside." Worst lie ever. She'd be amazed if he bought it. "If you don't mind."

"Sure." He paced to the door as he dug in his pocket for the keys. Giving her a final wary (disbelieving?) glance before unlocking the store, he shut off the alarm code and let her in.

So. Here they were. Sadie made a show of looking for the imaginary "something" she needed badly enough to insist on coming in. She vanished behind a shelf to collect herself. Boxes were lined up in neat rows, the front window display orderly. There wasn't so much as a discarded pen or scrap of paper lying around.

She crossed to the counter, where Aiden leaned against the cash register, waiting for her. There, peeking out of a drawer was a form. A Midwest price sheet. *Good enough.* She came behind the counter, latched on to a corner, and pulled it free.

"Here it is," she announced brightly. Now she could leave with her dignity intact.

"You needed your own price guide?" Doubt clouded Aiden's eyes. Evidently, his BS-o-meter was in working order.

"I…" Sadie flagged. "I don't have one at home. I don't want to go back to the office."

Aiden's expression said he wasn't buying it. Was it too late to pretend she was drunk? She could stumble to the front door. Of course, then he would offer to drive her home and she'd get to replay that *Will he kiss me or not?* nightmare all over again.

"Well, if you have everything you need…" he drawled. The low timbre of his voice galloped down her rib cage like a troupe of Riverdancers.

He didn't mean to speak so seductively. She must have imagined it. Like she imagined the hand that looked a lot like hers fisting the front of his shirt. Like she imagined the voice that sounded like a huskier version of her own, saying, *There was* one *more thing*.

Only it wasn't her imagination.

Sadie's out-of-body experience ended the moment she pressed her lips against Aiden's for a very solid, full-on lip smash of a kiss. It was a little longer than the peck she'd given him at Rick's party. And a lot more needy. She pulled back and flattened her hand against his solid chest, her stomach flopping like a dying fish.

With a clumsy smile she hoped would disguise her rattling nerves, she said, "Thanks for driving." She'd taken one step toward the finish line—the glowing red EXIT sign over the front door—when Aiden caught her wrist.

"No, no, no," he said as he brought her to stand before him again. "That was not an acceptable good-night kiss."

Embarrassed, Sadie blurted out the first thing that popped into her head. "Why not? What was wrong with it?"

He clasped on to her other wrist and tugged her close, so close her thighs bumped his. "*Wrong* is such a harsh word."

Sadie heard herself snort-laugh, not because it was funny but because her nerves were rattling like a game of Boggle. "Like you can do better?" she asked, her voice weak and edgy.

His grin was slow, sliding into place as he held her eyes. "Definitely."

He released her wrists and skimmed his palms down her sides to the flare of her hips. His hot palms burned through her jeans as he bent and gripped the backs of her thighs. She sucked in a breath of anticipation at what might come next.

"Up," he breathed into her ear.

He lifted her and Sadie let out a yelp of surprise and held on to his neck for support. Aiden deposited her on top of the counter. She pulled her arms from his neck and attempted to put them at her sides. She bumped the cash register with one wrist and the credit card machine with the other before giving up and holding them in front of her awkwardly.

Aiden's lips twisted in amusement. "Like you haven't kissed me before," he teased, moving her hands back to his neck.

"That was a long time ago," she said quietly, heart pounding.

With her arms locked around him, their faces inches apart, there was nowhere to look but into his eyes. Eyes erased of the trace of humor they'd held earlier, replaced by a deep, dark *want* she knew reflected in her own. Aiden wrapped one of her ankles around his waist, then the other, and tugged her until her butt was at the edge of the countertop. His big body settled between her legs. She crossed her feet around him, her breasts brushing against the front of his shirt, her body humming with excitement.

"Now, let's see if we can remember how this goes," Aiden said.

Lust plugged her throat, rendered her speechless. She nodded.

Aiden clutched her hips, kept his eyes on hers as he came nearer and nearer to her lips, his pace purposefully slow. When he finally dipped his head and touched her lips, a moan of approval sounded low in Sadie's throat.

This was no peck on the lips, no, no. Aiden was taking his sweet time, his speed downright leisurely, the pull of his lips hypnotizing. Sadie was pliant beneath him. She easily matched his rhythm, savoring the faint taste of beer lingering on his lips.

Oh yes, she remembered this. She remembered *him*.

The heat of his mouth, his full but firm bottom lip. The tiny bit of hair beneath it was new, and she enjoyed that, too. Enjoyed the prickling sensation against her chin as he slanted his mouth over hers and deepened the kiss.

He teased her lips with his tongue and Sadie gave in, all too willing to open to his exploration. He swept his tongue in her mouth and out again. Then in, then out, the mind-numbing tempo sending her hormones over the edge like lemmings.

If the heat between their mouths didn't make her orgasm where she sat, the feel of his wide hands might. He slid them from her hips to her ribs, his thumbs brushing her bare skin just under the hem of her shirt. She waited for the counter beneath her to reduce to ash. For the first time since the last time she'd kissed Aiden, she found herself not wanting to stop. She wanted him to keep going— to run those wide, slightly rough palms of his under her shirt and cup her full, sensitive breasts.

Sadie needed him closer. Wanted to kiss him until their teeth clashed and his stubble caused a rough rash on her jaw. She reached for his hair, to grab the length of it and haul him down to her like she used to, but she encountered prickly growth at the back of his neck instead. She'd forgotten he cut it. And she whimpered.

Actually *whimpered*.

Aiden smiled so wide her next kiss landed on his teeth. "It'll grow back," he said against her mouth, then finished her off with one final full-lipped kiss before sweeping her hands away from his neck. He brushed her fingers with the pads of his thumbs, his breathing far more even than hers. Sadie's chest rose and fell in a stuttering rhythm, like she'd just run a mile. Underwater.

"I can tell by your face you're not impressed." Aiden sighed.

Sadie felt her mouth drop open. Her entire body hummed like a speaker blaring too much bass, and he thought she felt...nothing?

He gave her a brief wink to show he was kidding. "Although..." He ran a thumb over her cheek. She felt heat bloom on her cheekbones. "Maybe I didn't fail entirely."

He stepped away from her, taking his warm, hard body with him. He held her hands and helped her down, only letting her go when she was steady on her feet. Well, as steady as she was going to get after a grade-A lip lock.

He swiped a finger and thumb over his mouth. *His delicious, juicy apple of a mouth*, Sadie thought, pressing her fingertips to her own lips.

"I should go." Sadie backed toward the door, unsteady, her knees Jell-O, her emotions tumbling like lottery balls.

Aiden followed, matching her every jiggly, backward step with a solid, forward one of his own. "If I knew you'd miss my hair so much, I wouldn't have cut it."

Remembering the needy sound that emitted from her throat sent a fresh blast of heat to her cheeks. "I don't."

"Oh, I think you do," he said, advancing.

Sadie reached the door and grasped the handle behind her. Aiden stood over her and she instinctively flattened her back to the glass and waited for him to kiss her again. She was so sure he would, it startled her when he reached over her head and flicked the lock instead.

"You're free to go." He backed away from her an inch, giving her room to breathe. Room she didn't want. An easy smile decorated his face. "Unless you want me to drive you home," he offered. "And tuck you in."

What was frightening was that Sadie paused for a millisecond to consider his offer. Before her skin went up in a blaze caused directly by the idea of this man in her bed, she shut down the fantasy. If she kept this up, she'd have to stop, drop, and roll to get her hormones under control.

"No," she said a little too loudly—letting them both know how edgy she was—"I'm good."

She turned the handle and nearly fell out the door, catching herself in a skip-walk. She continued briskly to her car without glancing over her shoulder, twisting the key in the ignition and hazarding a look in the rearview mirror. She was so sure she'd see Aiden's face peering back at her through the glass, but found the window blank and dark.

Sadie was tired of being surprised; tired of being off-kilter. She jerked the wheel, stepped on the gas, and headed home.

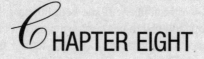

CHAPTER EIGHT

Aiden laid the bat over his right shoulder, muscles coiling as he trained his eyes on the pitcher. The machine released a baseball and he swung, smacking the ball with a satisfied *crack!* It shot into the back of the net covering the cage.

"Nice," Shane said from behind him.

"I have mad skills," Aiden said, prepping for the next pitch.

"So, you're what, dating Sadie now?" Shane asked as another ball shot out of the automated pitcher.

Crack! Not as fast, but still good.

Aiden hadn't meant to bring up the kiss after the bonfire, but since it'd been the only thing he could think about, he ended up blurting it out.

"I don't know," Aiden said, flexing his hands around the bat as he readied for the pitch. "Would you consider that a date?"

"The making-out part sort of counts."

Aiden swung, hitting the ball on the bottom of the bat. It hit the dirt with an unimpressive *thud*. He frowned at the ball, then at his smartass cousin. "Okay. Well, I guess we're *sort of* dating."

Aiden lifted the bat again.

"Do you love her?"

Whiff! Swing and a miss. The automated pitcher whined to a halt, signifying the final ball.

"That was going to be a home run," Aiden said, casting Shane an agitated glare.

Shane drank the remainder of his orange Gatorade rather than comment.

Aiden stepped out of the cage, tugging the glove off his fingers. "What do you know, anyway?"

Shane waggled the hand his wedding band rested on.

Aiden rolled his eyes.

A kid, probably thirteen or fourteen, stepped up to the cage entrance. "You guys done yet?" he asked, impatience outlining his every word.

"Yeah, kid, have at it," Aiden answered. He and Shane left the cages and walked across the park to a food stand. They took a seat at an empty picnic table and wolfed down hot dogs, washing them down with semicold beer.

"So, do you?" Shane asked, swallowing his next bite and lifting his eyebrows. "Love her?"

Aiden stopped chewing.

You do. Admit it.

"I don't think I ever stopped," Aiden heard himself say. He waited for Shane to lecture him for being stupid, or laugh for the same reason. Instead, he nodded.

"Crickitt was right." He swiped his napkin over his mouth, balled it up, and dropped it onto his plate. "How is she always right?" he marveled, looking a little peeved.

Aiden would have chuckled at the sight of Shane be-sotted over a woman, but the fact that Shane and Crickitt obviously discussed his love life when he wasn't around curbed the urge. "What do you mean? Did Sadie say something?"

Aiden had today off work, which had given him the morning to himself to replay the feel of her warm body against him, to recall the heat from her tongue tangled with his. And that moan. The needy moan coming from the back of her throat that nearly rendered him her indentured servant. It'd taken all he had to keep his cool, to let her walk away. To not follow her home—and follow her *in*.

Shane lifted his plastic cup and chuffed. "Like Crickitt would tell me what those two talk about? She knows it would get right back to you."

Aiden's frown deepened. That wasn't very comforting.

"But no, I don't think she and Sadie have spoken or seen each other since last week."

Aiden lifted his own cup and took a drink, but the alcohol was doing little to help him relax. His cell phone rang, and he pressed a button. "Yeah."

Axle's voice boomed from the other end. "I need you to come in today."

Aiden noted he didn't ask. Wasn't like Aiden had plans anyway. And Shane was on borrowed time, heading home within the hour to report for some unnamed husbandly duty. Aiden suppressed a smile when he thought back to Shane telling him he was looking forward to getting home to Crickitt. His loyalty didn't surprise Aiden, but that his self-proclaimed bachelor cousin was pretty darn good at marriage kind of did.

"I can be there in an hour," Aiden told Axle.

"Good." Axle ended the call without a good-bye.

"What's up?" Shane asked.

"Work."

"Well, good," Shane said, polishing off his beer. "You could use the distraction." Shane gave him a knowing grin.

The smartass.

* * *

Sadie stood in front of her full-length mirror, shoulders slumping as she evaluated her outfit. "How the hell am I supposed to dress for this thing?" She focused on the reflection of Crickitt, who perched on Sadie's bed in the background.

She shrugged. "I liked the black one you tried on first."

Sadie yanked the floral patterned dress over her head—far too festive for Celeste's country club birthday brunch—and tossed it onto the floor. If she dared wear anything other than blend-in-with-the-woodwork beige, Celeste would feel upstaged.

Snatching the black dress off the bed, Sadie slipped it over her head and tied the belt at the middle. It was low-cut and short, showcasing her large breasts and an ample amount of thigh. "I look slutty."

"You look beautiful."

Sadie turned from the mirror.

"And why not show Trey what he's missing?" Crickitt suggested. God, she looked happy. Like sunshine bursting from the clouds. Sadie was happy for her . . . and a smidge envious. Which was an awful, awful thing to think.

"Trey doesn't even *see* me when Celeste is around." Not that she wanted him to. Sadie was over him with a capital O-V-E-R. But her best friend knew her well, and because it stung to be discarded in favor of someone else, Sadie did kinda want to rub in the fact that she still had it. Just a little.

She strode to the bed, where jewelry was spread across her comforter. "Which one?"

Crickitt handed her a chunky, clear beaded necklace and bracelet. "These."

Sadie clasped the lobster-claw enclosure at the back of her neck and slid the bracelet onto her wrist. "When does the contractor come?"

"Two."

"When can we swim in it?"

Crickitt twisted her lips. "He's just there to do measurements. Then they have to enclose the room, dig a hole, fill it with water...probably not until late fall."

"You poor dear. Can't you throw another million at him and demand to have your indoor, heated pool by morning?"

Crickitt laughed, pushing herself off Sadie's bed. "I should try. Grease the wheels a bit."

Sadie faced the mirror again, swiped clear gloss over her lips, and smoothed her sleek ponytail for the umpteenth time. "There," she said, turning to Crickitt. "Do I look put together? Like nothing either of them say or do could break through my CoverGirl foundation?"

"You'll be great." Crickitt gave her a one-armed hug and gathered her purse. "I'm off to bribe a contractor," she called as she headed down the stairs.

With Crickitt gone, Sadie's smile faded. If Sadie

hadn't answered her mother's jolting early morning phone call, maybe she could've avoided this entire scenario today.

She could have slept in and continued the delicious dream she'd had about Aiden. One where he did all the things she wished he would have last night. Right there in Axle's store. On the countertop. Against the display stands.

She focused on her reflection, on the rogue glint in her eye, and blinked. There was the saucy, confident person she knew and loved. Funny how her mother, with a phone call, with one pointed barb, had managed to snuff out Sadie's self-assuredness. She sneered as her mother's words drifted back to mind.

Darling, do try and behave yourself where Trey is concerned.

Behave *herself*? Sadie *always* behaved herself where Trey was concerned. She was surprised she didn't resemble a Macy's Thanksgiving Day float after all the pride she'd had to swallow. She had friends who wrote off siblings for smaller crimes than fiancé stealing. Not that anyone in her bloodline gave her credit for taking the high road.

Sadie grabbed her purse and keys. She'd better get going if she hoped to find Celeste's gift (one-hundred-dollar limit so graciously set by Celeste herself), and get to Meyer Inn Country Club with enough time to down a glass of champagne before everyone arrived.

* * *

Sadie was late.

While shopping for Celeste's favorite perfume, Sadie

had been sidetracked. She stepped out of her car and smiled down at her new black and ivory peep-toed heels, complete with Swarovski crystals along the toes. The store didn't have her size, so she had to drive across town to another location to pick them up. Sadie slung her new Kate Spade bag over her shoulder—hey, a girl had to accessorize—and walked, head held high, Celeste's gift bag dangling from her finger.

Looking fabulous was half the battle won. The shoes were nonnegotiable.

Trey had brought Sadie to Meyer Inn countless times when they were dating. Usually to meet his parents for some pithy meal or other. For a passing second, she considered calling and asking Aiden to play her fiancé again. He'd done a stellar job at Rick's party, and she'd like to see Trey's face when she walked in with someone handsome and confident on her arm. In the end, she opted out. Not only would she have to deal with the aftermath of the countertop kiss, but she'd also have to deal with Celeste pouting over her birthday thunder being stolen. And Sadie introducing Aiden to her family would cause a *severe* thunderstorm.

Inside she spotted the back of her mother's coiffed platinum hair and explained to the hostess she'd walk herself back. She weaved around a waiter, past a flaming tray of Baked Alaska, and spotted Celeste and Trey. Smile pasted firmly on her face, she raised a hand to wave, the action frozen midway when the couple next to Trey came into view. Trey's mother and father craned their necks around to shoot daggers at Sadie. Sadie's smile dropped like dice on a Craps table.

She hadn't seen Trey's parents since Celeste and

Trey's wedding. They'd made it clear then whose side they were on.

Trey's. *Natch.*

Sadie survived brunch. Barely. She downed a mimosa, mumbled apologies to her mother, who repeatedly reminded her she was late for "Celeste's big day," and was tempted to order a second glass of champagne and orange juice. She refrained. Champagne gave her loose lips and, in her state of frustration, Lord only knew what might bubble out of her mouth.

After dessert was served—chocolate soufflé with raspberry sauce and white chocolate shavings—Celeste tapped her water glass with a fork. Her wide blue eyes were her father's, Sadie's stepfather's, but she and Celeste shared their mother's fair hair, fair skin, and petite figure that nipped in at the waist and swelled in all the right womanly places. Celeste was shorter than Sadie, which was a feat considering Sadie barely hit five two, and her hair was shorter, a sloppy pixie cut Sadie would have never been able to pull off.

"Thank you all for coming out for my birthday," Celeste squeaked in a small voice that made her sound cherubic and adorable, like an angel. *A fiancé-stealing angel*, Sadie thought with a snort. See? Had she ordered a second mimosa, she'd have announced that last thought.

"Trey and I asked you all here not only because I'm turning twenty-six—"

Bitch.

"—but also because we have a big announcement to make."

The raspberry Sadie popped in her mouth turned rancid on her tongue. There were only two words that could follow that kind of a statement, so it came as no surprise when Celeste said, "We're pregnant!" and *squeeeed* high enough for dogs to hear.

Expecting the announcement of a bun in the oven hadn't made it any more palatable.

Celeste dug out the blurry ultrasound pictures, and Sadie quickly planned her exit. Trey was glowing. Frickin' *glowing*. She realized then the reason it irritated her to see how happy he was with Celeste. His happiness further broadcasted how Sadie had failed to please him.

"It's got your nose!" Trey's dad joked about the indiscernible blob on the photo.

"Do you know the sex yet?" his mother asked.

"Not yet. We're only twelve weeks," Celeste said, nuzzling her husband.

Yeah. Sadie needed to get the hell out of here. She turned to say good-bye to Mother, but something about Miriam DeWalt's stalwart expression made her pause. Shouldn't she be weeping tears of glorious joy? Her perfect daughter had married the perfect son-in-law and they were having a perfect baby. Instead, Mother sat with her hands folded in her lap, a contented smile on her thin lips.

"You knew!" Sadie whispered the accusation, not that anyone could have heard her over the celebratory racket at the other end of the table.

Sadie's mother shrugged. "She had to tell someone, darling."

And not her, Miriam implied. Not the jilted, bitter older sister. As usual, Sadie was the last to know. Just like when Celeste and Trey had begun spending extra time together on the patio at her mother's house. Just like when Trey had asked Sadie's stepfather for Celeste's hand in marriage before he'd broken off the engagement with Sadie. Just like *now*, when Celeste had made sure Sadie was in a position where she was forced to behave while being skewered with the news that not only was her younger sister married *and* pregnant before her, but would hence be bearing the child of the fiancé Sadie had failed to keep at her side.

Sadie stood from her seat so abruptly, everyone at the table turned toward her. "I have an appointment," she muttered, silently adding, *with a very big bottle of wine.* "Happy birthday, Celeste."

Sadie dropped her napkin over her dessert while Celeste did her impersonation of downtrodden, *Woe is me* Eeyore. Sadie spared a glare for her turncoat mother before marching for the door. "Thanks for the meal."

She almost made it to the exit when Trey's voice rang out behind her. "You can't be happy for us, can you?"

She turned to face him, sliding her sunglasses onto her nose in the process. "I beg your pardon?"

Trey led her by the elbow into the coat closet. She let him. "Your sister just announced she's having a baby."

"Yes, I heard."

Trey let out a humorless laugh. "Don't you think the sisterly thing to do would be to offer to throw her a baby shower? Or, I don't know, say you can't wait to be an aunt? At the very least, offer your congratulations?"

"I'll send a greeting card," she snapped. "She should have told me. I should have known before today." And that was the key, wasn't it? The emotion causing her gut to swirl and her eyes to burn had nothing to do with the fact that Celeste was ahead of Sadie in life and had everything to do with hurt. Celeste hadn't come to her. Her only sister.

"This isn't being done *to* you, Sadie. Celeste and I are bringing a child into the world. This moment is about us."

Sadie ground her teeth but she couldn't keep from saying, "Oh, that part I got, Trey. It's *always* been about you and Celeste." When she'd learned of their affair, Trey had framed it that way, too. *Celeste and I didn't mean to fall in love. But we are. We deserve happiness.*

Meanwhile, Sadie deserved what? To be left at the altar? To dismantle the wedding she'd planned brick by brick while Trey enjoyed his new fling? Only it wasn't a fling. It'd turned into an engagement. A wedding. And now a baby.

Sadie turned to leave but Trey blocked the doorway with one outstretched arm. "Wrong again, Sadie," he said. "Things have always been about you."

"Well, this has been nice," she said, her voice dripping with derision. She pushed his arm away and he backed up, staying in front of her as she walked.

He lifted his hands. "Wait. I'm not berating you. Let me finish, please."

Sadie didn't want to let him finish, but she also didn't want him chasing her out of this coat closet and making a scene. If her mother and Celeste saw them arguing, they would pounce on Sadie in tandem. Resigned, Sadie crossed her arms and shot out one hip, letting Trey know he had a very, very limited window to dispense whatever speech he had in queue.

"When I asked you to marry me, I meant it," he said. "I know to you, it seemed very spur of the moment because it was a random afternoon in a mall, but I assure you, I'd had it planned for at least a year."

She blinked behind her sunglasses, digesting the new scrap of info.

"We got along well, were great friends, things were good between us. So I thought, why not now, you know? What are we waiting for? After dating for almost two years, I figured we'd end up married anyway."

Well. Not exactly a profession of undying love, but then, what did she expect?

"But after the engagement, Sadie . . . well, I don't want to use the term *bridezilla*, but—"

The word sent her defenses sky-high. Even as she uttered a harsh "I was not," part of her wondered if Trey had a small, barely discernible, itty-bitty smidge of a point.

"Our engagement turned into your project du jour, and you know it. The three-ring binder you had under your arm twenty-four seven was more your fiancé than I was."

Ah, the binder. She loved that binder. Tabbed markers separated everything from color swatches, flower ideas, dress designs, cakes, and the vows she'd written for both of them. She'd cataloged and detailed the menu choices and had chosen meals specifically based on the food intolerances of her guests. Sadie had made it her mission to have a complaint-free wedding. A perfect wedding.

"You were so wrapped up in the planning," Trey said, snapping her out of her memories *of* the planning, "I'm not sure you would have noticed if it was me waiting for you at the end of the aisle or someone else."

Sadie frowned. "I *had* to be wrapped up in the planning, Trey. You wouldn't lift a finger to help out."

"Not true." His calm, collected demeanor was grating her nerves. "Remember the appointment for the photographer? The appointments for *several* photographers? I went, and you steamrolled over me, choosing the package you thought was best, choosing the price point you thought was best."

"But you told me to spend whatever I needed," she said, clinging weakly to her position.

"And I meant it." He touched her arm. "It wasn't about money, Sadie. It was about the time we weren't spending together. Once you painted a bull's-eye on becoming my wife, you were so laser-focused, there wasn't any room left for me in your life. Cripes, we saw so little of each other, it was like we'd broken up. Remember the weekly dinners at your mother's house? When you bothered to show, it was an hour late, and you made calls on your cell phone half the time you were there."

Sadie shook her head, but the movement didn't hold much conviction. Probably because, while she wasn't about to admit it aloud, Trey was right. She hadn't attended many of Mother's Sunday dinners during that time. Once the fifteen-month marathon leading to her walk down the aisle had begun, there simply hadn't been enough time to do it all…

"It worked out for the best," he said, patting her arm. "I know you still resent me for ending it, but you should know it's because of you I found Celeste, the woman I was meant to spend the rest of my life with."

Ouch. Sadie was tempted to look down at her gut for a protruding knife. She sure as hell felt one there.

"Admit it." Trey slid his hands into his pockets. "You didn't want to marry me. The wedding was another task to check off your list, a chance for you to impress everyone you knew."

The knife twisted. She wasn't going to stick around long enough to have it removed and jabbed into her again. Sadie elbowed past him and encountered Celeste in the foyer.

"Darling?" Celeste said as Trey joined them. "Everything okay?"

"Peachy," Sadie answered for him.

Celeste frowned, a *darling* little line denting her forehead, and cradled her flat abdomen.

"Someday, Sadie," Trey said, pulling Celeste against his side and wrapping a protective arm around her, "we hope you will be a part of your niece or nephew's life. Even if you can't truly be happy for us."

Sadie turned her back on them and stomped outside before her brunch made an encore appearance.

CHAPTER NINE

Turns out one of Axle's friends-slash-customers was remodeling a 1957 Panhead and, in the process of dismantling it, realized he wasn't able to *re*mantle it. Axle had called Aiden in to close and gone out to offer his advice and expertise.

Aiden made a mental note to up his A game. When he was running Axle's someday—*think positive*—he wanted to keep the personal touches Axle added. Well, as personal as Axle got.

The remaining work hours had flown, and thoughts of Sadie had only managed to increase with the hours that passed. He was standing at the counter, where he'd kissed her rather thoroughly last night. So, yeah. *Thoughts.*

At five he locked up, looking forward to a lengthy ride. Somewhere outside of the city, where the trees lined the roads and the traffic was sparse. He thought about asking Dad to go, then thought maybe he'd just go by himself. Dad. Axle. Aiden was surrounded by men who didn't talk. He wondered how they'd become friends in the first place. Maybe they just pointed and grunted at each other.

Aiden swiped his keys out of the drawer where he'd tossed them, and his hand bumped into an object in its recesses. He pulled the square something out of the drawer, a pink cell phone with a sparkly pink case. He smiled. The ultrafeminine phone could only belong to one woman. A woman who had the shoes to match.

Aiden slid it into his pocket, deciding to stop by her apartment and drop it off. He'd like to see her today. Hell, he'd like to see her *every* day. Maybe he could talk her into joining him for a bike ride. Doubtful. He eyed a pink helmet on a shelf on the back wall. Same kind he'd bought and returned last year when she refused to climb onto Sheila.

Maybe this time she wouldn't refuse.

After he locked up the store and stowed his new purchase in a saddlebag, he rode the short distance to Sadie's apartment. As he knocked on her door, he recalled the moment he'd stood on this porch a year ago and kissed Sadie for the first time. She'd been feeling raw and vulnerable after all they'd shared; he could see it in her eyes. Aiden had felt more purged than exposed, and like he was ready to dive into the next stage of his life. Starting with the kiss he'd planted on Sadie Howard's lips.

Thoughts so mired in the past, Aiden was caught off guard by the elderly woman scowling at him from the other side of the door. She clutched her blue bathrobe and scowled some more. "Can I help you?"

"Uhh..." He rocked back on his heels and studied the number on the side of the town house. Yep. This was it. "Does...Sadie Howard live here?"

"Here, actually." Sadie hung off of the doorknob of the town house next door, leaning out over the stoop and smiling at her neighbor. "He's mine, Mrs. Norman."

Aiden couldn't keep the grin from his face. *He's mine.* He liked that.

Sadie's smile dropped when Mrs. Norman retreated back into her apartment. "What are you doing here?"

He shot a thumb over his shoulder. "I was so sure you lived at 1912."

"I did." Her eyebrows scrunched over a giant pair of sunglasses. "I moved into 1910 last year when they upgraded the kitchen."

He walked the three steps to her side of the stoop and stood in front of her, taking her in. Wow. Sadie was poured into a belted black dress hugging her curves and leading down to a damn sexy pair of high-heeled, open-toed shoes. He jerked his attention from her hot pink toenails to her face, pausing briefly at the swell of her breasts beneath the clingy material.

"You look amazing." He sounded awestruck. He was.

She rolled a shoulder. A small gesture, paired with the soft purse of her lips. "Thanks."

He met her eyes, or would have if he could've seen them through the dark lenses covering half her face. Her vulnerability was apparent in her body language. So was her impatience. "So, what do you want?"

"'Scuse me, Ms. Onassis. Should I have made an appointment?" Her nose wrinkled. Guess she wasn't in much of a joking mood. Before she shut the door in his face, Aiden extracted her phone from his jeans. "You left this at Axle's."

"Oh," she said, nothing in her tone revealing that she'd

noticed it was missing. She took it from him. "I must have dropped it when—I must have dropped it."

Aiden would have smiled at the memory of *when* she must have dropped it, but something was...off. From the slight slur in her words like she'd been drinking, to the sunglasses she was wearing, to the outfit better suited for public consumption than for sitting at home by herself.

"Going somewhere?" he asked, prepared to invite himself to go with her.

She ran her fingers through her untamed hair. "No."

Okay.

He couldn't leave her like this—all dressed up and nowhere to go. "Mind if I grab a glass of water before I head out?" Before she could tell him no, he made a face. "Think I swallowed a bug on the way over."

Sadie's lips tilted into the semblance of a smile and she slid the sunglasses into her mane of blonde hair. Her eyes were clear. So...she hadn't been crying. That was good. Maybe he'd misread her after all.

She dropped her hand from the knob and he followed her in. This town house was an exact replica of its neighbor, only reversed. The staircase ran up the adjoining wall, leading to the bathroom. The door was open, a Harley-Davidson shower curtain hanging from the rod. His Sadie, Aiden thought with a shake of his head. An anomaly through and through.

In the kitchen, Sadie handed over a water. "Bottle okay?"

"Perfect," he said, accepting it and cracking off the cap. "This"—he looked around the room as he took a drink—"is a kitchen worth moving for."

"You remember what my old kitchen looked like?" she

asked as she reclaimed her half-empty wineglass from the counter.

"No," Aiden said. "But I wasn't exactly checking out your cabinetry the last time I was here."

She pulled the sunglasses out of her hair then folded and unfolded them before setting them aside. Then she took a drink of her white wine, filling her cheeks with the liquid before swallowing it down.

No, he was right the first time. Something was up. "Are you okay?"

She met his eyes, her gaze clear, but not as sharp as he was used to. "Do you think I'm…" She shrugged as if searching for the right word. "Too driven?" she asked after a significant pause.

Aiden lifted his brow. A loaded question if he'd ever heard one. Wasn't like he could say yes, no matter what she put behind the word *too*. Too beautiful, too short, too *anything*. It was a bear trap waiting to spring.

"Too driven?" he repeated, stalling.

"Too controlling?"

Oh boy.

Aiden crossed to the counter and looked down at his hostess. There was a heaviness in her dark eyes, as if she'd lugged a significant load home from wherever she'd gone earlier. He slid a wave away from her eyes. "What's this about, Sadie?" he asked, loving the way her lips parted and her breath hitched when he touched her.

She turned away from him and stared into her wine. "Nothing."

"Talk to me."

She took a breath, her shoulders slumping even lower than before. "I guess I wanted a second opinion."

"On...?"

She looked up at him, her hurt a present, living thing. "Whether or not I am a self-centered, shallow bitch."

Anger tore through Aiden's chest at the word. He clenched his teeth together and struggled to speak through them. "Who told you that?" If it was that dickhead Perry, Aiden was going to effing kill him. Or at least cripple him.

"Easy, tiger." She grazed his chest with her fingers and smiled. Faintly, but it was there. "No one *said* it." She shook her head. "No one had to."

It killed him to see her like this—to see her so filled with doubt. She was amazing. How did she not see that? "Look at me, Sadie."

She did, but only after a long, slow blink.

He held her cinnamon-colored gaze. She needed to hear him. Really hear him. "You're not selfish. You're not self-centered. And if I hear you use the *b* word about yourself again, I'm going to wash your mouth out with Chardonnay."

Another smile. Progress.

He brushed her cheek with the back of his knuckles because he couldn't stand being this close and not touching her. "You're focused. You're determined," Aiden told her as he stroked her skin. "You know what you want. You stand up for what you want." He tipped her chin. "You are an incredible woman, Sadie. Don't ever doubt that."

Sadie turned her chin from his hand and muttered a soft "Thanks." Aiden wasn't sure if she was completely convinced, but he didn't mind hanging around to convince her if she'd let him.

"Wine?" she offered.

Hell yes. "Sure," he said, going for casual.

She pulled a second glass from the cabinet and filled it and handed it to him. Aiden took a sip from his glass as she emptied hers. She frowned at the cork sediment in the bottom like she was reading tea leaves.

"Trey said I wanted the wedding more than I wanted him," she said. "That I basically neglected him into my sister's arms."

Aiden was going to interrupt, but she inhaled to continue and he took it as a hint this was a monologue.

"I mean, I *was* busy planning the wedding. *Our* wedding." She refilled her glass, splashing wine over the rim and onto the counter. Aiden took the bottle from her and finished the pour before topping off his own. The more for him, the less for her, he figured. And she'd had just about enough.

Sadie lifted her glass and studied the pale yellow liquid. "A wedding has a lot of moving parts. You men don't know this because all you do is show up. In a tuxedo you *rent.*"

Aiden was married in jeans. In a courthouse. It had been about as romantic as a trip to the Bureau of Motor Vehicles. He thought better of correcting her and kept his lips firmly pressed together.

"I wanted to do it right, you know?" she continued. "I wanted to show Trey I would be a good wife. The best wife. And maybe I did get wound around the details, but is that bad, really? Isn't focus a good thing? Shouldn't he have been grateful he only had to sign the checks?"

She took another mouthful of wine, pointing a finger at Aiden as she swallowed. "Which, by the way, he says was not the issue. No, no. The *issue* was that I *ignored* him.

And when I stopped showing up to my family's house for Sunday dinner, he and Celeste started making out on the patio. Right under Mother's nose! He actually thanked me for ignoring him so that he could find his beloved Celeste," she said with a sneer.

It was hard not to laugh. He liked her Trey impression, the way she made him sound like a moron, which, obviously, he was. "I take it you had the displeasure of running into Trey recently?" Aiden asked.

"This morning," she said, looking for a chair. Aiden lifted off the one he sat on, slid it to her, and retrieved another for himself.

"So Trey...what? Called and unloaded a guilt trip onto your shoulders?"

Sadie snorted. "I wish. Today is my sister's birthday, and since Celeste always gets what she wants, we had a big, last-minute to-do at the country club."

Aiden couldn't imagine how hard it must be for Sadie to be around her fiancé and her sister and play nice. It wasn't fun to be left for someone else—he knew—and if it had been his brother who Harmony had left him for, Aiden thought he'd probably have fled the country by now.

"I left, but not before Trey followed me out to tell me I was being a bad sister." The pain in her eyes suggested she agreed. "I keep replaying what he said..." She paused, unshed tears shimmering in her eyes. Sadie was strong, a real suffer-in-silence type. But her control was flagging. She swallowed hard, blinking at the ceiling. When she met Aiden's eyes, hers were clear. "I think he was right."

He put a hand on her arm in a show of support. He

had so much to say, so many arguments to offer, he didn't know where to start. He'd never met Celeste but couldn't imagine Sadie's younger sister being more remarkable than the woman before him. Sadie was vibrant and challenging and sexy as hell. And if Trey couldn't see that then his head must have taken up permanent residence in his ass.

"I didn't congratulate her, you know." Sadie ran her fingertip along the edge of her glass. "I didn't hop out of my chair or throw my arms around her. I just sat there and felt sorry for myself." The tears were back, and finally a few spilled over when she confessed, "I didn't even see the ultrasound."

Whoa.

No wonder. Aiden imagined the scene unfolding. A table full of flowers and gifts, family members surrounding the guest of honor, and Celeste announcing she was pregnant. *With Sadie's ex-fiancé's baby.*

"Sadie," was all he said. Her mouth pulled at the sides as she choked back what he guessed was going to be a sob. Aiden lifted her chin. "Sadie," he repeated.

She blinked at him, stunned to have shown her real and raw emotions, and swiped her hands over her eyes to erase the evidence. She hopped off her chair so fast, Aiden had to catch it to keep it from falling over. He could almost hear her regrouping, the iron gates sliding down, the moat encircling her, the snapping alligators sliding into its depths... Sadie could shut down her feelings faster than he could say *Batten down the hatches.*

No one in her family cared to dig any deeper than the false surface she projected. It was easier for her mother and Celeste and Trey to write Sadie off as shallow and selfish and continue living their lives. They were the selfish ones, not Sadie.

Telling her that wouldn't crack her defenses and Aiden was running out of time. The first night he met her he'd accidentally lured her out from behind her stone walls. All it had taken was a confession of his own.

He happened to have a doozy.

"I feel like I could have done more to save my mom's life." Wow. Saying that out loud hurt more than he'd thought. It worked, though. Sadie stopped fidgeting with the belt on her dress and watched him instead. "When my brothers and sister found out I'd moved her to Oregon," he continued, "they were pissed."

Sadie gripped the back of her empty chair.

"Mom was convinced the center we moved her into would save her life. Angel, Landon, and Evan tried to convince me to get her back into chemo." He shook his head, remembering arguing with them in private, or via text, fighting with them as hard as he fought to keep their arguing a secret from Mom. "Mom didn't want to have chemo. I refused to hound her about it. I figured she was where she wanted to be, and she seemed a little stronger, definitely more hopeful. And seeing the hope in her eyes..." He blinked back tears of his own. "I just...I couldn't take it away from her, you know?"

Sadie rested a hand on Aiden's shoulder, her attention completely on him. *Selfish, my ass.* If she could see her face, she'd never for a second see herself as anything less than the radiant, supportive woman comforting him right now.

"When it was obvious she wasn't going to recover..."

He swallowed, felt like a bowling ball was lodged in his esophagus. "I brought her home." And then his mother, his beautiful, strong, amazing mother, lost her fight.

"She lived ten more days," Aiden said, feeling the pain of losing her spread across his chest like wildfire. "Landon, Angel, and Evan had barely had time to come home and visit before she passed." Some days he wondered if they still held it against him.

"I should have made her get chemo," Aiden said. He'd thought it a thousand times—a million times—since the funeral, but this was the first time he admitted it aloud. And hearing it now . . . *God*. He could hear the truth in his words.

He'd been thinking lately how he hadn't really fought *for* her. Sure, he'd sat in waiting rooms for acupuncturists, nutritionists, and even a hypnotist. He'd scheduled her appointments, pushed her thinning body around in a wheelchair; he'd filled out her paperwork and written checks and reported back to Dad. But he hadn't fought. Not *for* her.

"I thought I was doing the right thing," he told Sadie. "But all I did was sit around . . . and wait for her to die."

He was suddenly seeing things so clearly from his siblings' points of view. Whoever came up with the saying "the truth hurts" deserved an award for that golden nugget of accuracy. The truth *did* hurt, and right now it was slashing at his insides like Freddy Krueger.

Sadie put a palm over his forearm, and when Aiden tilted his chin down, a tear splashed onto the top of her hand.

* * *

Vulnerability was not Sadie's forte. If asked, anyone she knew would say she was as stoic as a Viking ship in gale force winds in the middle of a raging sea storm. And yet, Aiden had been here no more than ten minutes and she'd opened her case of secrets and laid them out like prized jewels.

Here you go, have a look at all my shit.

Like the last time she and Aiden had entered the bubble of safety that was her apartment, Sadie shared her unfiltered, uncensored feelings. And yes, she may have been lubricated with a glass of California white, but the moment he'd touched her face and complimented the hell out of her, she'd remembered that Aiden was a strong wall on which to lay her burdens.

When she'd first met Aiden, hot-handed, dead-sexy-smile, two-hundred-pounds-of-delicious-golden-muscle Aiden, he'd been to hell and back. Now he'd been to hell and back, and returned for one more round trip with frequent flyer miles. And he was still clawing his way out of the depths. Not that he'd burden anyone with the crap he hauled around with him. No, he was too busy making everyone else feel better about themselves.

But Sadie didn't have a problem coming to his rescue the way he'd come to hers. She kept her palm firmly on his arm and watched the single drop of salt water trickle off her hand.

"Aiden." Despite the silent promise she'd made herself not to cry again, her emotions teetered on a needle-thin point. "You did exactly what your mother wanted. In spite of what everyone else said. You were the strong one. You did the right thing."

She knew firsthand when a loved one got sick, how

hard it was to make clear-headed decisions. After Sadie's father's accident, she'd been too young to fully understand what was happening. Only that her father was in a coma and wouldn't wake up. Her grandmother had to make the gut-wrenching decision to turn off life support, and Sadie knew now that Grandma Howard had done the right thing for Daddy. In spite of Sadie's mother's instinct to hold on to him for as long as possible.

Aiden, in his own way, had done the same for his mom.

"I would have kept my dad hooked to a breathing machine forever," Sadie told him. "But you put aside your own agenda. You knew what your mom wanted. And it wasn't to spend her final days throwing up and losing her hair. It wasn't, Aiden. And you knew it." She squeezed his arm. "Didn't you?"

Aiden met her eyes. Pools of green swimming in unshed tears. Sadie's heart cracked when she thought about what Aiden had gone through in the last year. He'd put his life on hold to move his mother to Oregon, invested nearly all he had left to pay for her continuing treatment. How long had Aiden been setting aside his own wants and needs? Harmony certainly hadn't had a problem betraying him. And the strength it must have taken for him to stand firmly against his family and fight for his mother...

In a blink, she saw Aiden very clearly. Saw his abundant love for others, his deep compassion for people. His kindness. His unbreakable spirit.

Was it any wonder she'd fallen in love with him a year ago?

"God, Aiden," she whispered, stroking her fingers

through his hair. The tears came and Sadie stopped trying to quell them. "I'm so sorry. I'm sorry for all of it." Every heartrending moment of the last year, including the hard time she'd given him at Crickitt's wedding...He deserved her support. Then and now.

Sadie wrapped her arms around his neck and clung to him, unsure if she was comforting him or if it was the other way around.

CHAPTER TEN

$\mathcal{A}$iden clutched on to her shoulders, his big arms bracing her body, and buried his face into her neck. He took one ragged breath, then another, and while she didn't hear or feel the sobs wracking his body, Sadie felt his breathing grow slow and shallow, and a damp spot on her shoulder where he'd rested his cheek.

When he pulled away, he gave a mighty sniff and wiped his eyes on one shirtsleeve. In true Aiden fashion, he laughed. It may have been raspy and watery, but it was a laugh. A lesser man would be embarrassed, maybe even make an excuse to leave. Not Aiden.

"Wow." He coughed into one fist and, keeping his chin down, turned his eyes up to Sadie. "Was that sexy, or what?"

But it *was*.

"I don't make a habit of barging into attractive single women's houses and crying over my mother," Aiden said with another smile. His unflappable optimism had snapped firmly back in place. "I didn't mean—"

Sadie grasped the back of his neck and smothered whatever words he would have said with her mouth. This was a kiss of pure need. She *needed* Aiden. And she told him with her tongue in his mouth, her hands gripping his shoulders, and her breasts mashed against his chest.

Aiden latched on to her just as desperately, locking her in his arms, his tongue sparring with hers. Like he needed her, too.

I'm ready.

The thought came with so much conviction, she didn't even question it. Thirty years of waiting to have sex hadn't been easy. Being engaged and enduring a long-term relationship without getting physical had challenged her in a whole new way. After Trey dumped her for Celeste, Sadie had to choose how she felt about it—about herself. Either she could A) believe the only way to keep a guy around was to have sex with him or B) believe that if a guy couldn't go without sleeping with her, then he didn't deserve her anyway.

She chose B.

What may have started as a why-buy-the-milk-if-you-get-the-cow-for-free theory had morphed into another layer of protection. Sadie simply didn't *want* to get hurt ever again. Keeping sex out of the mix had been a no-brainer. But Aiden, while he had hurt her in the past, maybe even worse than Trey, had never once pushed her, pressured her, or been anything less than good to her. And *that*, she thought solidly, was worthy of the whole damn dairy farm.

Sadie pulled her hands over Aiden's solid chest, shivering with anticipation at feeling his hot skin against hers, of getting him out of his thin cotton tee. She lifted his shirt and ran her fingers over the bumps of his abs, then up to his nipples. They pebbled beneath her nails and Aiden clasped onto the material of her dress, his teeth raking over her lips as a low, guttural groan emitted from his throat.

Sadie smiled against his mouth, sure, *so sure*, of her decision. So sold on stripping this man of his clothes and dragging him into her bedroom.

She needed more. And she needed it now.

Fingers diving into the waistband of his jeans, she tugged him and he stood, bracing one hand on the counter, the other around her waist. He let her back him against the sink, keeping his lips fused with hers. His hip hit the edge of the counter, rattling the dishes in the drainer.

With the idea of making love with Aiden firmly planted in her brain, Sadie's actions came at the pace of a runaway train. Thrill bloomed in her belly, and lower, as she straddled his leg, rubbing her body against him while her hands explored his torso. She traced a circle around his belly button, plucked the stud on his jeans. When she reached for his zipper, Aiden's hand covered hers.

His lips curved against hers and he laid another damp kiss on her mouth before blowing out a warm, wine-scented breath.

Sadie opened her eyes, met his gaze. He watched her, his pupils wide and dark, want warring with intent. *Or maybe not*, Sadie thought suddenly. Maybe Aiden didn't want her. Maybe last night's kiss was just a kiss.

There was a sobering thought.

She stepped away from him, sliding her hand out from under his. He snapped his jeans, scrubbed his face with both hands, and ran them through his shorn hair. His tongue darted out to wet his lips and all of Sadie's girly parts sang his mouth's praise.

"My fault," he said, voice rough. "I didn't mean to..."

He didn't finish. He didn't need to. Sadie understood that he'd been responding to her and she'd gone too far. A kiss was a kiss, but sex was so much more. And Aiden clearly didn't want to invest quite as much in her as she did in him.

So...this was new. Sadie had never had a guy try and stop *her* from going too far. For the first time, she understood how frustrating it was to receive a cease and desist when things were starting to get good.

"No, geez, I'm sorry," Sadie said, rubbing her eyebrow with two fingers to partially hide her face. She gave Aiden a carefree smile and shrug, trying to play things way down.

Way, *way* down.

She straightened her dress and fished for an excuse. "The wine—"

"It's not that I don't want to sleep with you," Aiden said.

She hazarded a look up at him. He gripped the countertop with white knuckles, holding his body in check as he sent a longing gaze down hers.

Sadie shivered, the words *sleep with you* causing a flash of X-rated visions to dance merrily in her brain. Heat gathered between her legs.

"Believe me." Aiden lowered his chin, his expression

menacing in the sexiest way possible. "It's not that I don't want to."

She pressed her knees together in a vain effort to control the thrumming pulse at her center.

Aiden sucked in a breath and blew it out, as if recalibrating his thoughts. "But you have had a hell of a day, Sadie."

Right? And after the day she'd had, the very best thing for her—for both of them—would be to strip him of those inconvenient clothes and invite him up to her mattress. The thrumming quickened and Sadie wondered if anyone had ever died of lusty, sinful thoughts.

Aiden rested his hands on her upper arms and Sadie would have melted into him if not for the hand she raised and anchored against his chest.

"You're upset," he said, "you've been drinking, and I won't let you make a decision you might regret later."

Sadie huffed. Foiled again.

After he left, she was going to finish the bottle of wine they'd been sharing and open another. Maybe once she was slobbering drunk, she'd lose the needy ache pounding relentlessly along her every vertebrae.

"You'd be surprised how sober I feel," she mumbled. She took a drink, swallowed. Took another. "Sorry I attacked you."

Aiden laughed, a hearty *ha!* "Never, *never* apologize for *that*."

He was so easy to like. How did someone who'd been through some of the hardest things in life maintain his level of *easy*? Aiden brushed by her and Sadie turned to tell him good-bye. He surprised her by snapping up the wine bottle and emptying it into his glass. "Have any more of this stuff?" he asked, dropping the bottle into the recycling bin.

"Yeah. In the fridge."

"Good," he said, digging out a fresh bottle. "Because I'm going to need to come to terms with the decision I just made." He shot her a self-deprecating grin. "Parts of my body will never forgive me for turning you down."

Her smile returned.

"Only another glass or two," he told her. "If I have more than that I'll be tempted to make up a story about how I need to sleep on your couch."

She snickered and Aiden pressed a kiss to her mouth. It wasn't a long kiss and it wasn't overtly romantic, but it curled her toes inside her four-inch heels all the same.

He worked the corkscrew into the bottle and refilled her glass, sending her a wink that had her sagging against the counter behind her. Then he took both their glasses and swaggered his sweet ass into her living room.

Sadie knew because she kept her eyes on it the entire time.

* * *

Three hours later, Aiden was still trying to talk himself into leaving, and his feelings for Sadie into submission. The moment she wrapped him up in her sweet scent and came out swinging in his defense, his heart gave a dangerous squeeze.

Do you love her?

I don't think I ever stopped.

And then that kiss, and an offer he'd somehow been able to refuse. Good God, he was insane for turning her down. He was tempted to excuse himself to the kitchen and repeatedly bang his head against the refrigerator.

He wanted nothing more than to peel back that black dress and reveal her tight little body. To finally feel the warmth of her—all of her—sliding beneath him. To taste her nipples, find out what made her scream his name—

Aiden shifted, rearranging his going-for-the-world-record-for-endurance hard-on.

He'd like to convince himself he didn't love Sadie, that what he felt for her was lust, pure and simple. No doubt something any red-blooded man felt when he laid eyes on her.

He looked over to where she lounged on the opposite arm of the couch. She'd changed into low-cut jeans and a long-sleeved shirt, and had kicked off the shoes that could've doubled as weaponry. Her outfit was considerably less sexy than the clingy dress she wore earlier, but Aiden couldn't tear his eyes off her. Or those hot pink toenails peeking out from beneath the cuffs of her jeans.

He glanced toward the kitchen. Maybe after he banged his head on the fridge, he'd go a few rounds with the stove.

This wasn't just lust. There was more. There'd always been more. The way he got her to confess with no more than a word or two. How protective he felt of her. Even now, when he should be on his bike riding off his every horny thought, he didn't want to leave her. Like the night he tucked them into his bed last year. He hadn't wanted her to go then, either.

Maybe he should admit out loud, to both of them, that he loved her. But he was pretty sure, to paraphrase a famous movie, Sadie couldn't handle the truth. The thing was, Aiden *could* handle it. Handle loving her, handle slipping a gold band onto her finger, and certainly handle sliding into her bed. Not just tonight, but each and every night until they were so old they had to gum their food.

"I should go." Aiden stood suddenly, knowing if he didn't make that pronouncement soon, he wouldn't make it at all.

Sadie unfolded her legs and stood. Aiden caught a glimpse of her breasts as she bent over, the dark shadow of her cleavage and the flash of her black bra. He ground his molars.

"You sure you're okay to ride?" Sadie asked.

He nodded at the wine bottle on her end table. "My last glass was over an hour ago."

"I meant...in the dark," she said, twisting her fingers as she looked out the front window.

Aiden had ridden in more elements than she knew. Weather ranging from stinging needle-tipped raindrops to air so cold it frostbit his nose. He took a step closer to her, already anticipating a lengthy good-night kiss. "Why, you worried about me?"

"Just being polite," Sadie snapped, her tone saying *How dare you accuse me of caring*.

Damn. He did love her.

"I promise to be careful," he said. At the door, Aiden experienced been-there-done-that when he stepped onto her porch and told her good-bye. Light reflected in a halo around Sadie's golden hair. Her face was placid, angelic, and didn't reflect the heavy emotional toll the day had taken on her.

Aiden leaned in and pressed his lips to hers and Sadie

sighed into his mouth. The soft, feminine sound tore into his chest and pulled out his still-beating heart. Her fingertips grazed his stomach, lighting twin trails down his legs. He needed to end the kiss before he hauled her legs around his waist and pushed her up against the nearest wall.

God. This woman.

When their lips parted with a subtle smooching sound, Sadie uttered one word. A word that floated out on a breath, curled around his heart, and squeezed. "Stay."

His nostrils flared, his earlier good behavior incinerated by the jolt of lust hitting his gut like an electric shock.

"On the couch," she added, fizzling out the pornographic images in his head. "I promise I won't drag you to bed and make you take advantage of me."

She was teasing, but the part of him pressing painfully against his fly didn't know that. He glanced at the garden hose hanging on the brick wall behind her flower bed and considered sticking it down his pants and turning it on full blast.

"I am worried," Sadie admitted, her eyes going to Sheila, parked right next to Sadie's car. "I would sleep better knowing you were safe on my couch instead of wrapped around a tree."

The weather was moderate, the roads practically empty this time of night. Aiden didn't live all that far from her place. But those reasons paled in comparison to the gorgeous woman asking such a simple request.

"Okay," he heard himself answer. "I'll stay."

* * *

Sadie wasn't a morning person, but she found it impossible to sleep later than six a.m. knowing Aiden was sprawled across her couch.

She crept down the stairs, careful to skip the overly creaky one in the middle, and sat on the second to last step, peering at Aiden around the banister. He showed no signs of stirring, asleep on his stomach, his arm dangling over the edge of the couch. The sheet she'd given him was on the floor, his body bare save for the black briefs stretched over his amazing butt. She'd always thought of herself as a boxer kind of girl, but seeing Aiden laid out like he was had her fervently switching sides on the debate. She allowed her gaze to roam over all his tanned, tattooed flesh, liking how much space he took up, one leg nearly off the couch, his bare foot hanging off the edge of one cushion. His breathing was steady, his hair a mess over his forehead, his lips parted in the most seductive, tempting way.

She'd thought about waking him and dragging him back to her bed a hundred times last night. Just for sleeping. Just so she could snuggle against him. But last night had been volatile enough without her tossing gasoline onto an already steadily burning fire.

And she didn't want to look any needier (if that was possible). The last blow to her stinging ego would be Aiden rejecting her again. She could hear it now: *Are you still trying to get me to sleep with you?*

Aiden sucked in a breath and rolled over, his hand sliding over his flat stomach, then down to the impressive bulge hiding beneath the confines of his underwear. He adjusted himself and Sadie stared, mouth open, hand clutching her throat. She bet that part of him was as glorious as the rest of him. Oh, how she'd like to see it. Just once. She licked her lips and his hand moved away, his slightly amused voice slicing into the air.

"You keep looking at me like that and you may get more for breakfast than you bargained for."

Sadie's face went hot. She stood and wrapped her robe tighter, her movements jerky, and beelined for the sanctuary of the kitchen. "Want some coffee?"

Aiden caught one of the ties on her robe and pulled her onto his lap, where the part she'd been ogling earlier pressed against her hip. Keeping his hand fisted in the slippery material covering her, he watched her for a few agonizing seconds before his lips, rimmed in a sheen of sexy stubble, formed the words, "I'd love some coffee."

He released her and Sadie scuttled away like a frightened crab.

She popped the individual plastic coffee container into the single-serve maker and pressed a button, lamenting not having extra steps to busy her hands. The task of pulling out a filter, counting scoops of coffee, and measuring out water would have helped distract her from the fact there was a sexy, aroused man in the other room.

As it was, she could think of nothing but.

Were mornings after always this awkward? Seemed unfair to have an awkward morning after if she didn't get an exhilarating night before. How did anyone endure this unnerving, skin-vibrating tension?

Get the good part now, a newly awakened, wanton part of her crowed. Her pragmatic side agreed. She could return to the living room, drop her robe into a pool at her feet. Aiden was obviously ready to go. No doubt he'd be a willing participant in extracurricular morning activities.

Though, things might get weird after...when she had to shower and get ready for work. When he gathered his clothes and tried to make forced conversation as he backed toward the door.

Maybe it was for the best they hadn't had sex. Made love.

Whichever.

The coffeemaker finished its sputtering and she stared into the dark brew for a few seconds, recalling the morning she and Aiden had shared last summer.

"I take it black."

She turned to find Aiden standing in her kitchen, feet and chest bare, jeans riding low on his hips. And she was staring. Again. "I remember."

She slid the mug across the breakfast bar. He brushed his hand against hers as he took it. "Thanks."

Sadie's fingers tingled as she made herself a mug. She stared at the brewer rather than allow her eyes to parade around Aiden's incredibly beautiful bare chest. She didn't know how much longer she would last. This man was distracting to the nth degree. "You work today?" he asked.

"Yes. Yes I do." She emptied approximately a gallon of creamer into her mug. "You?"

"Yeah."

She blew on her coffee, took a sip, drummed her fingernails on the porcelain. Five seconds passed, then five more, circling them like sharks around an injured harp seal.

Aiden broke the tense silence. "Coming into Axle's?"

Ah, relief. A topic. "For a little while. I want to finish the display."

"Dad is dropping off my nephew around lunchtime. Care to join us at the park for a little while?"

"Park?"

"Yeah. Cordoned outdoor area with trees, grass, and the occasional jungle gym."

"Smart aleck."

Aiden smiled the sexiest smile she'd ever seen. And she bought *People*'s annual Sexiest Man Alive issue religiously. "He likes to play football. He's only five, but the kid's got an arm already."

A park. A park sounded harmless. Especially with a munchkin chaperoning them. She didn't have plans for lunch, other than eating a container of Yoplait and wrestling her hormones into submission.

"Sure, why not." She was trying to act casual, but as she lifted her mug and peered at him over the rim, she reconsidered her safety.

Five-year-old or not, with Aiden, a park was never just a park.

CHAPTER ELEVEN

Aiden's rambunctious nephew Lionel, Lyon for short—how cute was that?—tackled Aiden to the ground and roared in triumph. The kid had energy like he'd eaten a bag of Pixy Stix for lunch rather than the half a turkey sandwich and apple slices Aiden had brought for him.

Lyon may have his late mother's mocha skin and dark hair, but the unique blue-green color of his eyes resembled his uncle's. Man, he was gonna be a heart-breaker when he grew up. Aiden rolled out from under Lyon and waved his nephew farther out before he threw the ball. Sadie admired Aiden's strong legs, the sprinkling of fair hair, and the way the cutoff gray sweats cupped his butt.

In spite of the cool air, Sadie fanned herself.

"Sadie!" Lyon hollered, bounding over to her and interrupting her R-rated, heading for NC-17, thoughts. She replaced them with Disney-like dancing bears.

"Yes, sir," she said, "what can I do for you?"

"Catch!" She didn't think Lyon ever uttered a phrase that didn't end in exclamation points.

"You bet." Sadie held out a hand and caught Lyon's throw smoothly. She lined up her fingers and drew back to throw, feeling Aiden watch her, his eyebrow cocked curiously.

"You don't look like you need help with that pigskin," he said, lifting his hands to catch a pass.

Sadie pulled her arm back and tossed the ball, watching the impressive spiral slice through the air. Aiden had to back up a few steps and lift his arms over his head to catch it. His shirt rode up, flashing a stomach abbreviated by a damn sexy belly button. God bless her twenty-twenty vision. She would have hated to miss that sight for a pair of imperfect peepers.

"She's awesome!" Lyon hollered, throwing himself to the ground again.

Aiden jogged over to where she stood. "Yeah, I know." His eyes flickered to her mouth and her lips tingled. "Where'd you learn to throw like that?"

She shrugged a shoulder. "Oh, you know..."

Lyon tugged on Aiden's shirt, breaking their intense eye contact. "I'm throwing it," Lyon instructed, pointing at the ball. "You tackle Sadie, Uncle A."

"It's not nice for boys to tackle girls," Aiden said, casting Sadie a sideways glance.

"I don't know about that," she said. Which got his full attention.

Lyon ran back, ball in hand and turned. Aiden bent, hands on his knees, and Sadie narrowed her eyes at him and prepared to catch it before he did. Lyon's throw was short. The football hit the ground, wobbling in three directions at once.

Sadie reached the ball first, but as her hand grazed one pointed tip, Aiden lashed an arm around her waist and fell to the ground, bracing her fall with his body. The air whooshed from her lungs, and Sadie laughed. Before she knew how, Aiden had rolled her onto her back in the grass and straddled her.

Her laughter ebbed into a soft *hmm*.

"Gotcha," Aiden whispered.

She'd say.

Aiden lowered his head, taking her waiting lips with his. Sadie went loose beneath him, darting her tongue out and tasting the Coca-Cola lingering on his lips. He pulled away from her, something intense dancing in his eyes.

"Sadie," he murmured. "I—"

"What are you doing?" Lyon interrupted.

Aiden rolled to one side, leaving Sadie like a tree split by lightning. Sadie sat up and brushed grass from her hair and skirt.

"I, uh, was tackling her like you told me to," Aiden said. He stood and offered Sadie his hand. She took it, loving the buzz of electricity that shot up her arm on contact.

"Looks like kissing to me," Lyon grumbled, clearly unimpressed.

"How do you know what kissing looks like?" Aiden asked, winking at Sadie.

"Daddy kisses our neighbor sometimes," Lyon said with a shrug.

Aiden made a funny face and Sadie cracked up, holding her stomach as she laughed. She couldn't remember a time she'd felt lighter.

She wanted the feeling to last as long as possible.

They walked the short distance from the park to Axle's, Lyon insisting on walking between them, his hands in theirs. Aiden cradled the football and Sadie carried the food bag, and every once in a while, Aiden would look over Lyon's head and smile at her.

She wondered if she would have moments like this with her own niece or nephew when Celeste had the baby, or if the gaping distance between them would only widen.

In the parking lot, Aiden crossed to a car and a man got out. He was Aiden's height and build, with longish mostly gray hair and a scar on the side of his face. Lyon let go of Sadie's and Aiden's hands and yelled, "Grampa!" The man embraced Lyon, a proud grin on his rugged face.

"I'm going to go in." Sadie gestured toward the store.

"Not yet." Aiden clasped her hand and tipped his head in his father's direction. She tensed as they approached and Aiden must have noticed. He squeezed her hand and pulled her close. "Dad."

Sadie couldn't tell if the older man was happy about his son holding her hand or not.

"This is my dad, Mike." Aiden nodded at his dad. "This is Sadie."

Mike's face split into a smile, and the scar on his face pinched behind his sunglasses.

Sadie tried not to stare. "Nice to meet you."

"Never thought I'd meet you," Mike said with a sideways smile reminding her of Aiden's.

"He means he's glad to finally meet you." Aiden shot his dad a warning look.

"Yeah. Was sorry to miss Shane's wedding. Couldn't make it down." He pointed to his face. "Freak muffin tin accident."

"Dad," Aiden mumbled.

"I kid." Mike's mouth curved. "It was a pizza cutter." Sadie allowed herself to laugh. Clearly that was Mike's goal. Before Aiden could reprimand him again, he said, "I hear it was a nice wedding."

"Very," she agreed, feeling guilty all over again for the way she'd ignored Aiden. A fresh wave of embarrassment crashed over her when she recalled how much she'd drunk, how she'd asked Aiden to undress her. He'd not only undressed her, but redressed her and tucked her in. How could she have been so mean to him after all he'd done for her?

"You're as beautiful as he said." At Aiden's penetrating stare, Mike only shrugged. "Just tellin' the truth, son."

Four hours later, Sadie was sorting through the final box in the warehouse when she caught a glimpse of Goliath out of the corner of her eye. She tipped her head and smiled at the mountain before her. "Hi, Axle."

"Window looks good," he said.

"Thank you." While digging in the warehouse, she'd found the mannequin's missing arm and a female mannequin wedged in a corner behind some old signage. Sadie arranged the now fully limbed male and his new mate next to the custom Harley, placed a map on the seat, and drew a path with red marker. She accessorized with matching helmets and a stack of Midwest parts recommended for long-distance travel.

She wasn't sure if the burst of inspiration had come from finding the discarded mannequin, or the fact that hanging around Aiden reminded her how much better everything was with a partner. Either way, the display finally felt right. Complete.

"Well," Axle said. "Bye."

With that, Axle Zoller, man of few words, made his exit. Sadie followed him as far as the store when Aiden stopped her in the hallway. Something in his eyes warned her he meant business. "Can I talk to you for a second?"

"Um...no?" She smiled hopefully.

He tipped his head in silent reprimand and turned, walking into Axle's office at the end of the hall. Never one to chicken out, Sadie followed. Even though she was pretty sure this so-called talk had nothing to do with work. She entered the office and found Aiden fidgeting with a stress ball he'd found on Axle's desk.

"Shut the door for me?"

Panic pinged around her stomach like ricocheting BBs. She thought back to the park as she closed the door with a *click*. There'd been a moment, a tangible, meaningful moment when Aiden had looked into her eyes and started to say something. Something that started with *I*. She could only hope he wasn't planning on finishing the phrase with *you* and sliding a four-letter word in between.

I love you in any form was frightening, but an *I love you* from Aiden would be terrifying. Admitting her feelings when she wasn't sure what they were would make her more vulnerable to him than ever.

"Lyon's adorable," Sadie said to fill the void in the room.

"Yeah, he is a very cool kid." Aiden looked proud for a second, then his smile dropped. "About last night. I thought...maybe I should try to explain."

Oh no. Worse than the park thing. What did he regret? Staying? That she'd eyed him the way a hungry lioness would meat on a hook?

Aiden licked his lips and opened his mouth to speak. Sadie interrupted before he could.

"I know I was aggressive," she said. "I shouldn't have..." Shouldn't have what? She'd kissed him, unsnapped his jeans, asked him to stay. "Been so needy." She realized that was an apt description.

"No. No, that's not—"

"I just felt so sure, you know? I mean, I wanted it. I *really* wanted it."

Aiden gave her an anguished look.

Nervously, she continued. "It was the first time I'd ever—" Oops. Back up. She hadn't meant to go *there*. "I think I was overly excited."

"Sadie, I—"

"But propositioning you was wrong. Especially when you weren't interested in"—she gestured at his crotch with a wave of her hand—"you know. I can understand if you don't want to—"

"Sadie," he interrupted again, this time sternly. His expression softened, his eyebrows rising. "Please let me speak."

Well. She'd tried to head him off. She nodded her reluctant agreement.

Aiden ran a hand through his hair, looking none too happy about whatever he was about to tell her, which made Sadie more nervous. Maybe he'd decided he didn't want to see her any longer. What if he'd had a change of heart since the park?

"I want to." Aiden pinned her with a deadly serious

look. "Trust me. Where you're concerned, there isn't much I *don't* want to do with you."

Sadie's heart beat double time. She reached for her earring, spinning the stud in her ear and trying not to faint. That...might have been the best news she'd heard today.

"But..."

Or not.

"...I promised myself...ah, I sort of made a decision." Aiden dropped the stress ball on the desk and pointed an accusing finger at it. "That thing doesn't work." He sent her a sickly smile before sitting on the edge of Axle's desk and closing his eyes. "I made a decision," he said, his voice dipping an octave. "That the next time I make love to a woman, she will be the last one." He opened his eyes. "The last one ever," he clarified.

Sadie felt her brows lift. "Like..."

"She'll be my wife," he said.

"Oh."

"That probably sounds stupid, doesn't it?" Aiden stood and paced the short distance from desk to door in Axle's office. "I went through a lot of crap over the last year. And I thought maybe I'd try to do everything right instead of"—he threw a hand into the air—"effing it all up. I just...kind of wanted to start over." He winced.

Sadie was going to cry. Or laugh. Or laugh until she cried. "You're a...a born-again virgin?"

Aiden palmed his neck, looking uncomfortable with the label. Uncomfortable about everything. "Yeah, I guess."

Sadie laughed, a short, high bark she staunched by clapping a hand over her mouth.

Aiden's face pinched. "Thanks a lot."

"No." She touched his arm, which was as rigid as a steel pipe. "I'm not laughing at you." But that didn't stop her from giggling.

Her life was pathetically funny.

"Right." Aiden turned the doorknob. "Sorry I brought it up."

When he would have made his escape, Sadie said, "It's just ironic." He paused, turned his head. She swallowed and forced herself to continue. "That you aren't ready. And I am. Finally," she added quietly.

He narrowed his eyes as if trying to figure her out. Great. Just what she needed, Aiden seeing through her like a recently Windexed windshield. "What do you mean 'finally'?"

She gulped. "I—nothing. I don't even know why I said that."

He released the doorknob and walked over to her. "You mean you wanted to sleep with me at the wedding, but you are finally allowing yourself to admit it?" he asked, arriving at a very wrong conclusion.

"That's not what I meant by f-finally," she stammered, lifting her long hair off her neck. "It's hot in here."

"Then what did you mean?"

Sadie let go of her hair and flipped it over her shoulder. "Just that I'm ready"—*just say it and get it over with*—"to have sex."

"With me," Aiden said, a smile tickling his lips.

"With anyone!" she said a little too loudly. She picked up a manila folder and fanned her face. Wasn't she too young for hot flashes?

"Anyone at all, huh?" But Aiden didn't look offended.

He looked amused. The bastard. She fanned harder. She could tell by Aiden's expression that he thought she was busting his balls, keeping his ego in check.

Sadie *so* wanted to stop having this conversation. And leave Axle's sweltering office.

"You don't have to spare my feelings." Aiden took the folder from her and leaned in. "I get it," he said, his voice low. "You're a sexual person."

"Shh!"

"You have needs." His lip curved. "And here I am, unwilling to be your boy toy."

"Dammit, Aiden," Sadie snatched the folder and slammed it on the desk. Go big or go home, right? "That's not what I meant."

Her stern expression knocked the smile off his smug face. Aiden's lips flattened. "What *do* you mean, Sadie?"

With a Band-Aid-esque tear, she told him the painful truth. "I meant I'm finally ready to sleep with someone for the first time. Ever. In my entire life," she reiterated to be crystal clear. "And I was hoping that someone would be you."

* * *

Aiden had tried to speak once, twice, but only managed to emit a thin wheeze. He felt as if his throat had been lined with cotton batting, his tongue barricaded by bags of sand.

Was she saying…?

No way.

Sadie moved for the door and Aiden pressed a hand against the panel. "Not even Trey?" he rasped.

Sadie crossed her arms over her chest and met his eyes. "No."

Thank God. He didn't like the thought of her having sex with that philandering douchebag. Aiden didn't like the idea of her having sex with *anyone*. And she hadn't. Apparently.

"It's not that big of a surprise." Sadie looked at him through the veil of her lashes. Hiding.

"Wanna bet?" he choked out. He was beyond surprised. He was shocked. Although...when he'd helped her out of her dress at the wedding, Sadie had shown her modesty.

No peeking while I crawl into bed.

But how could she be a *virgin*? Sadie was completely irresistible. He would know. Every time he found himself alone with her, he was tempted to tie his hands to his sides to keep from touching her. She turned him on wearing high heels or tennis shoes, hair up or down, wielding a silly-saying key chain or a set of sparkplugs. How had she endured the many men who must have—*had* to have—tried and tried and tried again to get her to change her mind?

"I'm just tired of missing out."

"That's what this is about?" Aiden asked, disappointed. "Experimental?"

Sadie shrugged. "What else?"

How about because she was precious? Because she was loved? Because she was worth waiting for?

"This is exactly why I didn't tell you!" Sadie dropped her arms against her legs with a slap. "You're looking at me like I'm some rare, legendary creature."

You are, he thought but was smart enough not to say.

"It's not a big deal," Sadie insisted.

Maybe the best thing to do here was downplay his shock. "I know."

Some of the steam went out of Sadie's voice. "Oh. Well. Good." She leaned on the door, hands behind her back. "I guess I just think it's silly to save it. To wait."

Aiden wasn't sure which of them she was trying to convince at this point. He reached up and brushed her cheek with the back of his hand. God, she was beautiful. Everything he ever wanted—could ever want.

She stared at her shoes. "It's just sex."

He tilted her face and pressed his lips to hers for a slow, soft kiss that drew an answering moan from the back of her throat.

Cradling her face in his hands, Aiden bent to meet her eyes. "Not with me, it wouldn't be."

* * *

Aiden hung his motorcycle keys on the metal hooks that spelled KEYS hanging beside the back door. "Hey, Pop," he called, alerting his possibly snoozing father that he was home.

Instead of hearing a rattling snore followed by the sound of the recliner returning to its upright position, his father hollered back, "In here!"

"Uncle A!" Lyon burst through the kitchen before Aiden could make his way into the den.

"Hey, buddy, what are you still doing here?" Aiden said. Evan usually didn't stay this late, especially since Aiden had moved in. Evan avoided him as much as possible. It's why Aiden had asked to have lunch with Lyon. Otherwise, he might never see him.

"Me and Dad are staying the night," Lyon said, running off again. "I have new jammies! Wanna see?" He took off for the staircase without waiting for Aiden's answer.

Aiden walked into the den. Evan sat on the couch looking none too glad to see him. Of course, Evan never looked happy to see him.

"Hey, brother," Aiden said.

"My son said you were kissing a girl in the park."

And this chafed Evan for some reason?

"Sadie somebody, Dad says."

Aiden shot his father a look. Mike shrugged. "Didn't know it was a state secret."

"K-I-S-S-I-N—"

"And Lyon says you make out with the neighbor." Aiden interrupted Evan's chants. "So why don't you lay off?"

Dad rolled his eyes. "You two sound like a couple of idgits."

"Evan started it."

"You started it," Evan barked. "When you refused to bring Mom back from Oregon. When you lied to Dad about how much of your own money you were putting up to keep her there."

"Enough!" Mike's booming voice garnered both sons' full attention. "We are not going to assign blame for your mother's sickness."

"Death, Dad," Evan corrected.

Aiden scowled at him. Mike's eyes sank closed at the word.

"You're right, Ev," Dad admitted softly. "Death."

The room grew eerily quiet for a moment. Until Lyon

burst back onto the scene. "Jammies!" He was wearing only his underwear and waving the pieces of clothing around his head like a helicopter.

Aiden caught a pant leg before he lost an eye, and helped his nephew dress. Lyon chattered about a super-hero movie, growing more animated when he described the "'splosions and battles."

When he was dressed for bed, Lyon clambered away from his uncle. The kid's darker skin and mass of coffee-colored curls were his late mother's, but his light eyes and build were his father's. "I'm gonna get the football!"

"Not now, Lyon," Evan told his son. When Lyon whined, Evan gave him his sternest dad look. "I'm talking to Grampa and Uncle Aiden. Go watch your DVD and I'll tuck you into bed in a few."

"A few what?" Lyon asked with a frown.

"Child," Evan said, lifting an arm to point. "Go." Lyon groaned and lurched into the kitchen. Eventually they heard him stomping up the stairs, followed by the rumble of the television.

Mike slapped Evan's knee. "You're a good dad."

The hurt showed through Evan's pride. Lyon, and any reminder that Evan was a father, reminded Evan of Rae. When she died two years ago, she left Ev with a three-year-old and a hole in his heart the size of the Grand Canyon. Aiden couldn't imagine what his brother's life must be like in the lonely, quiet hours at night.

"I love that kid," Aiden told him.

"He's his mother," he said.

"He's you, too," their father said. Then he stood. "Beer?"

"Yeah," Ev said, then cast a glance at Aiden. "And bring Aid one, too."

Aiden figured that was as close to a reconciliation as they were going to get today.

He'd take it.

$\mathcal{C}$HAPTER TWELVE

$\mathcal{L}$andon. Aiden's oldest brother. Who lives in Chicago?" Crickitt spoke slowly, making Sadie feel like the dimmest bulb in the chandelier.

"I know who Landon is," Sadie said. She was just distracted, that's all. Distracted by her admission to Aiden, and by his sultry promise after he kissed the brains right out of her head. "Oldest brother, started his own advertising firm in Chicago. Millionaire." She gestured at Crickitt with a flourish of her fingers. "Go on."

Crickitt tore apart a breadstick and mopped up the remaining marinara from her plate while Sadie sipped her iced tea. "Well, Landon and Shane have been referring clients to each other for years. Shane to Landon's firm for their advertising needs and Landon to Shane for their logo design and general business consulting. But today"—Crickitt dropped her breadstick to rub her hands together—"Shane and Landon have officially partnered!"

"That's great," Sadie said flatly. She didn't mean to

sound so disconnected, but she was. Her mind was wandering along the fray, and definitely not here with Crickitt and the lunchtime crowd packing Giovanni's outdoor patio.

"It is great," Crickitt said, smile faltering. "It's a big deal for August Industries, for Shane and me. For all of us, really."

Sadie was happy for her friend. She was. So why couldn't she muster up anything other than a thin smile of support? "I'm so glad," she said, sounding less than convincing.

Crickitt frowned. "Oh my gosh. I'm bragging, aren't I?" Crickitt swiped her mouth with her black cloth napkin. "I've gone and married a wealthy businessman and turned into a desperate housewife."

"No, no you haven't."

"Yes, I have. I can't believe it. Pretty soon I'm going to have plastic surgery and a drinking problem to go with it."

"Crickitt, that's not what I'm thinking." Sadie smiled over at her friend. A real smile.

"Don't let me buy a little dog and carry it around in a purse, okay?" Crickitt wrinkled her cute nose.

"Okay." Sadie leaned in. "I have to tell you something."

Crickitt's eyes rounded. She leaned over the table.

Sadie kept her voice down, but spoke loud enough to be heard over the din of dining patrons. "I want to sleep with Aiden, but he won't sleep with me because he's decided to take a vow of celibacy until he gets married." She didn't know Crickitt's eyes could get wider until they did. "I'm tired of being a virgin," Sadie added, because, well, why not admit it all? *The truth shall set you free.*

Crickitt's mouth dropped open. Sadie leaned back in her chair and watched her friend stare across the table at her.

"I know. I should have told you a long time ago," Sadie said. "About the virgin thing, I mean. I don't even know why I would want the man who left me an aching, devastated mess a year ago. Your plastic-surgery-wine-addiction is sounding pretty good right about now compared to the woman I'm becoming. I don't want to be a doormat."

Crickitt walked around the table and hugged her. "Oh, this is so great!" When she released Sadie, she was blinking away tears. "I always loved the two of you together."

"Did you hear anything I said?" Sadie asked as Crickitt returned to her chair. "About my being a"—she mouthed the word—*virgin*?

Crickitt waved a hand and reached for her water. "Oh yeah, that. I had my suspicions."

Sadie sat back in her chair. "Really?" She worked so hard to come off as worldly.

"It's neither here nor there. The point is you and Aiden are back together," she cooed.

"We're not...together." And evidently they wouldn't be *getting* together if Aiden wasn't having sex until his wedding day. What was Sadie supposed to do, marry him to get some? She snorted to herself.

"Why *aren't* you two together?" Crickitt asked, reclaiming her abandoned breadstick. "What are you afraid of?"

"Are you kidding me? How about him calling from across the country to dump me over the phone?"

Crickitt tilted her head. "He regrets that, Sadie. More

than you know." She finished chewing and patted her lips with the napkin. "Don't get mad at me for saying this."

Sadie felt herself getting angry already, but willed the emotion away. Crickitt was her best friend. She wouldn't tell her anything she didn't need to hear. Even if she didn't *want* to hear it. "Say it."

"I think you've gotten all the mileage you can out of that phone call."

"Mileage?" Sadie asked, struggling to keep her tone even. "You mean, like, pity?"

Crickitt shook her head and kept her hand firmly over Sadie's. "It was a terrible, awful, devastating phone call from a man who was going through a terrible, awful, devastating time. Aiden is a good man, Sadie. And you"— she lifted her hand and gestured to Sadie—"you're an absolute ten in every way. Let it go. Forgive him. And let yourself be happy."

Sadie thought about that for a second. Crickitt made it sound so easy. *Was* it that easy? "But what if I can't?"

"What if you *can*?"

Sadie blinked at her empty plate. A second later, it was whisked away by their waiter.

What if she could?

Did she dare put herself on the line again?

* * *

Aiden managed not to fidget with the pen in his hand, but his foot bounced up and down like a sewing machine needle. He'd spent the last ten minutes explaining his plan— his creative financial plan—to purchase all five Axle's stores. Axle remained silent the entire time, his eyes flat black stones, his face impassive.

The day Aiden had taken Sadie to lunch, she'd given him invaluable advice. *Find out what he wants*, she told him. Did Axle want to open a smaller store elsewhere or never look at another motorcycle again? Did he want to continue custom building bikes and advertise locally or collect soda cans in Key West and live in a hut?

Since that lunch, Aiden had slipped in questions whenever he and Axle had a moment alone, mentally taking notes and planning his pitch. Turned out Axle had no plans to move to Florida, and he wasn't about to give up building bikes. Axle wanted to stay in Osborn, build replicas of vintage motorcycles, and sell to local stores who would in turn resell them for profit. Axle's business plan was solid, his talent for crafting custom-made bikes impressive. They'd sell like hell. But Aiden didn't want him to sell to anybody. He wanted Axle to sell to him.

Exclusively to him.

Aiden hoped the offer he'd pitched—giving Axle all of the profits from the sale of his bikes, and a percentage of the profits from this, his largest store for two years—would appeal enough to get his agreement. Aiden needed to get some more money together to get the loan for the stores. After extensive number crunching, and adding in the increased business Axle's coveted replicas would bring in, Aiden figured two years was more than enough time. By then he could buy the stores outright and Axle could continue his hobby and bank a hefty lump sum when the sale closed.

Aiden just needed Axle to keep the stores in his name for those two years.

"Done deal," Axle said.

Aiden blinked the mountain range in front of him into focus. "Really?"

Axle's mouth cracked into a barely there smile. "Yup."

Aiden burst out of the guest chair like his pants were on fire. "Thank you, Axle. You won't be sorry. I'm—" Aiden cut himself off when he realized Axle was grousing up at him. "Thanks."

Aiden ran into Sadie on her way to the office from the sales floor. He grasped her shoulders and backed her into the supply closet, flipped on the light, and closed the door behind them. Sadie's eyebrows were up, lips poised, probably to ask him what he was doing.

Aiden lost sight of the answer.

Sharing his news took low priority with Sadie's lips this close. He pressed her against a shelf filled with paper, boxes of pens, and rolls of receipts, and kissed her. She kissed him back, stroking his face with cool, slim fingers as she moved her mouth against his. He pulled away to find a satisfied smile on her face, her lids at half-mast. Mmm. His favorite look on her.

"Um...thank you?" she said.

"Thank *you*," Aiden said in a thick husk. "I'm buying Axle's." He briefly explained the details. "He loved the idea."

"Loved?"

"Well, loved it like only Axle can love anything," Aiden said.

She grinned up at him. "Congratulations."

He could kiss her again. Would have if he didn't suddenly become aware of the haphazardly stacked supplies over her head, the dust tickling his nostrils. "I'll let you out of here now." But he didn't move, lowering his head for one more brief kiss after all. "Unless you don't want out of here."

Sadie flattened a palm on his chest. "I was coming to find you to say good-bye, so yeah, probably we should get out of here."

"I'll walk you out." Aiden popped open the door and practically smacked into Axle, who slid them a strange glance as he lumbered by.

Aiden walked Sadie to the parking lot. She paused before settling into her car. "Um...so Axle's is completely stocked with Midwest parts."

"Great," Aiden said. And soon he'd be running the place. He needed to hire someone else before Axle left. Or maybe two someone elses. Axle wouldn't be easy to replace.

"And the window is done."

"I saw." There was something in Sadie's face. Distance. Maybe a little sadness. Aiden digested what she was telling him, focusing on the words *completely* and *done*. "You aren't saying good-bye for the day," he said. "You meant..."

She shrugged. "I'm done."

Aiden nodded. That sucked. "Okay. Great." He'd sort of forgotten she was only around temporarily, had become accustomed to seeing her almost every day. He liked running into her in the hallway, talking to her in the store when they were slow. He liked finding her alone in the break room at the vending machine. And now she was "done." He frowned.

Sadie shut her car door and rolled down the window. "I'll be glad to get back to the office." She slipped her sunglasses on and sent him a grin.

Was she telling him the truth? Was she glad to be done? Glad to go back to sitting in her cubicle for most of the day? Aiden had watched her in the store, interacting with customers, setting up displays, chatting with employees. She liked it, was good at it. Her ease with people was the driving force behind her success.

"I'll miss you," Aiden said. When that hurt too much, he corrected, "I mean, miss your help. With everything." He gestured at the store. "In there."

Sadie's smile remained, which bothered him. "I'll miss it, too. It's a cool store, Aiden. You'll do well with it."

Why was this starting to sound like reunited high school friends promising to meet up for drinks before the next ten years passed them by? Had their attraction only been one of proximity? Convenience?

Sadie turned the key in the ignition and Aiden realized if he didn't make plans with her before she left, he never would. Convincing her to go out with him, to do anything with him, always worked better when he was face-to-face with her.

He leaned into her car window. "Hey, before you go…" She tensed slightly, so he put his hand over hers on the steering wheel.

Aiden briefly explained his brother's and Shane's partnership, and the celebratory cocktail party scheduled for this weekend. "Landon will be there, and my sister, Angel. Shane invited Evan and me, I think so we wouldn't feel left out." He wished he could see Sadie's eyes. With sunglasses hiding half her face he wasn't sure what was going on in that pretty little head of hers.

Stop stalling.

He squeezed her hand and shot her a smile. "Come with me, Sadie. Be my date."

* * *

Sadie rested the statuette on her desk. A few coworkers poked their heads into her cube and congratulated her some more. The awards ceremony took up the entire afternoon and now most of Midwest's employees were filing out to the destination of happy hour.

Sadie had worked so long, so hard to achieve number one in sales at Midwest. She studied the gold placard with her name engraved on it, and thought she should feel more of a...she didn't know...an *oomph* or something. Feel more powerful, or successful. Ready to tackle her job with renewed fervor.

Instead, she felt sort of *meh*.

Maybe the cloud overshadowing her achievement was the invitation from Aiden on her last day at Axle's. Not only would tomorrow be her first real, official date with Aiden since last year, which, face it, she wasn't a hundred percent certain was a good idea, but the party was also a very classy affair. Crickitt and her billionaire husband would be throwing the soiree at Diamond Crown Hall, and that place was *fancy*. Sadie should know. She'd booked her wedding reception at Diamond Crown.

She wasn't sure if returning to the site of her former reception-to-be was what was making her skin crawl, or that she'd finally be meeting Aiden's siblings. All of them. The sister from Tennessee, the brother from Columbus, the other brother from Chicago. She had no idea how she felt about that...or how she'd be received.

When she thought of seeing Aiden, however, a satisfied little smile curved her lips. She missed him, missed seeing him at Axle's, missed him taking up her space. She'd thought of him often, while running her sales appointments, or at random times during the day. Her mind had been on him more than not.

When Midwest's new catalogs had come in earlier this week, she'd used the excuse to pop in and see him. But when she'd gotten to Axle's, Aiden had left for the day. She'd stayed and made small talk with Axle—*very* small talk; this *was* Axle, after all—but she'd kept one eye on the door on the off chance Aiden might walk through it.

They'd sort of left their...relationship?...on eternal pause. He'd asked her to the party, she'd said yes, and that had been that. But now instead of *that* there was *this*. This unsatisfied...*this* she felt now that she hadn't seen Aiden for a week. She glanced at her calendar. Had it only been a week? It felt more like a month.

Her eyes went to her cell and she thought of calling him. She didn't have his number saved into her phone any longer, but she could call Axle. He would give it to her if she made up a good enough story. She wondered if Aiden had kept her number. Surely he'd call before tomorrow.

Perry walked into Sadie's cubicle and she stopped staring at her phone. No amount of "using the Force" would make the dang thing ring anyway. Perry folded himself into a bow, his tie swinging back and forth between them. "I hereby renounce my feud for number one," he said. He rose and looked at his watch. "For the next thirty-six hours. Then it's on."

She had half a mind to brain him with her trophy.

His smile faltered and, for a moment, she was sure

she'd said that out loud. "I'm sorry I was a prick," he said. "You won fair and square, and I'm a horrible, terrible person during competitions."

"Only then?" she asked drily.

He chuckled and pointed an *Oh, you* finger at her.

Sadie gave him a composed smile. She was pretty sure his recent attitude adjustment could be credited to Aiden. Just thinking of the way Aiden stood up for her honor at Rick's party made her want to fan herself. She would have smiled, but she didn't want to smile at Perry.

"I'll take whatever reprieve you offer. However brief," she told Perry.

"Truce?"

She regarded his outstretched hand before folding her arms over her chest. "For now."

* * *

Aiden called.

Saturday afternoon, Sadie had been hobbling around with wet toenails and cotton weaved between her toes when her phone rang. She had to run on her heels to avoid smearing her pedi.

Hearing his voice made her heart swell, had memories cascading over her. Memories of kissing him, holding him, and the way he looked sprawled on her couch wearing nothing but his skivvies.

Which is precisely why Sadie used the excuse of an errand so she could drive herself to the reception hall. She was too nervous to have Aiden come to her place. Where she'd missed him in her space yesterday, today the idea of him in her apartment felt like a bad idea. She wasn't sure why, but the pressure had mounted. Before, there was none, but now, she felt as if a pipe had burst and she was hip-deep in it, a dangerous undercurrent threatening to tow her down.

It was just a feeling, really. A pit-of-her-stomach gut call she couldn't make sense of.

Sadie followed the signature patterned carpet of Diamond Crown Hall past smaller rooms hosting various celebrations as she looked for the August-Downey affair. The Klepps' reception, Jim and Nancy's fiftieth anniversary party, Jillian's Sweet Sixteen...Finally she reached the room Shane had booked for his gathering and her heart sank. It was the very same room Sadie had booked for The Wedding That Never Was.

She steeled her spine and plowed forward. It wasn't as if the site were haunted by unpleasant memories. Although, in a way, it kind of was.

Sadie may not have had her garter removed in here, or sliced her eight-tiered red velvet cake, but this was where her life was *supposed* to start. The marriage to Trey would have put an end to her single life and marked the beginning of the rest of her life.

Or so she'd thought.

When Trey and Celeste had married each other instead, Sadie's forward progress had ground to a halt. And now she was...What was she doing? Perpetually bobbing along...randomly dating?

Aiden and I could date.

Excitement flitted through her veins.

What a brilliant idea.

Not that it hadn't occurred to her before now, but whenever the thought arose, she shoved it back down again. Now that she thought about it—*really* thought about it—she liked the idea even more.

Aiden admitted he wanted her, and if she had any doubts, she couldn't deny she'd felt the press of his manhood against her hip a time or two. As much as she hated to steal his reclaimed virtue...well, hell, who was she kidding? She didn't mind at all.

Maybe she should apply a bit more pressure tonight. And a bit more the next date. Dating Aiden would be fine, wouldn't it? Dating and sleeping with Aiden sounded finer than frog hair, as a matter of fact. She could stop fretting once and for all. *If* she could convince him to take her to bed, she thought with an evil smirk.

Oh yes. She liked this plan.

Music drifted from the double doors of the main ballroom. Soft notes of the piano, the rasp of cymbals, the smooth cadence of horns. The sign out front read AUGUST INDUSTRIES & DOWNEY DESIGN GALA. Sadie gripped the handle and let herself in.

Shane knew how to throw a party. From the candles and vases of live flowers scattered around the room, to the low light cast on the walls, every square inch of the room spoke suave sophistication. Since this was a Black and White Party, the guests were asked to dress accordingly. The waitstaff was dressed in black and white, but wore ties in August Industries' signature bold blue and silver to differentiate them from the guests.

Sadie used the excuse to purchase a short white dress with a black lace overlay. The ornate black chandelier-style earrings and beaded black bracelet were also new, as were the four-inch satin high heels with lace overlay that matched her dress.

Matching lace overlay. She hadn't been able to resist.

She spotted Aiden standing with a man who could only be his brother. He was a few inches taller than Aiden, his hair the same dark shade of blond, but his was a much crisper cut than Aiden's careless shag.

Both men wore black on black, but Aiden's suit was playful, the cut casual. He didn't wear a tie and his shirt hung open at the collar. The very picture of easygoing. Conversely, the other man's outfit was made up of razor-sharp lines, matching his angled, clean-shaven jaw, and a black tie sliced down the center of his shirt. As if he felt her eyes on him, Aiden turned and waved Sadie over.

When she reached him, he took her hand. "This beautiful woman is with me, if you can believe it," Aiden said, his eyes shining as he smiled down at her. "Sadie, this guy, despite his appearance, is not a celebrity. He's just my brother Landon."

"Nice to meet you." Sadie extended a hand.

"And you," Landon said with a regal tilt of his head. He took her hand in a corporate handshake. He was handsome, no doubt about it. From his stylish black-framed glasses to the enviable cheekbones beneath them. But the seriousness in his eyes and his firm, flat line of a mouth made him less approachable than Aiden. She turned back to Aiden, his familiar smiling face like a blast of warmth.

"Would you like a Blue Martini?" Aiden asked, moving her hand to his arm. "They're the signature drink of the evening."

"Please." Happiness trickled molasses-slow down her spine. She liked being here with him. She'd probably like being anywhere with him. She may as well loosen up and have some fun, especially since she planned on convincing Aiden to have some fun, too. The kind of fun that wouldn't require a scrap of the clothing he wore now, she thought with a devilish grin. But first, she had to play the game. They were on a date. Sadie was good at dating. She practically had a 4.0 in dating.

"Your brother seems very . . . professional," she told him as they meandered through the well-dressed crowd.

Aiden chuckled. "He's a serious guy. Brilliant head for business. He and Shane will make good partners."

Shane had a brilliant head for business, too, but according to Crickitt, he managed to keep a firm hold on his playfulness. Landon struck her as the type to ream the waiter if his martini wasn't precisely chilled to a preferred temperature.

Blue drinks in hand, Sadie and Aiden made their way to one of the chairless tables scattered around the room. There was an occasional stuffed sofa or ottoman along the wall, but they were full.

"They don't want people lounging, do they?" she asked.

"They don't want them to eat much, either." He cast a dubious glance at the table of plated tapas in beautiful but miniscule portions.

"The prosciutto bruschetta looks delicious," Sadie said.

"It is," Aiden said. "I've had about fourteen of them."

She laughed, but Aiden didn't join her. His smile dropped, shoulders tightened. She followed his eyeline to the man approaching. He was dressed in black pants and a white shirt, and his sleeves were pushed over forearms decorated with tattoos. This had to be Aiden's other brother. His facial features were a mix of Aiden and Landon, but his hair was several shades darker. The bump on his nose was his own and hinted that this Downey brother had lived a rougher life than the other two. A shock of dark hair dropped over his forehead when he nodded at Aiden, his mouth set in a hard line.

"Sadie," Aiden said, his tone careful. "My brother Evan."

Evan gave her a curt nod but kept his hands in his pockets. She retracted the hand she'd held out for him and clutched her purse under her arm instead.

"Lyon is a great kid," she said. To her surprise, Evan's face broke into a small smile.

He shrugged one shoulder. "He's his mother."

She cast a sideways glance at Aiden. A muscle in his jaw ticked and Sadie inched closer to him, brushing his arm with hers. Aiden wrapped an arm around her waist and took a breath, calming some now that she'd reminded him she was here.

Tension strung between these two in a practically visible cord. Sadie remembered what Aiden told her in her kitchen, about how his brothers held Aiden responsible for having taken their mother to Oregon. Half of her wanted to lecture Evan and defend Aiden. The other half of her knew exactly how Evan felt. She'd been betrayed back then, too. No matter how righteous Aiden's reasoning, Sadie had been hurt. And recovering would take time, because hurt...well...it *hurt*. There wasn't much anyone could do besides wait it out.

Evan took his hand from his pocket and ran a hand through his hair. A tattoo of a bird decorated the inside of his forearm. She grasped his wrist, startling him, but he let her look. Not just a bird, then, she thought as she turned his arm to get a better look. A sparrow. Holding a string of hearts in its beak. One heart had snapped from the rest and was broken in two.

"Lyon's mom?" she guessed.

Evan's mouth turned down as he studied the artwork on his arm like he hadn't looked at it in a while. "Yeah."

She kept her hand on him, letting her palm warm his skin. When he met her eye, she said, "I'm sorry."

His eyebrows met over his nose in a brief flinch. "Thank you," he said with a nod.

Sadie released his arm. She knew Lyon's mother had passed away, but Sadie wasn't sure if she and Evan were a couple when she died. It was clear from the anguish darkening Evan's blue eyes that they were. And it made Sadie's chest ache to see how much the loss still hurt him.

As badly as she and Aiden's breakup had been, at least he was here next to her. She could touch him, look into his eyes, talk to him.

A bit of ink peeked out of Evan's sleeve and a design tracked up his other arm. "I like your tats," Sadie said, hoping to steer the conversation onto smoother terrain. "Aiden's is really good. Did you do it?"

Evan's mouth turned down and he cast an angry look at his brother. "You have a tattoo?"

Oops.

"When?" Evan demanded.

"After Mom..." Aiden didn't finish, his posture going rigid.

Sadie tipped her head in Landon's direction, hoping the mention of their oldest brother would end this conversation. "What about him? Does he have any?"

"If he did, I'd have done them," Evan grumbled.

"Ev." Aiden's tone was a warning.

Sadie looked over at Landon again. A glaringly beautiful woman approached, her long honey-colored curls dripping down her lithe, lean frame. She turned and Sadie nearly swallowed her tongue. *Lissa Francine?* Lissa, a lingerie model and runway queen, was here in the enviable flesh. Sadie would trade her entire shoe collection to have a body like hers. Lissa leaned in and said something to Landon. Sadie didn't think it was possible for him to look less comfortable until his face twisted into a grimace. He followed her woodenly across the room in measured, reluctant steps.

Sadie was about to point out the celebrity in their midst when Evan muttered, "Nice to meet you," and brushed by them, wandering toward the food.

"He's cheery," Sadie said.

"You should have seen him after Rae died," Aiden told her. "I actually think this *is* him being cheery."

"Sorry about the mentioning the tattoo."

His mouth relaxed and he palmed her back. "You didn't know." He slid his eyes down her body and back up, tucking her closer to whisper into her ear. "You look good enough to eat."

Her knees nearly buckled.

"Speaking of eating," he said, backing away from her, "if you expect to get a meal out of these hors d'oeuvres, you'd better grab 'em before someone else does."

After Sadie had eaten her weight in mini crab cakes and was on her second blue drink, Aiden went to the bar for a refill. Sadie chose to hang at a table rather than go with him. She sent a wave across the room to Crickitt, who shrugged in apology as she hobnobbed with a few of the company's muckety-mucks. Sadie waved her off with a shake of her head. Shane had made Crickitt full partner; Sadie understood that she needed to work the room.

"You must be Sadie."

Sadie turned to find a woman with chestnut-colored hair and kind blue eyes smiling at her. She was Sadie's height, and in flats no less, Sadie realized as she scanned her simple, attractive black dress and shoes. "I am."

"Angel Downey-McCormick." She shook Sadie's hand. "My brother's been hiding you from me all evening."

Sadie emitted an uncomfortable laugh. "I—"

"Thank you."

Sadie blinked at her. "For?"

Angel licked her lips as if debating whether or not to say what she was thinking. "Dad told me Aiden is a different person since you came back into his life. Better. Happier. I imagine it must have taken a lot to forgive him for the way he treated you last year."

Sadie felt the gratitude swell in her chest. Angel... understood. She didn't seem to be giving Aiden the benefit of the doubt. "I'm still working on it," she said thickly.

Angel's attention went to Aiden, who approached, fresh drink in hand. Before he got close enough to hear, Angel winked at her. "Keep working on it." She beamed over at Aiden. "Hey, baby brother."

"Evan's the youngest," Aiden argued, clearly not liking the nickname.

"You're all babies to me." She patted his arm. "Nice to meet you, Sadie." Then to Aiden, "I like her. Don't screw it up this time."

Aiden bit his lip and looked the slightest bit chagrined.

Sadie grinned. "I like your sister."

"Yeah." He put his drink down. "I bet you do." Aiden's attention went to the back of the room. "PDA alert."

Sadie turned to see Shane butt into the gaggle of suits surrounding his wife and put a protective arm around her waist. He tugged her against him and, heedless of professional company, Crickitt allowed him to tow her away. Shane leaned in to whisper into Crickitt's ear and Crickitt tossed her head back to laugh. Something warm and gooey pooled in Sadie's belly. *I want that.*

They were happy together, perfect for each other. Who wouldn't want that? In a world where marriage ended more often than it endured, Sadie hoped against hope that her best friend and Shane beat the odds.

"Dance with me."

Aiden's warm breath against her temple sent goose-flesh popping up on her arms. She turned to find him smiling down at her. "I know it's not 'The Electric Slide'"—he nodded to the jazz band in the corner—"but I think we can handle it."

Aiden led her to the floor and pulled her against the hard wall of his chest. She put a hand on the shoulder of his jacket and swayed to the music. The last time they'd danced together was at Crickitt's wedding. Sadie hadn't been very nice to him that night. Aiden had been apologetic and exposed and so... Aiden. Again she felt a wave of regret for not treating him better.

Keep working on it.

"Relax," Aiden murmured against her cheek. His palm splayed across her back, pulling her closer. "You smell so good." His voice rumbled against her chest, sending her hormones into fan-girl hissy fits.

That she and Aiden hadn't tumbled into bed the night they met had to be some sort of miracle of biblical proportion. Though technically, they'd tumbled into bed the *next, next* night, but they hadn't gotten physical. Another miracle. The attraction between them had always been—and continued to be—dangerous. Combustible.

She thought back to the evil-slash-brilliant idea she'd had on her way in. The idea of seducing Aiden once and for all. Of finding out what sex was like when she gave herself over to the connection between them. Sadie was all out of hidden aces. She didn't want to wait, didn't want to date, didn't want to pussyfoot or beat around the bush any longer. She wanted Aiden. Period. And she'd bet with the right approach...Aiden would fold like a cheap suit and have her out of this dress faster than she could say *Do me*.

Only one way to find out.

Sadie moved the hand not clasped in his from his shoulder and rested it over his heart. "I do wish you'd reconsider your stance on premarital physical relations." She tilted her chin down and peered up at him through her lashes.

Aiden's muscles went taut and his hand squeezed hers hard before he realized it and eased up on the pressure crushing her fingers. Sadie's lips arched into a dirty-girl grin. She had his attention. And while she'd never taken teasing this far before, she felt herself ease into familiar territory. She was a good flirt. And she hadn't even dialed it up halfway.

Sadie walked her fingers up Aiden's suit and let them trickle down his open collar, brushing the flesh at the bottom of his neck with her nails. "Imagine," she said, leaning close to his chest and smelling his skin, "what we could spend the evening doing if you changed your mind."

Aiden came to a halt and Sadie lifted her eyes, flitting her lashes again. His jaw was set, eyes dark, nostrils flared. He looked like he might devour her, and Sadie got a little thrill low in her belly at the thought. As if he just realized they were standing stock-still in the center of the dance floor, Aiden began moving with her against him again.

Sadie bit her lip to hold in the triumphant giggle. Instead of a devil on one shoulder and an angel on the other, she had a pair of pitchfork-holding twins on her back. And they were both chanting the same tawdry suggestion.

Sadie lowered her voice and pressed her body against Aiden's, going in for the kill.

"What do you say?" she asked in her sultriest voice. "Would you like to take me to bed tonight?"

CHAPTER THIRTEEN

Aiden needed a drink. A big one. One the size of the bucket of Gatorade football players dumped over the coach's head after a game. Though he doubted iced-down sports drink would cool the heat slowly consuming him, even if he poured it in his pants.

Sadie made him an offer he wasn't sure he could refuse.

And why would I?

Great question.

Ever since Harmony cheated on him with Daniel, Aiden hadn't exactly been looking. Then he met Sadie. And after last year—losing his mom, ruining what he and Sadie had together, and learning he was completely unsuccessful at getting over the blonde in his arms now—Aiden decided not to get involved with a woman until he was serious.

Serious, serious.

It wasn't a pact he'd taken lightly. Lord knows he'd

had the opportunity over the last year to go to bed with a woman—even casually—but he had zero desire to satisfy his body's impulses.

Since his mother's diagnosis, Aiden's life had stopped being his own and had become one of service to others. It was why he'd moved to Oregon. And why he'd moved in with his dad. And why he'd taken the job at the factory temporarily. But now Aiden was slowly reclaiming himself. He'd found the part of him that wanted things just to want them. The idea of saving himself until marriage was probably unfashionable and archaic, but dammit, that's what he wanted. Or maybe that's what he told himself so he wouldn't get involved with a woman at all.

Aiden probably never would have considered marriage again if he hadn't met Sadie—would've probably been more against it than she claimed to be. He'd been burned as badly as she had. He knew how she felt. He also knew how he felt.

He loved her.

Sadie was the only woman he trusted to walk down the aisle at his side and not betray him. He could trust her. He'd always trusted her. He *still* trusted her. It wasn't just love; Aiden had sunk like he was wearing a pair of cinder block shoes. He was a fool if he believed the whole marriage thing would work with anyone but this woman.

All he had to do was get her on board.

Aiden looked into Sadie's cinnamon-colored eyes, long lashes sweeping over them as she attempted to seduce him. A slow smile curved his mouth. Sadie was trying to get her way. A common theme. He wanted what she was offering, but he had terms.

Terms including a ceremony and the key phrase *I do*.

But this wasn't a game. Not any longer. If he was being honest with himself, hadn't he been making plans since Sadie reentered his life to include her in his future? When he pictured himself moving out of Dad's house, hadn't he imagined buying a place big enough for a family? In two years, hadn't he pictured celebrating with Sadie on the day he closed the deal and owned all five Axle's stores?

And in the wee, small hours of the morning, when Aiden lay awake in bed, his mind too busy to allow sleep, didn't the family he envisioned feature a little girl with Sadie's cherubic face and fair hair?

Yes. To all of the above.

Aiden's heart beat erratically in his chest as he stared at the woman in front of him. He loved her; he knew that. He'd *known* that. But not until this very moment had he seriously considered what he was considering now.

He glanced around the full room. Shane, Crickitt, his brothers...Angel over in the corner with her husband. Was he really willing to risk asking Sadie here? Risk that she might—hell, probably *would*—say no? Asking would be a leap of faith. Without a net.

"Cat got your tongue?" Sadie purred. She was an exquisite, naughty angel. A beautiful winged creature with tiny horns poking up out of her blonde curls.

Aiden's brow quirked in challenge. Yeah. He was willing. She deserved no less than to be called out on her sexy antics. And he deserved no less than Sadie in his life. Forever.

God, that sounded good.

Aiden pulled Sadie against him and spoke roughly, "I think you know my answer. Now don't move out from in front of me for a minute or the entire party will know it, too."

Sadie may have had the upper hand, but Aiden saw her resolve slip as he pressed against her. Desire bloomed in her brown eyes, and her lips parted as she took in a breath. Aiden nearly smiled.

Not so composed and in control now, was she? He loved when she dropped her guard, when she had no choice but to be led around by her emotions like the rest of the human population. It was a small triumph, but enough to spear him forward.

"I'll make you a deal," Aiden murmured into her ear, keeping her tightly against him as he steered her in another circle on the dance floor. "I'll make love to you," he said against her cheek. "And I'm talking about the kind of long, slow, agonizing, so-good-it-hurts love."

She shuddered in his arms. Aiden nipped her earlobe and whispered, "I'll make love to you until your toes are permanently curled."

A small sound escaped her throat. One he'd bet she didn't mean to let loose. He licked the curve of her ear with the very tip of his tongue. "Until you're too weak to move…"

Sadie's fingers fisted the front of his shirt, wrinkling it all to hell. He couldn't care less. Nothing thrilled him more than the sound of the sharp intake of air between her teeth. Proof that her control was shattering into a million pieces.

"But I have stipulations," he murmured, sliding his hand as low on her back as he dared.

Sadie's feet moved to the music, but the rest of her body was still. "Oh?" she breathed.

"Mmm-hmm. Want to know what they are?" Aiden abandoned her ear and pressed a kiss onto her neck.

"Uh-huh," Sadie said. It wasn't a yes, but he hoped she'd give him one next.

Aiden pulled away so he could look at her and moved her hair over her shoulder. He stroked the back of his knuckles down her cheek and came to a stop in the middle of the floor. Her eyes widened slightly.

"Marry me."

Sadie's throat convulsed as she swallowed hard. "That's not funny, Aiden."

He expected her to be nervous. He remained calm, moving them to the music again and holding her gaze. "I'm not kidding, Sadie."

She blinked a few times and gave him a shaky smile. "We can't get married just to—just to—"

"Make love for hours on end?" he finished, allowing his smile to break free.

Sadie tried to narrow her eyes, but she didn't quite make it. Instead, her cheeks grew pink and she darted her eyes left then right before landing on his face again. "That's not a good reason to get married," she whispered, angling an uncomfortable smile at the couple dancing near them.

But they weren't close enough to overhear. And in a second, the whole room would know his intentions. He just had to get her past this part, make a confession...*the* confession.

"You're right. That alone isn't a good reason to get married," he said with an intentional sigh. "I have another reason."

Sadie shook her head, just barely. "Aiden."

It was a plea he ignored. She deserved to know. He deserved the chance to proclaim it. "I love you, Sadie. I always have. I never stopped."

She inhaled. Held her breath. Bit her lip.

Well, she hadn't run from him. That was a good sign. "We're good together, you and me," he said. They were. They complemented each other in a way that was both synchronized and opposing at the same time. "We can talk for hours," he continued. "We can kiss for hours," he said, resting his cheek on hers and lowering his voice. "And I bet we'd be great at the long, agonizingly slow, making love part."

He pulled back to face Sadie. She licked her lips, desire prevalent in her wide, dark eyes. Then she squeezed them shut. "Be serious, Aiden."

He was. As a heart attack.

"Okay," he told her. "I will."

He took both of Sadie's hands and stepped away from her, even though he saw the panic on her face. Now or never. It was time to find out whether he was wasting his time...or if Sadie felt the same way about him as he did her.

In front of God, his brothers and sister, his cousins, and over a hundred guests, Aiden dropped to his knees in the middle of the dance floor. He said a silent prayer and squeezed her hands before making the offer of his life.

"Sadie Ann Marie Howard, will you be my wife?"

* * *

Oh God. He did it. He actually did it.

Sadie didn't know what was worse, the pure sincerity

on Aiden's face as he waited, chin raised, for her response, or the fact that she was going to have to tell him no.

Eyes, dozens of pairs of eyes, were trained on them. The other couples on the dance floor had stopped moving to the music, though (thank goodness) the band continued to play. They were watching, though—the band as well as the dancers. Everyone in the room waited for her to say yes, for Aiden to stand and embrace her, so they could applaud and shout their congratulations.

Aiden was waiting for a yes, too.

Regret was a snake coiling around her heart. But she couldn't say yes…not here, in the room she'd once reserved for her and Trey's wedding reception. Not now, in front of his family, in front of Crickitt, in front of gawking strangers. They weren't even dating! What was he thinking?

Regret turned to panic and Sadie's heart jackhammered against her rib cage. She pulled her hands from Aiden's, shook her head, and offered him as gentle a smile as she could muster. "I'm sorry."

Sadie slipped through the crowd, head down, and walked as quickly as her four-inch heels would carry her. Outside the double doors, in the brightly lit hallway, her chest felt less constricted, her pulse less erratic.

How could he do this to her? They hadn't talked about this, hadn't eluded to it. They were friends. Coworkers. Well, not anymore. But what had given him the idea of m-m-*marrying* her?

She couldn't even think it.

She heard her name being called and quickened her pace until the wide chandeliers overhead were flashes of light in her peripheral and her feet a blur over the red and gold carpet.

Aiden chased her. *Awesome.*

"Sadie!" He caught her easily, snagging her elbow and pulling her into one of the open, unoccupied rooms along the hallway. The room was dark; the only light came from the hall and sliced across the floor at an arc. Aiden steered her behind the open door, out of sight from any passersby.

He released her arm. She wouldn't look at him. "Sadie."

It took every drop of her dwindling courage, but she finally lifted her eyes to his.

"That's it?" he asked, his mouth a grim line. He'd taken his jacket off before coming after her. She idly wondered what he'd said to everyone in the room when he left.

She blinked at him, feeling a flash of fear and regret that soon morphed into anger. "You asked, I said no," she said, her voice shaking.

"Actually, you said you were sorry."

She sighed. "I am." Because she couldn't marry Aiden. She couldn't marry anyone. She was a hopeless wreck where men were concerned and—

"So my only options are to take you to bed or lose you forever?"

She blinked at him. "Are you quoting *Top Gun*?"

"Maybe." The corners of his lips tipped into a cautious smile. "Are those my only options?" he asked, his voice quiet.

"I can't marry you, Aiden," she whispered, closing her eyes so she wouldn't have to look at the disappointment swimming in his.

She felt his hand caress her shoulder and a moment later was enveloped in heat as he stepped into her comfort zone. Only, when Aiden was in it, she felt more comfortable, not less.

"Okay," he said, stroking her face.

She opened her eyes.

"You win."

His eyes held no clue as to what he meant by that. "What?"

"Did you mean it when you asked me to take you to bed tonight?"

Her heart slammed into third gear. He wasn't serious... was he? She made the mistake of challenging how serious he was moments ago. She'd been dead wrong. Now he was suggesting... oh. Wow. But that was before... before he'd proposed to her. Before he'd forced her into a tight, dark corner where she couldn't breathe. "Aiden—"

"I want you to ask me again." He walked her one step backward. Then two. She allowed him to advance until her butt bumped against the wall.

She shook her head, but there was no conviction in it.

"Ask me again," he repeated, looking scarily serious. His hands were heating her hips through the material of her dress. He kept his stormy eyes on hers, refusing to allow her to escape. "But only if you still want me."

Her breaths came in short pants. "I do."

"Then ask."

When he was this close, she couldn't fight. But maybe... maybe she didn't want to fight. Not about this. She wanted him; she couldn't deny that. And he'd be worth it, she knew. Being with Aiden here, or anywhere, would be better than going home alone and reliving the pain of turning him down. But Aiden wasn't arguing about his marriage proposal. Which made this decision that much easier.

Sadie licked her lips, took a breath, and asked the damn question. "Will you...take me to bed?"

His hold tightened on her hips. "Yes" came his gravelly response. "To bed." He kissed her lips. "To your car." He kissed her neck. "Up against this wall." He leaned into her body, his erection pressing firmly against her belly.

Sadie dropped her head against the wall. She couldn't think beyond agreeing. First time or not, she'd make love to this man on a park bench in the middle of a Fourth of July parade if he asked.

She nodded like a bobblehead, managing to eke out one word of agreement. "Okay."

Aiden's mouth hit hers hard, swirling her senses and stealing her next breath. Kissing him had a drugging effect. Left became right, north became south. What she thought she knew became muddled in a confusing whirlwind of sensations: Aiden's mouth on her skin, his hands pushing up her dress and cupping her rear end in his palms.

Sadie clasped on to his neck as her tongue met his. Unlike the proposal that had caused her to panic, she knew the decision to make love to Aiden was the absolute right one. She wanted him. He wanted her. She'd wanted him for so long. This part was very, very overdue.

Aiden lifted her leg and hooked it over his hip while he devoured her mouth. She dug her heel into his thigh to pull him closer, but he didn't complain, leaning hard into her while his hand slid over her dress. She wasn't wearing a bra, and his thumb found her nipple. He cupped and rubbed her as her panties grew damp.

This was what she wanted the night he stayed at her house, when she'd attacked him in her kitchen and flicked the stud on his jeans. She wanted Aiden wild, out of control for her. And finally, he was. Sadie felt his hardness at her center. He ground against her, one hand stroking the underside of her thigh as he held her leg over his hip, the other sliding from her breast to belly, to her waist, to—*oh!*

He stopped kissing her to look into her eyes, squatting to hold her in place, his body shaking, no doubt from the lust saturating his bloodstream. She could relate.

Eyes on hers, he trailed his fingertips along the lacy waistband of her underwear, then past the silken barrier. He slipped a finger against her as his forehead collapsed against hers. He muttered a harsh curse, another sign of his losing control.

She loved it. "I thought you weren't swearing," she teased, back arching as he continued to touch her.

He buried his face in her neck and said it again and Sadie's face broke into a smile. Briefly. When he lifted his head and ran his tongue along her bottom lip and slid a finger into her, her smile turned into a soft gasp. "So wet," he murmured in appreciation.

His harsh language, the dark look in his eyes, the increasing tempo of his fingers and thumb over her most sensitive spot... all of it a lethal mixture. Sadie was going to slide right over the edge in a wave of ecstasy. A few more kisses, a few more strokes, and Aiden's green eyes trained on hers, and she'd be a goner.

He kissed her softly, gently, all while sliding in and out of her body. Then he hit *the spot*. He didn't let up, his hold on her tightening, pressure increasing until Sadie was shaking and whimpering. He kissed her neck, bit her ear, and she tumbled over with a sharp cry, one that he swallowed with another kiss as her inner muscles clenched around his fingers and she clawed onto his shoulders with both hands.

He kissed her lips, her jaw, her neck, then murmured into her ear, "You're a screamer."

And Sadie, so relaxed and tingly, *laughed*. It felt good to laugh. It felt good to be this loose, this comfortable, this amazingly sated.

Aiden slipped his hand away and lowered her leg, holding her steady. Good thing. If he weren't half propping her up, she would have slumped in a heap to the floor. Sadie had given herself orgasms before, but nothing like this one—brought forth by the rough feel of Aiden's hands on her body, the smell and taste of him on her tongue, and the words he'd breathed into her ear.

She shuddered as aftershocks washed through her, and gripped his shoulders for support. She hadn't opened her eyes yet, hadn't been able to lift her head from the wall behind her. She felt, rather than saw, Aiden tug her dress down and smooth it over her thighs.

He kissed the corner of her mouth. "You should lie down." His voice held a note of mischief and innuendo, and Sadie smiled, wondered if she'd ever *stop* smiling.

"Mmm." She rubbed herself against his tented pants. "Find the coat closet."

He chuckled and because they were breast to chest, the vibration of it reverberated in her belly, making her feel as languid as a cat that had drunk its weight in warm cream. Her lids were heavy, her body as pliable as taffy.

She opened her eyes to find Aiden wearing a satisfied, proud male smile. He stroked her hair from her face and tilted her chin. "Sorry, beautiful. Your first time isn't going to be in a closet."

A shudder tore through her that had nothing to do with the release he'd blessed her with. Sadie had temporarily forgotten about her "sacred" first time. No surprise there; she'd temporarily forgotten her name. Sadie something. She knew it had two syllables...

She took in the darkened room they were in, the slice of light across the floor, the various *other* doors around the room. Anyone could have walked in on them. Could have caught Sadie, dress hiked to her waist, being braced against a wall by Aiden.

She was fairly sure part of her was trying to be appalled by her ribald behavior, but she couldn't find the strength to do anything other than smile warmly at the man who had taken her to heaven in under sixty seconds.

Aiden. Only Aiden could take her to the very pinnacle of desire and make her forget who she was. Or maybe, she thought in a burst of insight, when she was with Aiden she was more herself than when she was without him.

"Come with me somewhere," he said, taking her hands in his.

There was only one answer.

"Anywhere."

CHAPTER FOURTEEN

Sadie's steps aligned with her heartbeat as she walked hand in hand with Aiden out the side door and down the sidewalk. So wound up in the passion preceding their little jag, she didn't notice he was leading her to his motorcycle until they stopped in front of it.

Sheila sat under a streetlamp at the front of the lot, her orange paint gleaming. Sadie ground to a complete halt, blood freezing in her veins. She met Aiden's sea green eyes and shook her head. "I can't."

He took her face in his palms. "You can." There was his easy smile again. "Trust me, Sadie."

She did trust him. She trusted him implicitly. If she didn't, she wouldn't have lost herself in his arms moments ago. For once, she hadn't tried to hide behind her inner wall of safety. And it'd been so worth it, the freedom of it, like rolling around on decadent cotton bedding—

What do you have to lose?

They could wreck. They could get injured...And in

the banquet hall, they could have been caught. They could have been kicked out. But they weren't. It was a risk, but in a way, a safe one.

Again, she was struck by how she hadn't overthought it. About how she had zero regrets now. She'd experienced something exhilarating she'd never experienced before. It was *worth* it, and it felt wonderful letting Aiden take care of all the worrying for her.

Her eyes tracked to the bike.

Aiden would take care of her. He would make sure she was safe. And maybe this would be exhilarating, too … and lead up to the most exhilarating time of her life. After what just happened, how could tonight be anything less than mind-blowing?

She looked into Aiden's familiar, handsome face. Of course it would be. Instead of giving him an answer, Sadie pulled her skirt high on her thighs and approached Sheila. "Think I can ride in these shoes?"

"Sadie," Aiden said, pride evident on his face, "I think *you* can do *anything* in those shoes." He pulled a helmet from one of the saddlebags. It was pink.

She opened her mouth to ask how long he'd had it. He must have seen the question in her eyes. He answered before she had the chance to ask. "Bought it the day I dropped off your phone. I thought I might try and convince you to ride with me then."

"And you kept it," she murmured as he settled the helmet onto her head.

"You never know." He adjusted the strap on her chin and laid a soft kiss on her lips. "You'll be fine."

"I trust you," she said. But just in case, she closed her eyes and said a quick backup prayer.

Aiden put his own helmet on. "You need instructions?"

She opened her eyes. "Hold on tight, lean into the curves, and keep my legs away from the tailpipe."

He shook his head, his answering smile spreading warmth through her entire body. "I didn't think so."

Aiden got on first and Sadie climbed on after him, settling against his back and snuggling in. She wrapped her arms around his waist as he backed them away from the curb. Before he sped off, he clasped one of her hands in his and lifted it for a kiss. Sadie smiled against his back and closed her eyes.

They'd get safely to wherever it was he was taking her. After waiting thirty years to lose her virginity, *they had better* get there safely.

Or Saint Peter was going to get an earful when she reached the pearly gates.

* * *

She said *yes*.

Aiden felt like throwing his arms in the air and whooping for joy. Granted, she didn't say yes to his proposal, but Sadie had given in an inch in that darkened, empty room back at Diamond Crown Hall. And she'd given in another when she climbed onto the back of Sheila.

Wind beat Aiden's cheeks as he took the side streets to get home. No way was he draining Sadie's limited well of trust by zipping down the highway at seventy miles an hour. Despite wanting to get her home as quickly as possible.

She felt good nestled against him, her hands at his stomach, her body warming his back. He liked her there, liked her conceding control and letting him take care of her. That's why he'd proposed. That's why he'd asked her to ride. He wanted to take care of her. Wanted Sadie to see she could trust him. With her body... and with her heart.

One step at a time, he reminded himself. Even if they were slightly out of order.

Stubborn as she was beautiful, Aiden shouldn't have been surprised when Sadie ran from his proposal. He'd stood and assured the crowd, "That was a maybe." He'd been vaguely aware of his scowling siblings, and Shane and Crickitt's looks of concern. No doubt they'd ask for an explanation later.

Well, they could wait.

He'd run after Sadie, understanding too late he'd pushed her too far. Understanding that Sadie wasn't the kind of woman who reacted well to being pushed. He'd known that about her, but had thought maybe she was ready and didn't know it yet.

Wrong.

He could only hope her languid, agreeable nature would continue after he got her home. Because getting Sadie into bed was only the start of what he had planned for her. After he got her to shout *yes* followed by his name at least a dozen times tonight, he intended to propose again... eventually... and get a similar response.

They were meant to be together. And if he hadn't thought so before he'd made her come and mewl and grip on to him moments ago, seeing her guard drop so solidly at his feet would have convinced him.

And because Sadie was who she was, Aiden realized it may take longer for her to arrive at the same conclusion.

Hell, Aiden, on some level, had known he wanted her for forever the first night he met her. All he needed was her undivided attention for a little while and he knew he could get her to see it, too.

It wasn't as if he was coercing her. Sadie was the one who wanted to take him to bed, who'd made it her mission to seduce him tonight. He couldn't think of a better way to show her how serious he was than to prove their connection was way beyond friendship, way beyond physical. To show her just how much he loved her. And he did. God help him; he loved her until it hurt. Tonight, he planned on peeling back her layers until she saw the same undeniable truth.

That she loved him, too.

He pressed a remote to open the garage and pulled the bike in. He parked and kicked the stand as Sadie let go of his middle.

"Where are we?" she asked

He allowed Sadie to climb off first, then he followed, pulling off his helmet.

"My dad's," he told her as she pulled off her helmet and smoothed her hair. "But not for long."

* * *

Aiden unlocked the back door and Sadie slipped off her heels and followed him in. The kitchen was dark save for a light on the range above the stove, the only sound a ticking clock counting away the seconds.

Seconds until she'd be in Aiden's arms again. A shiver of hair stood on her nape.

"My room's through the den," Aiden told her, his voice

hushed. "Bathroom, too. Give me a minute." He kissed her forehead and Sadie clutched her shoes to her chest.

Give him a minute to what? Find his dad and tell him he'd brought a girl home? There was a thought. She cringed, feeling sixteen and unsure of herself all over again.

Sadie scurried into the den, decorated in deep, forest-green carpeting and burgundy and cream plaid wallpaper. A rolltop desk and bar stood on one side of the room, a large leather wraparound couch and fireplace on the other. It was a guy's space, furnished by Aiden's dad, she guessed, given the deer head mounted on the wall. *Ew.* She made a face and entered the adjoining room, closing the door behind her with a quiet click.

This looked more like Aiden's space. The furniture was more feminine than it should be—picked out by his late mother, she assumed—but Sadie could tell Aiden spent his time here. His shoes were lined against the wall, workout clothes tossed over the back of the desk chair, and a sleek black laptop rested next to a lamp near his bed.

His bed.

Never before had an unmade bed—with rumpled black bedding—looked so inviting. If Aiden could make her eyes roll back into her head in the corner of a banquet room, what could he do with all this space and a closed door?

Tonight she'd find out. She dropped her high heels on the floor and padded over the neutral gray carpet to the attached bathroom to freshen up. After she used the facilities, washed her hands, and repaired her helmet-head with damp fingers, Sadie stepped back into his room.

Aiden was sitting on his bed, but stood when he saw her, rubbing his palms down his suit pants in a nervous gesture. "Hey."

"Hey."

"I have everything ready." He pointed to a rolled sleeping bag and duffel on the floor.

Sadie approached the pile of gear as warily as she would a cobra in a basket. Camping? *Please, not camping.* Sadie's idea of camping was a cheap motel.

Aiden lowered his eyebrows as he studied her. "What's wrong?"

"This makes it look like we're braving the elements." She gave him a pleading smile. "Can't we just stay in here?"

He shook his head, stalking toward her with dark intent in his eyes. He glanced at the ceiling. "My dad's room is over this one," he said, keeping his voice low. "And I do not want your screaming to wake him up."

Sadie's eyes went wide. "Screaming?"

Aiden leaned forward and kissed her, a rough, possessive kiss as he slid his hands beneath her dress. His palms cupped her bottom and he lifted her, settling her onto his lap as he sat on the edge of the bed. She clutched his neck and straddled his legs. "You don't strike me as a girl who can keep it down during sex," he whispered, his hot breath in her ear sending trails of goose bumps down her arms.

He moved his lips to hers.

"I can control myself," she breathed against his mouth.

He kissed her again, deeper, with tongue.

"I mean, I *think* I can," she breathed when he pulled away.

"Think so, huh?" Challenge flared in Aiden's eyes. There was nothing she liked seeing more. He reached behind her and unzipped her dress, then slid her top to her waist. Sadie's breaths came rapidly as he revealed her breasts. He stared for a few seconds before running his hands over her nipples. They peaked in response.

"Beautiful," he murmured, leaning forward and laving her skin. His tongue circled one nipple, leaving it to cool as he moved his head to work on the other.

Sadie's head dropped back on her neck. His fingers gently pinched one nipple as he suckled the other. It was too much. It wasn't enough. She wiggled against him, aware of the high mewling sounds emitting from her throat as he tongued and pulled her. The pulse between her legs grew to a painful throb.

"Aiden," she whispered. Or squeaked. She couldn't quite get her vocal cords to do what she wanted them to.

He extracted her nipple with a soft *pop*, then darted his tongue around the bud, biting her ever so softly. She pressed her lips together to keep the cry from pushing out of her throat. Aiden smiled against her skin, knowing he had her, and did it again, this time pinching her other nipple in tandem. She bucked against him and let out a brief whimper she was powerless to hold in.

He took the sound as encouragement to continue and dove back in, pinching, licking, suckling, and pulling as Sadie clutched on to the back of his head for support. Then she was flying apart, releasing his head to cup her mouth with both hands to keep from wailing Aiden's name at the top of her lungs.

She collapsed against his shoulder, one arm hooked around his neck, one palm secured over her mouth. She dropped her hand only when she was sure she wouldn't yell the word *more!*

Aiden swept his hands up her back and held her against him. When she finally had the strength to lift her head, she found him grinning to beat all.

"Fine," she said, giving in. "Let's go camping."

* * *

Aiden had brought Sadie to the tree house behind his parents' house last year. She hadn't seen what he'd done to it since and he found himself excited to show it to her.

But he was more excited for what he'd get to do to her after.

She climbed the wooden slats to the top, commenting they were easier than the rope ladder she'd scaled the last time she was here. He let her go ahead of him, shouldering the duffel and sleeping bag as he kept his eyes securely fastened to her butt as she climbed.

Every inch of this woman was more beautiful than the last. Aiden could hardly wait to have her completely nude and beneath him tonight. And on top of him. And in front of him. He didn't want Sadie in *any* way...he wanted her in *every* way. Heart, soul, body, and mind. With any luck, this trip to the tree house would pave the way for getting what he wanted long-term, too.

She entered through the floor and he heard a soft gasp and climbed in behind her. "Oh my God, Aiden."

He could get used to hearing that a lot tonight.

Aiden stood to his full height, the recently remodeled tree house easily six inches over his head. He dropped their effects on the smooth wooden floor as Sadie took in the room. She swiveled her head toward the windows, the ceiling, the floor that latched and locked, to the mattress, easy chair, and footrest. It wasn't expansive—he could walk the width of the room in five steps—but what it lacked in space, it made up for in privacy.

"The last time we were here, this was a dusty, cobwebbed shell," Sadie said.

He and his brothers and father had originally built the ramshackle hideaway when Aiden was twelve. It hadn't aged well.

"When I moved in, Dad and I made the remodel of this place our project."

After Mom passed, his father was at loose ends. And since Aiden couldn't get the man to talk about her, he'd suggested they redo the tree house for Lyon so Dad had something to do besides watch television until he fell asleep in his chair. After the place was rebuilt, Aiden had spent a few nights out here himself. Nights when the house felt a little too familiar, or the grief a little too oppressive.

"We'd come out here every night after work until the weather got too cold," Aiden told her, referring to the brief, miserable stint when he'd worked at the factory with his father. "We finished it in the spring." He smoothed a hand along the wall until he found the switch for two small sconces on either side of the bed. They blinked to life, bathing Sadie in a soft, yellowish glow.

She quirked a brow at him. "Impressive."

"Has everything but a bathroom."

She wrinkled her nose. "But the house is so far away."

He crossed the short distance between them and

clutched her hips. "Yeah, which means you can be as loud as you want."

Sadie tucked her fingers in his belt loops and pressed against him. "Yeah, well, so can you," she purred up at him.

He bent forward and took her waiting mouth, backing her to the bed before forcing himself to stop. "You probably want a blanket on that bare mattress," he reminded himself aloud. He could have thrown her down on it as is. He made quick work of spreading out the sleeping bag and propping open the windows. A cool breeze and the soft chirp of crickets wafted through the screens.

This was her first time. He wanted it to be as perfect as possible. He didn't think it could get more perfect for him. Especially when Sadie sat on the edge of the mattress and unzipped her dress.

Aiden knelt on the floor in front of her and watched. There was such a vulnerable, open light in her dark eyes. She kept her focus on him as she shimmied out of her dress, revealing the breasts he hadn't gotten enough of and the triangle of black panties he'd felt but hadn't yet seen. Scalloped lace edges swept over her hips—beautiful, curved, rounded hips that led down to a pair of creamy thighs. Hips he'd kneaded beneath his palms, but until just now had never laid eyes on.

She reached for his shirt and unbuttoned it, one button at a time, keeping her eyes on his. He didn't dare look away from the openness of her face; the sheer look of trust that would have brought him to his knees if he wasn't already on them. This was all he wanted. Sadie. One-hundred-percent willing, pure Sadie.

She ran her fingers along his chest, exploring him with

her eyes and hands while his breaths shortened. When she tugged the shirt from his waistband, he stood and joined her on the mattress.

She worked his belt, sliding it aside and unbuttoning his pants. "This is where you stopped me last time," she whispered, a hint of mischief in her eyes.

"Not going to happen," he rasped.

She snort-laughed and he fell a little more in love with her. He hadn't even known that was possible. Sadie slid the zipper down and Aiden made quick work of shucking his pants, underwear, socks, and shoes, leaving them in a ball on the floor. He hovered over her and reached for her panties. She leaned back on her elbows and lifted her hips and he pulled them down her legs.

Finally, he was seeing Sadie in all her nakedness. His heart collided with his ribs like a battering ram. His hands shook. His brow broke into tiny beads of sweat. How long had he waited to have Sadie in his bed? How long had he wanted her? How many times had he gnashed his teeth over the thought that he'd lost her forever?

Yet here she was.

Gloriously naked and spread before him, trust and desire mingling in her eyes. And she was his.

Almost.

He moved up her supple body, taking a nipple in his mouth as his fingers found her center. She was wet and warm and ready for him and he groaned around the tight pink bud on his tongue. Sadie's hands went to his short hair and she guided him, arching her back and squirming beneath him. He lifted his head, laving first one breast then the other, mentally promising to return to them later.

But for now, he had to kiss her.

Aiden slanted his mouth over hers and Sadie raked her fingernails through the hair at his nape, causing him to shudder. She could turn him on completely clothed, with just her nails against his scalp. When her hand left his neck and found his cock, he was surprised the top of his head didn't shoot into the stratosphere.

"Now," she breathed into his ear. "I need you now."

Her lids were at half-mast, her mouth damp from his kisses. He held her gaze as he brushed a hand down her body and slid a finger inside her, thrilling as those same eyes grew wide and dark. Then he added another, moving gingerly within her, preparing her for him.

"I don't want to hurt you," he said, closing his lips over her neck. As badly as he wanted to be inside her, be encased in all her warmth, Aiden would sooner die than cause her any pain.

"You won't." She lifted his face and kissed him softly, her words coming out on a heated breath. "I trust you."

Her trust was an elixir for his soul and all the encouragement he needed. He left her body with an apology and dug a condom out of his discarded pants. There were five more in the duffel bag he'd carried up, and if he could physically walk—or crawl—after making love to Sadie, he intended to spend as many of them as she'd let him use.

He knelt beside her on the mattress and rolled the latex on.

Sadie watched him hungrily. "Wow, I had no idea you were . . . wow."

He grinned. A feral, ego-driven grin he couldn't help. "I'll go easy on you."

She chuckled, a throaty sound, then arched an eyebrow and said, "I hope not."

Aiden hovered over her, feeling the happiest he'd felt in...God. *Ages.* Just being with her like this, completely bared, and joking, and smiling—it was all he could ever want.

He coaxed her legs open with his knee and leaned into her, massaging her entrance with the tip of his arousal. Sadie clutched on to his shoulders, her smile fading as she pulled in a short breath. Aiden leaned on his elbows, threaded his hands through her hair and watched her closely as he slid in an inch.

Sadie closed her eyes and threw her head back. Her cheeks were pink, her lips swollen from his kisses. She was the most beautiful thing he'd seen, maybe ever. Aiden pulsed within her, gritting his teeth and wondering how the hell he'd hold out long enough for her to come first. He was halfway there already.

Clenching his jaw, he slid into her another inch and Sadie gripped his shoulders, her nails digging into the flesh of his back. He held himself tightly in check, grinding his teeth into dust and reminding himself that a gentleman should last longer than a few hot seconds. He slid in a little farther...then a little farther, agony and excitement merging into one.

Sadie emitted a soft cry, her eyebrows pinching together, and Aiden halted, afraid he'd hurt her, gone too fast too soon. He loved her too much to go any farther if she was ready to stop. He cradled her face in his hands and through a harsh breath managed to ask, "Do you need me to stop?"

Sadie's eyes flew open, fire sparking in their dark

depths. She grabbed on to the back of his neck and hauled him closer, and gave him the best warning of his life.

"Don't you *dare*."

* * *

Sadie didn't think a dimple could cause an orgasm… until Aiden's mouth curved into a half smile and the divot appeared on the side of his cheek.

But before she could unravel, he sealed his mouth over hers and kissed her. Distracting her with his tongue, he slid in to the hilt in one, smooth motion, effectively shifting her focus to the sensation of the absolute fullness, the absolute *rightness* of Aiden being inside her. It was nothing like she'd ever imagined. Nothing like she'd ever dreamed.

He'd been right about one thing. This wasn't "just sex" at all.

Aiden froze above her, his breathing high and tight. "Okay?" he asked, nodding his encouragement. She wondered if he could speak more than that one word, because she didn't know if she could speak any.

Sadie nodded instead. She was more than okay. The slight pain had faded, replaced with so much pleasure she wouldn't ask him to stop if the tree house caught fire. Not right away, anyway.

He backed out slowly and, just as slowly, slid back in while Sadie made noises she hoped sounded like approval. She didn't know how Aiden had been so sure, but she was beginning to think he was right. She was a screamer.

She dug her heels into the backs of his solid thighs,

urging him forward at every thrust. Gauging her reactions, he kept his eyes on hers, his hands on the side of her face as he pumped into her, quicker and quicker. She lifted her hips to accommodate all of him, knowing on some basic level that no one else could have felt this good, this right. Knowing she'd waited for the right moment, the right man. This man.

Aiden's handsome face contorted, his eyebrows pulled together, teeth bared as he tried to hold out. She couldn't wait any longer. The friction, the smell of his sweat, seeing the pleasure she'd given him evident on his face...It was all so *hot*. It was too much.

He thrust again, hitting a spot deep inside her, and Sadie came undone, clasping on to Aiden with her arms and her inner muscles as she let out a sound she was pretty sure, by anyone's standards, was a scream.

His chest hair brushed her nipples and the sensations continued to ripple through her. His breathing grew shallow, labored, as he thrust into her once more, twice more, then shouted his own completion in her ear before falling silent and sucking in one harsh breath after the other.

Aiden braced himself on one elbow to keep from crushing her and dropped his forehead onto his arm. She clasped his bicep, feeling the quake in his muscles.

I did that.

What a completely heady, amazing idea...that with only her body, she'd brought this Adonis to a shuddering halt.

Aiden laid there, head down, for a few breaths, while Sadie stroked his short hair, his shoulders, and ran her fingers over the ridge of the scar on his back.

The scar. The tangible reminder that Aiden wasn't

bulletproof. And a reminder to Sadie of just how precious he was, how very much she cared for him.

With everything I have. But she couldn't let him *become* everything, she reminded herself. Everything was too much.

Aiden's lips pursed against her shoulder and he kissed his way up to her neck, unaware of the direction of her thoughts. He pulled out of her and Sadie felt more empty than she had in her entire life. Even when his lips closed over hers. Even when his fingertips stroked her hair.

Some part of her told her she was past the point of no return.

She met his sea green eyes only to find them brimming with emotion. "I love you, Sadie." He kissed her again, breathed her in. "I love you so much," he whispered.

She'd heard him proclaim it once already. It meant so much more now. Now it meant everything. And that's what scared her down to her toenails.

Everything was too much to trust to any one person.

CHAPTER FIFTEEN

Aiden and Sadie had sneaked back into his father's house in the middle of the night like a couple of teenagers to sleep in Aiden's bed.

He knew his father had picked up a Sunday shift, so after he heard his car rumble out of the garage early this morning, Aiden slid down Sadie's body and pressed one kiss to her inner thigh, then another, before feasting on her in the morning sunlight, her shouts of ecstasy wrapping around him like a warm blanket.

He'd felt her go rigid beneath him last night when he told her he loved her. He vowed not to say it again, not to crowd her. But dammit, part of him stung that they'd experienced something so incredible and still she resisted admitting what he knew she must feel. How could she not?

He'd felt the effing *earth* move after he'd rocked into her one final time. She was perfect. She was all he'd ever need. *But.* He'd play it cool. Convince her one orgasm at a time if he had to.

A challenge he was up for.

They picked up her car at the conference center and he followed her home and into her apartment, even though she hadn't technically invited him in.

Sadie was thumbing through her phone as she opened her door. She pulled the keys from the lock. "Crickitt texted me last night to let me know she has my purse and ask if I was okay." She grimaced. "She said Shane has your suit coat. Guess they know."

He shouldn't smile. But he did.

Sadie slapped his arm lightly. "You'd like that, wouldn't you?"

"I didn't say anything."

"You didn't have to." She fidgeted with her key chain, studying him. "You have this, like, postcoital glow about you."

"Me?" He snuggled her close, his hands finding her hips on their own. "You could power a sports stadium." She shoved him but he could tell she was teasing, so he kept her close and lowered his mouth to hers, kissing her until she moaned low in her throat. "Do you want me to go home?" he asked, moving his lips to her neck.

"Um…"

He palmed her breast, his thumb unerring in its search for her nipple. He knew her body. After only one night. He *knew* it.

"You're not playing fair," she breathed, her fingers slipping into his hair. "Please grow your hair out," she whispered before sliding her tongue into his ear.

He clasped on to her butt as he nipped her neck. "You like it long?"

A chuckle in her voice, she gripped on to him through his jeans. "And thick."

He backed away so he could see her face. "You want some more, beautiful?" he asked, stroking her cheek. He did. God help him. Maybe he'd never get enough of Sadie. Sounded like the best life plan *ever*.

"If you can handle it." She tried to smirk, but he thumbed her nipple and her lips dropped open into a pleased sigh.

Oh, he could handle it. Definitely. He kissed her hard, lifting her off her feet as he kicked her front door closed with the heel of his boot. Then he climbed the stairs for her bedroom and made it his mission to get her to scream so loudly the neighbors filed noise complaints.

* * *

The last two nights had been indulgent. Like an all-you-can-eat buffet, or Thanksgiving dinner.

Sadie knew she *should* stop, she just couldn't convince her appetite otherwise. Same was true of the man she'd woken to sprawled across her mattress.

Every part of her was deliciously sore and humming, tingling. She was awash with sensitivities. Aiden barely touched her and she called his name. She'd be lucky if her neighbor Mrs. Norman didn't file a noise complaint with the landlord.

The problem was, the sensitivity didn't end at her body. Her emotions were running high, her heart weak and overflowing at the same time. Come Monday, Aiden had to work. So did Sadie, and she found herself looking forward to having her space back for a few minutes.

She couldn't escape Aiden. He was in her bed, in her kitchen, on her sofa... and this morning he'd brought his sexy, scarred, tattooed body into the shower and turned her five-minute spritz into twenty minutes of slippery heaven.

She wasn't complaining, but his constantly being around was making it hard for her to think a straight thought. She felt as if there was something that needed sorting. Something she couldn't sort with him clogging the room with his infectious, dimpled smile.

He promised to return after seven and bring dinner, then kissed Sadie until she slumped against the kitchen counter. She couldn't escape him. Which excited and terrified her at the same time. Sadie had to get her head around things, around where things were going, what this meant.

After work, she dropped her purse and keys onto the sofa and sat. She still didn't know what she wanted more—for Aiden to come over and light her skin like a handful of sparklers, or stay away so she could wear frumpy pajamas and eat ice cream out of the container.

She was full and empty at the same time. Hot and cold.

She had to tell him how she felt.

Just as soon as she decided whether to keep him near or push him away.

* * *

"Take lots of pictures," Aiden told Sonya Rollins and her husband as they left the store. They'd come in and bought matching T-shirts for their road trip to California.

Aiden glanced over at the stack of shirts and wondered if Sadie would wear a Harley shirt and ride with him across the country. She hadn't *hated* riding Sheila back to pick up her car yesterday morning. She hadn't even complained.

Much.

He chuckled as he recalled the small wrinkle in her forehead. *How am I supposed to hold on to you after all that great sex? I'm going to look like a wind sock, flapping behind you on the air.*

She turned him on in the weirdest ways sometimes. He shook his head to himself as Axle lumbered into the store. Aiden looked at his phone. "It's not seven yet."

"Go," Axle said, gesturing to the door. "Finished early."

Aiden didn't have to be told twice. He pulled his keys from the drawer, his mind on Sadie.

"Why are you smiling so much?" Axle asked, eyes narrowed.

Aiden looked up at him, more than a little shocked that Axle noticed. "I, uh...I'm happy." He gave him a slightly embarrassed smile. "I guess I haven't been happy for a long time."

Axle surprised him further by leaning on the counter and crossing his arms over his big chest. "Yeah. Your family got served a shit sandwich last year." His mustache twitched and his expression turned somber. An expression on Axle was alarming. All Aiden could do was stare. "I loved your mom. She was like a sister to me. Your dad like a brother. I know he doesn't show it, Aiden, but he grieves. Men like us just grieve different, is all."

Aiden was struck dumb. This had to be the longest conversation he'd ever had with Axle Zoller.

"You worry about him, but you shouldn't," Axle continued. "He's your dad. Let him worry about you, not the other way around." He glared down at him. "Okay?"

Aiden nodded, speechless for a moment. "Okay," he managed.

Axle palmed Aiden's shoulder and gave him a brief shake. "I'm glad you're happy. Now go." His mustache curved into a genuinely warm smile. "Tell Sadie I said hi."

Outside, Aiden replayed the conversation with Axle with a chuckle and a shake of his head. Maybe he had been worrying too much about everyone around him and not enough about himself. Since he'd turned his focus on buying the stores, and on Sadie, Aiden felt more whole than he ever had in his life.

Things were coming together. Life really did go on. And while he'd never forget his mother, he didn't want to live in the shadow of losing her for the rest of his life, either.

Neither did Dad. He could see that now.

Aiden straddled Sheila and scrolled through his phone for the number for the Chinese place near Sadie's house. He planned on ordering at least six different things and crawling into bed to feed her a bite of everything. Then he could stash the rest in the fridge for a midnight snack, or a three a.m. snack—whenever they woke famished from the workout he had planned for them tonight.

He couldn't get enough of that woman. He loved her so much his chest ached with it. He didn't want to get over her...and he knew after one miserable, failed attempt, he'd never be able to.

He wanted to shout with victory.

Aiden had never felt this way about anyone. Not even his ex-wife. He may not have broken any vows during their short marriage, but he hadn't known what it meant to be married. Not really. He'd never before wanted to give absolutely everything, strip himself bare—literally and figuratively—for another person.

Sadie made him feel everything at once. Made him feel like he had all he needed, even as he gave her all he had. She also made him want to walk down the aisle sooner than later. Make this thing official so he could start the next part of his life. He didn't care where he lived—her apartment, a new place they picked out together—as long as he was with her. Aiden didn't want to go home anymore. To him, she *was* home.

He pocketed his phone and started his bike. Maybe Chinese in bed wasn't the best idea. Maybe a better idea was a nice restaurant, candlelight, and a small velvet box.

He sped down the road, trying to remember where, exactly, he could find the closest jeweler. Saturday, Sadie had turned him down. But that was before all they'd shared. Aiden knew Sadie was right for him. Knew it deep in his bones.

He thought back to the shower this morning, where he'd washed her and stroked her and told her he loved her in every way but saying the words. She had to guess where this was going. He wasn't in this halfway. She had to know that he wanted it all.

After giving himself so completely, there was only one gesture left to make.

He'd get a ring. And he'd ask. Again. But this time, he thought as he spotted the jewelry store, she'd say yes.

He knew it.

* * *

Sadie growled and dropped her phone. She'd gotten Aiden's voice mail three times in a row. Her fretting had turned into frustration.

Soon he'd be in her living room, crowding her, turning her on...and she would melt into him, of course she would. How could she not? He was sexy and perfect and turned her into a wanton sex goddess.

And yet she felt utterly buried, smothered by him. It didn't make any sense.

Maybe she just needed time. An evening, a *morning* to herself to process. She'd made herself a very big promise last year—to never trust Aiden again, to never show her vulnerability to him again. And boy, had she broken that vow. He'd seen her more vulnerable, more exposed—in more ways than one—than anyone ever had. And now the boundaries she used to trust in were blurred beyond recognition.

Sadie tried to heed Crickitt's sage advice to stop holding the sins of the past against Aiden. She tried to forget the phone call last year, tried to forget how his dismissal of her had torn her heart out. She tried to forget the weeks following, the weeks when she'd ignored his calls before they'd stopped completely. She tried to ignore the terror she *still* felt at the idea of losing him. He wouldn't ever cheat on her, or leave her for her sister, but he could wrap his motorcycle around another tree...or go skidding into a field with an exposed water pipe like her father had...

Her hands shook as she pulled her phone out of her purse and dialed his number again. Then she heard it: the low rumble of Aiden's motorcycle.

And her hands shook harder.

CHAPTER SIXTEEN

Aiden adjusted the collar of his shirt. He'd made reservations at Triangle after his purchase and had run home to change into a blue button-down shirt and black pants. He hoped to God not to make an ass out of himself in a fancy-pants restaurant, he thought, sweeping a hand through his hair. But he couldn't very well propose to Sadie in a steak house.

Though they did make love in a tree house...so maybe it was a safe assumption Sadie wasn't into the five-star scene, either. He didn't know why he was suddenly so riddled with doubt over the right way to ask her. Then again, yes, he did. Sadie spooked as easily as a wild mare. He didn't want to blow his chance at spending the rest of his life with her because she didn't like crème brûlée.

She opened her apartment door and Aiden's fears evaporated. Seeing her there, dressed in a smart black skirt and pale pink top, her heels as high and impractical as ever, reminded him he had nothing to worry about. He *knew* her. Knew what she wanted, what she needed, before she even knew it herself.

"Change of plans," he said, stuffing his hands into his pockets. He clasped on to the ring he'd purchased tonight. It wasn't hard to pick out at all. The moment he saw it, it practically shouted *Sadie*. "We'll take your car. You're dressed perfectly for where we're going."

It was then he really looked at her face. The wide, sorrowful eyes, her full lips drawn into a pout. He held out a hand to touch her and she stepped out of his reach. The threshold of her apartment seemed to be a barrier he wasn't supposed to cross.

"Axle says hi," he said, his voice thin.

She crossed one arm over her middle and clasped on to her elbow, bracing herself—for what, he had no idea.

Fear and anger mixed in his throat, making his next words a demand rather than a question. "Sadie, what's going on?"

She shook her head, dropped her arm, and squeezed her cell phone between both hands. "I thought I could do this."

His vision blurred and he grabbed the doorway for support.

"I mean, I don't think we need to stop seeing each other," she continued. "Just…you know. Maybe a little less…"

Faint. He was going to fucking faint.

"I appreciate you offering to take me to dinner, Aiden, but—"

"You *appreciate* it?" he asked, incredulous. "What am I, your coworker?"

She frowned, rolling her shoulders back. "No, of

course not. I just think you and I went from zero to a hundred and skipped all the numbers in between. I need a—a break. From you. For a night or two," she was quick to clarify.

Like that was supposed to make him feel better? "A break," he repeated, his chest constricting.

How many times had he done this with Harmony? The start, the stall, the start, the stall. She'd ease off, come back, and he'd accommodated her each and every time. Marriage took work. Marriage took trying. And he got that, he did.

But just how much of the "trying" was supposed to come from him?

"I don't want to stop seeing you," Sadie continued, hell-bent on making her point. "If we could...slow down..."

"Slow down." He was numb. From the hand that clutched the ring in his pocket to the legs somehow holding him up. "How is that even possible?"

"We don't have to stop having sex," she added as a caveat.

Okay, he wasn't going to faint; he was going to puke. "You think that's what I want? To have sex with you a couple times a week?"

She nodded, clutching her phone, and looking so hopeful it made Aiden's stomach toss. "I want that. Don't you?"

He bit the inside of his lip and leaned against her doorway frowning down at the welcome mat.

Welcome, my ass.

"No, Sadie," he said, lifting his head to meet her eye. "I don't. I want more, not less. I want every day, not every other. I want marriage, not dating. I want it all. I want you. In every way."

She blanched. She looked as sick as he'd felt when she'd told him she wanted to back off. Only he had suggested the opposite. And her reaction was telling.

A smile—the same fake smile she'd given to Garrett at the wedding reception a few months ago—curved her mouth but failed to reach her eyes. "Aiden, we'll get there—we'll get—"

"I love you." Where was her smile now? Sure as hell not on her face.

She blinked at him.

"I said I love you, Sadie."

"I know."

He laughed, but the sound was hollow. Empty. "And you don't love me."

"I didn't say that."

He pushed off the doorway, the ring in his pocket a leaden weight dragging down his soul. "You didn't have to."

He stalked to Sheila as the rain started. And when he climbed on his bike, he felt the same kind of echoing anger he had the night he'd wrecked on I-75.

Like that night a few years back, Aiden gave himself to the road, and the piercing raindrops on his face. Anything was better than feeling betrayal...this time from Sadie, who couldn't have hurt him more if she'd stabbed him in the heart with one of her four-inch high heels.

* * *

Aiden paced the width of Shane's office while his cousin finished his phone call.

Aiden had sweet-talked his way past Keena, Shane's secretary, at the front door, and Shane had waved him in while he wrapped up with whoever he was talking to now.

Shane ended the call and stood from his desk. "To what do I owe the honor?" He held out a hand and Aiden embraced it, bringing it in for a half hug. "Haven't seen you in a while…"

"Since I asked Sadie to marry me at your party?"

"Something like that."

Shane had sent a text to Aiden a day later. A simple "What's up?" to which Aiden replied, "Working on it." He hadn't talked to him since.

Aiden had been standing in front of a bookshelf on the far wall, studying the books and trinkets lining the wood. He turned back to it now and pointed at the three mismatched monkeys, all covering their mouths with their hands. "Why do you have three Speak No Evil monkeys?" He picked one up. It was *pink*, for God's sake.

Shane took the effeminate monkey from his hand and put it back on the shelf, careful to line it up with the others. "Crickitt gets them for me," he said. Followed by, "Don't ask. What can I do for you?"

Aiden paced away from the shelf to the center of the room before turning around and facing Shane. "You can buy me out of the Axle's contract so I can get the hell out of town." Aiden had lashed himself to the motorcycle shops in every way. Now he had a sudden longing to move back to Oregon. Or China. Or the moon. But he couldn't. He was stuck.

"What are you talking about? You love that place. This is going to be your final score. Your retirement plan."

Aiden blew out a breath.

"Sadie," Shane guessed. "Didn't work out?"

He would never cry in front of Shane. Even though he felt the humiliating burn behind his eyeballs. He shook his head and bit his tongue.

Shane sighed and ambled to his desk. He collapsed into his executive chair and gestured for Aiden to sit in one of the guest chairs. He did, sinking into it like a sulking kid.

After a moment of silence, Shane said, "Falling in love with Crickitt scared the shit out of me."

Aiden's eyebrows rose. Shane wasn't one to admit weakness. Wore his stiff upper lip as proudly as the tie knotted around his neck. Shane loved Crickitt, obviously, but to hear him admit he was...scared? It was...Aiden didn't even have a word to describe what it was.

"You have my attention," Aiden told him.

"You're not like I am, Aiden. You're okay with this"—he waved a hand—"feelings stuff." Shane leaned forward in his chair and folded his hands on his desk. "Maybe Sadie's more like I am. Less...sure of herself." Shane frowned like he hated to admit that.

Aiden watched him, his mind spinning. Partially because he'd never thought about Shane *not* being sure of himself in any capacity. He had it more together than anyone Aiden knew. Shane was a *billionaire*, for God's sake.

But Shane wasn't the focus. His cousin was suggesting that Sadie wasn't sure of herself, that *she* was the one not okay with this "feelings stuff." Wasn't it more important for her to place her trust in Aiden? Faith, trust—that's what this whole thing was about. Yet the faith Sadie had placed in Aiden had petered out almost immediately.

Aiden shook his head. "Doesn't matter. I can't do this again."

Shane's phone buzzed and Keena announced into the intercom, "Mr. Alberts is here."

"I'll be down in a minute," Shane answered. He let go of the button. Aiden stood to leave. When he reached the door, he halted at the sound of Shane's voice.

"Crickitt gave me one more chance than I deserved," he said. "Just one."

Aiden swallowed hard and nodded without turning around. Then he opened the door and let himself out.

* * *

"Drinks at Bo's Tavern," Perry said, leaning into Sadie's cubicle on Friday evening. He frowned at her. "What's wrong with you?"

She was numb, that's what was wrong with her. This time, when Aiden walked out, she hadn't cried. Hadn't curled into a ball and wept like last time. Also unlike last time, she hadn't had to ignore his calls and texts, because none had come. He'd shut her out completely.

And the horrible, awful truth was that she understood why. And she didn't blame him one bit. He'd been nothing but transparent and loving and she'd been her normal, obstinate self, hiding behind her Great Wall of No Emotion. Which may have been cute when she'd first met Aiden. May have been endearing after they'd spent a little more time together. But now? Now that sex was in the picture...now that Aiden had declared his love for her...yeah, not so much.

Perry cleared his throat and Sadie mumbled something

about having plans tonight. She gathered her things, left the building, and climbed into her car. But instead of going home for the fourth lonely night in a row, she drove to Crickitt's house. Maybe if the pool was installed, Sadie could drown herself in it.

She knocked on the front door, still unsure of what she'd say, and pretty sure Crickitt already suspected something was up. Aiden was Shane's cousin, after all. Word had to have traveled.

Crickitt opened the door, dressed in a casual cotton dress. "Sadie. Hi." She frowned, gave Sadie a once-over. "Were we supposed to go out tonight?"

"No. I just stopped by."

Crickitt conked her head. "Brain not functioning lately, I'm telling you." She stepped aside and Sadie walked in, admiring what Crickitt had done with the place. She'd moved into Shane's monochrome world and infused it with color. From the paintings on the walls, to cherished knickknacks, Crickitt's eclectic style was showcased in each room.

They crossed to the kitchen, and Crickitt opened the narrow wine cooler on the far wall. "Red or white?"

"What will get me drunk the fastest?"

Crickitt slid her a smile and extracted a bottle, using an electric wine opener to uncork it. She poured Sadie a glass of red and joined her at the counter. "All right. What's going on?"

Sadie looked at her glass and frowned. "Aren't you having any?"

Crickitt shook her curls. "I have to write up a proposal tonight. I'd better not. So...?"

Sadie took a drink from her glass. The wine sat in her

mouth, flavorless, tasteless. Like everything else in her life since Aiden had walked off her stoop and rode off into the rain. Even the sun didn't feel warm on her skin anymore.

She blinked over at Crickitt who sat, eyebrows elevated in anticipation.

"Aiden and I had sex," Sadie blurted. "A lot of sex."

Crickitt smiled and inhaled, probably to *squee*, but then her face fell. "You don't look happy about it. Was it...bad?"

"What? No. It was amazing. I mean, I don't have anything to compare it to, but if it got any better, he would've had to poke me with a stick when he finished to see if I was still alive."

Crickitt laughed but sobered quickly. "I don't understand. You look miserable."

"I *am* miserable." Sadie gave her the rundown. The abandoned ballroom, Aiden's bedroom, the tree house, her apartment...all the way up to the part when he demanded to know how she felt about him. "I couldn't say it, Crickitt. I couldn't say it because I don't know. I knew once...but then Aiden hurt me so badly..." She shook her head. "And Trey...I thought I was in love then, but how could I love someone who would do that to me?" She took a breath. "Aiden"—saying his name hurt, but she said it again anyway—"Aiden keeps *saying it*. That he loves me, that he loves me so much. He looks into my eyes and into my soul and—"

Sadie's breath hitched and fat tears escaped her eyes. She covered her mouth as she sobbed. Ah, there they were. She knew they were in there somewhere. A few minutes under Crickitt's shimmering, doe-eyed stare and

Sadie loses all control. The woman could bring water from a rock.

Crickitt palmed Sadie's shoulder. "Of course he loves you, Sadie," she said matter-of-factly, her voice terribly calm. Sadie blinked away the tears blurring her vision in time to see her best friend smile. "Aiden would never have proposed if he didn't love you with all he is."

Sadie shook her head. "Which is why he left when I asked him if we could see each other l-less." Oh goody, the hiccup-cry. Because this wasn't humiliating enough as it was.

"He left?"

Sadie nodded, and—what the hell—cried some more. "Have you heard from him this w-week?" She mopped her face and wiped her hands on her skirt. "When he left my apartment, it was raining and he was on the bike and he was s-so angry."

She'd been sick with worry but refused to call. Aiden was safe. He was always safe. Except for the one time he wasn't. And what were the odds of him getting into two wrecks?

Crickitt bit her lip. She looked worried. Which made Sadie panic. "Has Shane seen him this week, Crickitt?"

"If he did, he didn't mention it." She was quick to add, "But Shane doesn't see him every week."

Sadie slid off the stool, holding onto the counter to keep her legs under her. "What if . . ."

"No, honey." Crickitt stood, too, putting her hand on Sadie's back. "Don't even think it. We would have heard from Mike. Or from Landon. Or from Angel or Evan. We would know by now."

Okay. Okay, that made sense.

Crickitt rubbed circles on Sadie's back as Sadie's world sharpened to a very finite point. Where her world's edges had blurred earlier, now she saw them. Crystal clear.

"I love him, Crickitt." Sadie waited for the overwhelming feeling of dread to wash over her, to tie her into knots and cause her life to tailspin out of control. The dread didn't come. She felt light, not heavy. Full, not empty. "I want to marry him," she said, trying out the words on her tongue. Again, the heaviness didn't come. She smiled, laughing through her tears.

Crickitt was crying. "Oh my gosh, I'm so glad," she sobbed, waving her free hand to dry her tears on her cheeks. "I always pictured Aunt Sadie and Uncle Aiden, and now—" Her eyes widened, her face blanked. "I mean..." She shook her head, even as her hand strayed to her stomach.

Sadie's mouth dropped open. "You're pregnant?"

Crickitt nodded and Sadie looped her arms around her best friend's neck. "We're not supposed to tell," Crickitt said, her voice muffled by Sadie's hair. "Not yet."

Sadie pulled back. "I won't tell." She thought of her sister's baby, and how poorly she'd behaved when she heard the news. She had some making up to do in that department. But first, she had to go and find the man she loved. Which scared her to death.

Sadie held on to Crickitt's shoulders, hoping to extract some of Crickitt's strength for herself. "Do you think he'll forgive me?"

"Only one way to find out." Crickitt smiled.

The front door opened and closed and Sadie turned to find Shane home from work. He dropped his jacket over the chaise lounge in the front room and strode over to where they stood.

"Hi, honey," Crickitt said.

He flicked a look from Crickitt to Sadie. "You told her. I win." He held out a hand. "Five bucks. Aiden was in my office yesterday and I didn't—"

"Aiden?" Sadie's heart dropped. "You saw him? How is he?" She balled her hands into fists.

"He loves you," Shane said simply. He lifted his eyebrows at Crickitt. "I'm going to change." He kissed Crickitt's lips, then paused in front of Sadie, bending over so she was forced to meet his amber-colored eyes. "Go to him, Sadie. One way or the other, you have to put the bastard out of his misery." Then he kissed her forehead and squeezed her arm. Shane headed to the other side of the house, calling over his shoulder, "Five bucks, Crickitt. Pay up!"

"He's right," Crickitt said. "You have to go to him."

Sadie swallowed. And she'd thought admitting to herself she loved Aiden was hard. Telling him would be even harder.

CHAPTER SEVENTEEN

"He's out," Aiden said, hoisting his thumb over his shoulder. Lyon had made him read *Green Eggs and Ham* three times, but finally, he'd fallen asleep.

"Thanks, man," Evan said. "He's had a big day."

Evan had come into town for the weekend. And for some reason had been in a really good mood. Maybe he wasn't interested in maintaining their ongoing feud. Whatever epiphany he'd come to since the party, when they'd seen each other last, must've been a good one.

"Scotch, Aid?" his father asked, serving himself and Evan.

Aiden had done enough drinking over the last week to justify a lengthy stay at Betty Ford. He'd better lay off before he had a bigger problem than his swelling liver. "No, thanks. I was thinking of going for a run."

Evan cast a dubious glance out of the window. "Tonight? You're crazy."

"It's pouring, son," Mike said.

It was. Rain beat the roof, the windows, but there wasn't any lightning, and the temperature wasn't too cold. Since his chat with Shane yesterday, Aiden had some extra steam to burn off. A run in the cool rain might be just the thing he needed.

Shane's proclamation that Crickitt had given him one more chance had burrowed beneath Aiden's skin. And last night he'd lain awake in bed and actually, foolishly, considered going back to Sadie and seeing if she'd take him back.

Maybe he didn't need a stay at Betty Ford; maybe he needed a padded cell with a locking door.

He woke this morning recalling everything she *hadn't* said while he'd stood outside her door spilling his guts. Her continued silence spoke volumes. She hadn't called him this week. He'd given her what she wanted, then she'd drawn the line in the sand. Not that making love to Sadie was a hardship for him, but they'd made love on her terms. If he had his way, he'd be engaged by now.

"I'm not made of sugar," Aiden said, watching the rain hit the window behind his brother and father's head. He spun his ball cap so the bill covered his eyes. "Be back soon." He left his father and brother in the den and snagged his black waterproof running jacket on the way outside. Under the small front porch, he watched it pour, reconsidering that glass of scotch.

A memory of Sadie's übercool shrug the night he was going to propose—the casual way she suggested they have sex a few times a week—pissed him off enough to propel him into the storm. He splashed through a puddle, then another, keeping his head down as he found his pace.

This last week had been one of the hardest Aiden had ever endured. And that was saying a lot, since the last woman he'd committed to spend a lifetime with had left him for someone else. But as bad as it was to learn Harmony had chosen his best friend and business partner over Aiden, at least now Aiden could look back and see things had turned out for the best. When he looked back, or maybe forward, at the life he and Sadie could have had, he didn't see it as a dodged bullet. He felt as if he'd taken two to the chest.

He loved her. *Still* loved her, dammit. And when pretending he was okay didn't lessen the pain of losing her, or drinking to forget her hadn't made her the least bit fuzzy in his memory, he knew he was in trouble. In trouble and there was absolutely nothing he could do about it. He didn't know why he'd thought he could get over her this time. It wasn't like he'd been able to get over her the last time. The pain of losing her was dull, but still there. Like the pain in his back now, reminding him of the night he'd wrecked his bike.

He wondered if loving Sadie would ache in the same way. If it'd be a persistent reminder that never fully healed. If she'd remain a lingering, distant memory regardless of who came into his life next. A small, dark part of his heart knew she would be there forever. And that made him want to go to her and give her—and himself— one final chance to be who they were meant to be.

But he wasn't going to beg.

It wasn't a matter of pride. It was a matter of needing to get used to not having her around. Because casual wasn't going to cut it for him. Not where she was concerned. He loved her with every fiber of his being. It was the only way he knew how to love her. He couldn't do half measures. Not where Sadie was concerned.

And, yeah, maybe he wasn't going to her partially out of self-preservation. He was afraid if she did talk to him, she'd suggest they "see where it goes." But Aiden had figured out a long time ago that with Sadie, he knew exactly where he wanted it to go. And while he wasn't sure he could ever feel exactly this way for another woman, he *was sure* a truncated relationship with Sadie wasn't a good solution to his problem.

And so here he was, alone. Running in the effing rain.

But he wasn't alone, he reminded himself. He had plenty to be grateful for. His brothers, his nephew, his sister and her dorky husband. And yeah, he missed his mom. Losing her made him appreciate his family, and the time they had together, that much more.

The ache in his heart would subside. He may be crying into his beer (or Jim Beam or vodka tonic) for the remainder of his days, but he couldn't let this crush him. He was being melodramatic yesterday when he'd told Shane he wished he could run away from home. That was kid stuff, the running away. Axle's was Aiden's legacy. Aiden was equipped to run those stores better than anyone, and he'd be damned if he'd turn away from it now that everything was lining up the way he wanted.

Almost everything, anyway.

Aiden slowed to a walk, pressing a hand into his side. Pain radiated down his back. Damn, that hurt. He'd been running too much lately, hoping the pounding of his feet on the pavement would drown out his thoughts. At least the pain quelled them.

Then again, maybe not, he thought as he turned the

corner and saw Sadie's car parked in front of his father's house. He almost reached up and rubbed his eyes to be sure she was really there. But that was her, all right, climbing out and shielding her eyes from the relentless rain.

Her hair soaked through and went flat on her head in the seconds it took for him to walk to her. She waited, her white dress shirt plastered to her skin and giving him a peek at the lacy bra underneath.

His heart clenched. She was exquisite. Beautiful. He missed her so much.

She doesn't love you.

Yeah. There was that.

Her lids fluttered as stray raindrops splattered against her face. Either that or she was crying. He steeled himself for the possibility. Even if she wept, he couldn't let it break his resolve. He'd come this far—had nearly a week under his belt. It would get easier. Hopefully.

"What are you doing here?" he called over the driving rain.

"I came to see you," she called back. She gestured to the car. "Take a drive with me?" An uncomfortable smile. "My treat."

Aiden had imagined Sadie coming to him. And in every imagining, he had said yes no matter what she'd asked. He'd pulled her into his arms and kissed her senseless and promised to love her forever. But now that she stood in front of him, the memory of her pushing him away was too fresh. Too painful.

"No, thank you," he told her. He hazarded a glance at the wide front window of his father's house. The living room light was out, Dad and Evan likely still in the den.

Unable to let Sadie stand in the downpour any longer, Aiden tipped his head toward the awning and led her to the porch.

She scaled the steps in a pair of tall red heels and it took everything in him to keep from grabbing her hand and helping her up. If he touched her, it'd be over. He'd probably crush her against him and kiss her and forget every assurance he'd just given himself.

Sadie smoothed her hair, which was already starting to curl on the ends. He recalled the morning—*the last morning*—they'd shared a shower, how she'd towel dried her hair, leaving the strands in damp waves, her face scrubbed free of makeup. Had she known she didn't love him then? He gave the memory a violent push.

Don't go there.

"What's up?" he asked, hoping to get to the reason why she came, and get her out of here as soon as possible. Preferably before Dad and Evan noticed. He cast another look at the house. Still dark.

"I saw Crickitt today," she said as she rubbed her hands together in a nervous gesture. "She and Shane had some news—"

"Sadie." Aiden's patience was thin ice. Maybe thinner. "You didn't come here to talk about my cousin."

He wouldn't let her dance around this. Not again. Not after he'd been nothing but forward and honest. He deserved the same from her. He deserved at least that. Harmony had been the queen of the start and stall. She'd leave him, then come back, and he'd let her, only to watch her leave again. How long until Sadie's next freak-out?

Love shouldn't be this hard.

Love wasn't hard for him. Love was simple. Love was

yes, followed by a hundred more yeses. What was so
damn complicated about that? He understood Sadie was
afraid—hell, *he* was afraid. He knew how betrayal could
kill a relationship. And he knew how death could sepa-
rate you from a loved one for forever. So did Sadie, he
realized, as he watched the water dripping from her chin.
She'd lost her father. She'd lost her fiancé. And yet she
refused to open herself up to Aiden. Despite the firm hold
Sadie had on his heart, he wouldn't allow himself to go
through the pain of losing her again. No matter how good
it felt to take her back in the moment.

"You have one minute," he said, ignoring the painful
squeeze in his heart, "before I say good-bye and go inside."

His heart squeezed even harder when Sadie pressed
her lips together and acquiesced with a nod. "Okay, that's
fair." She pulled in a breath, lifted her shoulders, and
crossed her arms over her see-through shirt. He'd seen her
this vulnerable before. The night he'd driven into her, his
name rolling off her lips on a cry of ecstasy. The night
he'd told her he loved her while he cradled her face in his
hands.

Don't go there, dammit.

Right. He was an impenetrable wall of granite.

"The day you called me from the airport in Oregon,"
she started. "When you were with your mom."

Shit. Impenetrable, he reminded himself. *Effing impenetrable.*

"You told me you were moving there. And we couldn't
be together anymore."

Aiden shot a longing gaze at the front door.

"I loved you then."

He snapped his head back to her. Blinked. "Why are you telling me this?"

"Because I still love you."

It was all he'd wanted to hear for as long as he could remember. The unflappable optimistic part of him wanted to scoop her into his arms and bury his face in her wet hair, tell her he loved her, that he'd love her until he died. Maybe longer. And if this were a movie instead of his life, if the screen faded to black, and the cameras ceased rolling, he'd do just that. *The End* would appear in curly script, and they'd live happily ever after.

But this wasn't a movie. And this wasn't *The End*.

In the real world, there'd be a tomorrow and a day after tomorrow. And in a week, or a month, or a year, when Sadie got skittish—because, face it, that's what she did—she'd bolt and he'd be left to pick up the pieces. How much more would it hurt then?

He didn't want to know.

"Aiden." She took a step toward him. He stepped back. Tears swam in her eyes and he barricaded his heart. He was doing the right thing. "I love you," she said.

"Stop saying that, Sadie. Please."

She retreated, just one step, and nodded. Actually nodded. Her easy acceptance was harder to take than if she'd crumbled at his feet and begged. Not that he wanted her to. God, just her being here had flipped his world. He didn't know what he wanted. Minutes ago, he'd been so sure, so solid on his decisions...and now...

He had to get away from her. Away from her beautiful face and the emotional one-two punch of her confession and her pleading eyes. "I'm sorry, Sadie. I can't," he gritted out.

He opened the front door, waiting for Sadie to call his name. She didn't. And when he went inside and looked out the front window, he was almost surprised to see her run for her car and close the door. The engine turned over. The headlights came on.

She was leaving.

And Aiden hoped to God he'd done the right thing.

CHAPTER EIGHTEEN

Aiden turned to walk away from the window—there was no way he could watch her drive off—and nearly plowed into his dad's broad chest. Evan raised his eyebrows in a quick show of apprehension before skirting the both of them and launching up the stairs.

Just like when they were kids and Dad was about to yell.

Aiden stood eye to eye with his father now, but the sight of Dad's scar puckering as he scowled still scared the bejeezus out of him. Not that Aiden was about to let it show.

"Not now, Dad." He started to push past him but Mike blocked his path. Aiden pulled his hat off and shook some of the water off of it before putting it on again. "I'm serious." He tried again but his father stepped in front of him.

"Sit down." Dad's face was angry. His scar twitched.

Aiden knew he was pushing his luck. He unzipped

his jacket and dropped it by the door, then sat on the edge of a chair, wishing he could follow Evan up the stairs.

Mike lowered himself onto the sofa with a heavy sigh. "I'm guessing that was Sadie."

Aiden took off his cap and twisted it in his hands. "Yeah."

"What did she want?"

He shrugged, refused to meet Mike's eyes. "I don't know."

"You're a terrible liar."

Aiden said nothing.

"Your plan is to let her go, then?"

Aiden's anger sparked. "She let *me* go, Dad." Shouldn't everyone be able to see that? "I *proposed* to her, and she said no."

"Yeah, well, you still brought her to your bed, didn't you?"

Aiden ducked his head. "It's what she wanted. It's *all* she wanted."

"Yeah. I'm sure you didn't want that." The sarcasm in Dad's voice was thick.

Aiden lifted his chin, nostrils flaring. Mike had no right to corner him. He was the hurt party, here. And anyway, shouldn't he be able to count on his own father taking his side? "I went through this with Harmony once already," Aiden said, launching into the internal speech he'd given himself earlier. "The start and stall, the way she'd leave and come back—"

His father yanked the soapbox out from under him before he could finish.

"Dammit, Aiden! Stop being so stubborn."

Aiden closed his mouth, and stared into his father's simmering eyes. Eyes the same color as his.

Mike pulled a hand through his shaggy gray hair. "You don't know how long you have with someone in this life, you know. You may get them for a few months, or you may get them for thirty-seven years." He leaned over and rested his elbows on his knees, but didn't take his eyes off his son. "You don't know. That's the point. Life isn't laid out in neat little squares like some goddamn checkerboard," he said, his voice gruff. "Your mom…" He paused, lifting his chin.

Aiden kept quiet and waited.

Mike cleared his throat. "Your mom," he said in a titanium tone, "was supposed to grow old with me. That was the plan. That was always the plan. You may think I look old, but I don't *feel* old. And she's gone a lot sooner than I ever planned.

"When the accident happened"—he pointed at his face—"she told me she was scared to death she might lose me. Told me she hadn't thought about losing me so soon, if ever."

He was talking about the factory accident. It happened before Aiden was born. Mike's coworker had gotten caught in one of the machines and when Mike pulled him loose, a piece of metal shot out and nearly took his eye. The scar his dad liked to make jokes about was caused by an accident that could have ended his life.

"I didn't remember how she'd cried back then until she was diagnosed with cancer the first time," Dad continued. "Then I remembered. 'Cause I was doing the same for her. I realized what I was up against: losing her. Sooner than I expected." He gave Aiden a hard look. "I never took her for granted after that." His hands clenched into fists. "I held on to each minute I had with her with both hands. You've been through hell, son. You were with her in some of her darkest hours. You lost her. We all lost her." His voice wavered, but his face stayed strong.

"You have a chance to be with Sadie—to be with the woman who loves you. She came to you, Aiden. She came back," he reiterated as Aiden felt guilt punch a hole through his chest. "She wants you and you're sitting here like a jackass."

Aiden blinked at his dad. Mike was a good father, a tough father, but not since Aiden was fifteen and cheated on a final in school had he heard him speak to him with such authority.

"Do you love her?" he demanded.

Hearing Shane's question repeated after all he'd been through with Sadie stopped Aiden's thoughts in their tracks. Of course he loved her. Of all the excuses he'd made about not taking her back, not one of them had been because he didn't love her. He loved her with all he was. That was the problem.

Wasn't it?

He pictured Sadie, shivering, her shirt soaked through, her hair dripping, mascara running. Her eyes had been filled with fear, but her voice even when she'd told him the best news of his life. She'd bared her heart, confessed her feelings, and begged him to come back.

And he sent her away.

"I'm a brainless bastard," Aiden muttered.

"And she loves you anyway." Mike's scar crinkled when he smiled. "Man doesn't get any luckier than that."

An emotion swept over Aiden and in a rush, he named

it. *Certainty.* The kind he'd possessed when he hadn't hesitated to pack up his mother and move her to Oregon. The kind of certainty that had led him to sell his house and motorcycles to continue paying for her care behind his family's back. The kind of certainty that made it impossible to ever feel regret.

And he knew if he didn't act on his decision to go after Sadie, he'd regret this moment forever. And forever was a long time. He pushed to his feet and turned to open the front door.

"Don't come back without her!" Dad yelled behind him.

Aiden spared him a smile and pulled on his ball cap before taking off at a run for the garage. It'd be a painful bike ride in the rain to catch up with her, but he'd—

He froze midway across the drive when he spotted Sadie's car idling at the curb two houses down. But he only stilled for a moment. And then he ran to her.

Like his very life depended on it.

* * *

Sadie hoped she wouldn't have to sleep here. It'd be embarrassing to be outside Aiden's father's house in the morning with red, puffy eyes and an empty box of tissues on the front seat. She grabbed another Kleenex from the crushed box she forgot she had in the car. She'd found them under the seat with a petrified french fry and about two dollars in change.

She'd be able to drive in a second, she assured herself. The tears hadn't stopped, exactly, but they were no longer a constant flow. She watched the windshield wipers swipe the flooding water off the windshield. It filled before the wipers lifted to swipe the water away again.

Her tears were kind of like the rain. And her face kind of like the windshield.

She couldn't blame Aiden for pushing her away. Not really. She'd waited too long; she'd made her proclamation too late. Last year, she'd ignored his phone calls and walled herself up, promising to be hard and uncompromising where he was concerned. And when she saw him again at the wedding, she arranged a number of hoops for him to jump through. And dammit if he didn't jump through every one of them.

But it was Sadie, at the end of the day, who couldn't be bothered to leave her comfort zone. Sadie, who'd looked at all he'd given her and thrown it away.

Aiden looked as sad and broken as she'd felt when she'd told him she loved him. It was why she'd left his porch. He was hurting and needed to heal, and she was picking at his wound and dumping salt in it while she was at it. Sadie knew how hard it was to heal. How devastating it had been to lose him the first time.

So, she'd leave him alone and he could forget about her.

This part sucked.

She swiped her eyes again, closing them and pulling in a breath. She had to go home sometime. Now was as good a time as any.

The windshield wipers pushed the rain away, but this time, she spotted a soaking wet figure wearing a ball cap standing in front of her car. Her heart thudded out his name, but she refused to think it. She wanted him too badly. This had to be a dream.

But it wasn't, she realized when her driver's door opened. Aiden stood dripping wet and holding out a palm for her to take. Sadie put her hand in his and was swamped with familiarity, with the absolute rightness of the way they fit together.

In every way.

He pulled her to her feet and kissed her and she decided this wasn't a dream after all. She'd died and the Almighty was giving her a taste of heaven. When she moved to get closer to him and the cap got in the way, Aiden tossed it to the ground, pulled her against him, and kissed her harder. Like he needed her. Like he *loved* her.

She didn't want to stop. Ever. She just wanted to stand here, shivering in the rain, and kiss him. This moment was perfect. This moment was what she'd imagined when she'd pulled into his driveway.

He wiped her wet hair from her face. "Look at you," he said, his voice low. "I'm so sorry I made you cry."

Which, of course, made her cry again.

He wiped her tears, the rain, from her cheeks with the pads of his thumbs. "If I tell you I love you, will you stop crying?"

She smiled but shook her head.

He smiled back, his dimple denting his cheek and catching a droplet of rain. "If I let you punch me in the nose, will you stop crying?"

She chuckled. "Maybe."

"Maybe, huh?" He bent and kissed her, his tongue warm against her cold lips. She held on to him and thought how they must look, clutching each other, making out in the rain, desperate not to let go. She liked that. No, she loved that. She loved *him*.

He pulled away and clasped her hand, then ducked into her car and came out with the keys. He clicked the key fob to lock the door and led her to the back of his father's house and into the kitchen.

Aiden's father was cracking open a beer when they entered. He spared Sadie a smile and Aiden a wink, then scuttled through the doorway and up the stairs.

Aiden tightened his hold on her wet hand and pulled Sadie through the den and into his room, shutting the door behind them. Remembering the night he'd sat on this comforter with her in his lap was almost enough to buckle her knees. She never thought she would be in here again. But here she was.

He didn't let go of her hand until they stood in front of his dresser. She surveyed the items on the surface. A coffee mug full of change, a ball cap, a magazine, a key chain...

She smiled down at the cartoon of a bride and groom, and the words that read UNDER NEW MANAGEMENT. Her smile faded as her eyes tracked to what was attached to the chain.

Not a key.

Aiden lifted the key chain and dangled the platinum engagement ring in front of her. "This," he said, his voice tight, "is what I had planned for the night I came to take you to dinner."

Sadie stared as the ring swayed back and forth. "The night I blew it." She had, too. He'd stood there proclaiming how much he loved her and how he'd always loved her, and he'd had *this* in his pocket. She'd completely blown it.

"No more crying, remember?" he said as he unhooked

the ring from the chain. "And you didn't blow it." He held out a palm. "Give me your hand."

Heart pounding ninety miles a minute, Sadie did as he instructed.

"You only delayed it," he murmured, clasping her fingers gently in his. "Marry me, Sadie."

She snort-laughed and covered her mouth to muffle the sound.

Aiden's lips quirked. "I forget, is it one snort for yes, or two?"

She laughed as she swiped at her leaking eyes. "One," she managed. He grinned as he slid the ring home, a perfect fit. Like him, she thought. She threw her arms around his neck. "I love you," she said into his ear. "I'm sorry I didn't realize it sooner. I'm sorry I ruined everything."

He pried her away from him and tipped her chin. "Look at me, Sadie. Do I look ruined?"

No. He looked devastatingly handsome. His hair wet and mussed, his face damp, water droplets hanging off the longer scruff on his jaw. She raked her fingers through it, the rasping sound making her shiver. "Make love to me."

Aiden's smile vanished.

He dipped his head and took her lips, gingerly unbuttoning her wet shirt and dropping it with a *plop* at her feet. Then he peeled his own shirt away, revealing his damp, bare chest. He seemed to consider something, before moving to a radio on the nightstand. He turned it on.

"Maybe they won't hear you over the music," he said, standing in front of her again.

Sadie palmed his jutting erection. "Me?" she teased, enjoying him looking down at her with hungry, ever-darkening eyes. "You're the one who's going to have to try and keep it down tonight."

She was grinning, a big, stupid, happy grin that felt so much better than the agony she'd felt moments ago. Biting her bottom lip, she slid her fingers beneath the band of his running shorts.

Aiden dropped his head back on his neck and groaned before fishing her hand out and undressing himself. Sadie simply stared at his naked body, his damp, golden skin, broad shoulders, taking all of him in, and feeling so grateful to be here with him like this.

He undid her bra, slowly slid it down her arms, his fingertips trailing along her exposed flesh. Sadie shuddered at the intensity in his eyes. He unzipped her skirt, dropped it to her feet. When she bent to take off her high heels, he shook his head. "Leave them on."

She obeyed and Aiden dipped his head to take her nipple with his tongue. His hand slipped between her legs and when she brought her hand to the back of his head, the diamond on her ring finger glinted in the lamplight. He sensed her hesitation and lifted his face, still stroking her below, his other arm braced at her back.

"Tell me," he commanded.

She was disintegrating beneath his touch, but she managed to whisper, "I love you."

He dropped his forehead on hers and closed his eyes. "I love you."

And then he proceeded to show her how much.

*E*PILOGUE

*S*now drifted down from the sky, blanketing the front of Mike Downey's yard in a few inches of the stuff. Sadie stood at the front window, clasping her arms around herself and watching the serene picture outside.

The neighborhood was quiet, the holiday lights strung white on some houses, red or blue on others. It made for a twinkling, happy backdrop to the happiest time of Sadie's life.

"Here you go." Crickitt handed over a hot mug of cocoa. "Yours has Bailey's in it." She took a long, appreciative sniff and rubbed her protruding belly. "I'm so jealous you get to drink alcohol. Does that make me a horrible mom?"

"Not at all," Sadie said, palming her best friend's arm. "How are you feeling? Better?" Dinner tonight had featured a slab of perfectly seasoned, red, juicy prime rib. Crickitt had turned green at the sight of it and Shane and Aiden had whisked the platter back into the kitchen before Crickitt's unborn baby kicked the food right out of her stomach.

"Better." She rubbed her tummy. "I might have to stick to fish and chicken from here on out."

Deep laughter rumbled from the den, and Sadie's arm broke into goose bumps. Aiden was in there, she could hear his distinct chuckle apart from the others.

"You've never looked so happy," Crickitt said.

Sadie smiled at her, shrugging her shoulders to downplay her emotions. Love was a vibrant light and Sadie emitted it like the Gloworm she'd bought for Celeste for Christmas. Well, for her niece or nephew currently incubating in Celeste's belly, anyway.

Aiden had come with her to her mother's Christmas Eve dinner last night. It was the first time he'd met her mother and stepfather, her sister, and Trey. Sadie was a nervous wreck, despite having mended things with Celeste last month.

Celeste's pregnancy had been a rough one, and that had brought out Sadie's kind side. She saw Celeste several times a week, either to bring her food or magazines, or just to sit and talk to her about things they should have resolved long ago.

Yes, she and Celeste were a-okay...it was Aiden she'd worried about around Trey. She shouldn't have worried. Aiden had glided into her mother's house and greeted her family like he'd known them for years.

When he met Trey, he pulled Sadie flush against his side and rubbed her arm as he talked to her ex, simultaneously calming her and letting Trey know unequivocally that Sadie was his. Not that Aiden needed to claim her, but she'd appreciated his protection—so much she'd pulled him into a back bedroom after dessert and made out with him for several minutes.

"I've never been this happy," Sadie told Crickitt, belatedly responding to her statement. Aiden meandered into the living room from the direction of the kitchen and suddenly Sadie was even happier. Crickitt excused herself as Aiden ambled his way over to Sadie and stopped in front of her.

His hair was getting longer, just brushing his jaw. A piece fell over his cheek and he moved it aside. "Hello, beautiful." He embraced her, resting his hands on her hips the way he always had. They fit there like she was made for him. She'd begun to believe maybe she was.

"Hi." She held her mug out of the way. Aiden took it from her hands, setting it aside. "I love you," she told him.

There went his dimple. "I love you."

She beamed, no doubt lit up like the decked out Christmas tree standing behind him. She couldn't get enough of Aiden. Couldn't get sick of him no matter how hard she tried. Once she'd flipped the switch and allowed herself to love him, it had become impossible to flip it the other direction. She was his, through and through. There was no going back.

She never wanted to.

"One week," Aiden whispered in her ear before pressing a kiss to her neck. "And then you'll be mine. We can finally have sex legally."

Sadie laughed at his joke. Their wedding wasn't going to rival the royals, but it wasn't going to be at the courthouse, either. They'd settled on something in between, something that suited both of them. A small church Aiden and his family used to attend would perform the ceremony, with the reception being held at Shane and Crickitt's house in Osborn.

Sadie couldn't wait to become Mrs. Aiden Downey.

She stroked the scruff quickly turning into beard on his face. How did he look mouthwatering clean-shaven or hairy? Long ponytail, or short hair? *Oh, right*, she realized as he grinned down at her. The dimple. She stroked her hands down his arms. The biceps weren't hurting matters, either.

"I'm ready," she breathed, trailing her hands up his body and linking her fingers around his neck. The ends of his hair tickled her wrists, making her shudder.

"And then," he snuggled her closer and whispered, "babies."

Sadie's breath caught.

Aiden's fixed smile remained in place. "You're freaking out," he observed.

"No, I'm not." Yes, she was.

"Yes, you are."

She bit her lip. "A little."

"Why don't we start with one baby, and then work our way into multiples?" Aiden stroked her back as he held her, his face growing serious. "You are going to be an amazing mother, Sadie." Then he kissed her, and she melted into him, pretty sure he could talk her into absolutely anything.

"Come *on*, you guys." Shane's exasperated voice lifted through the living room.

Aiden's lips left hers. "Go away," he told Shane, not taking his eyes off Sadie's.

"Gift exchange time."

Sadie pulled her hands away from Aiden's neck and clapped. "Oh! I have the best gift! You'll want to end up with mine," she assured Aiden.

"No, you want mine," Shane told Aiden. "It's an island," he deadpanned.

"Yuppie."

"Hippie." Shane drained his scotch glass and grimaced. "Come on, Aid, your dad's making me drink this, and you should have to, too."

"Right behind you," Aiden told him.

Shane wandered into the den, calling, "Yeah, yeah," over his shoulder.

Aiden faced Sadie again. "You're going to want to get my present."

She pursed her lips and pretended to consider. "I don't know . . . I really could use an island. What'd you bring?"

"Remanned carburetor."

She grasped the waistband of his jeans and tugged. "Ohh, sexy. You know what I like."

Aiden's eyes darkened and a feral spark lit the sea of green. "I do know what you like."

Sadie's heart kicked up about three hundred notches.

"I bet we could sneak out to the tree house and be back before they start the gift exchange," Aiden said. Another whoop came from the den, and Sadie imagined everyone tossing back another mouthful of scotch. "They'll probably forget we were ever here."

He kissed her neck as she sighed and weaved her fingers in his hair. So sexy. "But it's freezing out there," she protested weakly as his rough jaw abraded her neck.

"I'd keep you warm," he murmured into her hair, his fingers sliding just beneath the edge of her sweater.

"I bet you will." She gave him a gentle shove. "Let's go to the den and open presents."

He curled his lip in protestation.

"And afterward, we'll check out the tree house."

Landon entered the living room next, swaying slightly, probably caused by the drink in his hand. Sadie had never seen him so loose. He looked more approachable with his hair mussed, wearing a casual V-neck sweater. "Shane bought an island? Seriously?" He frowned, gave them assessing glances. "You two at it again?"

"Leave us alone," Aiden growled, but his eyes danced with humor.

"I've never seen my brother so horny until he met you," Landon told Sadie. "And I knew him when he was fourteen."

Sadie covered her mouth to stifle a laugh. Aiden looked murderous.

"This one time, our neighbor—" Landon started, then his eyes widened as Aiden tore through the living room after him. Sadie followed. When she reached the doorway of the den, Aiden and Landon were scrapping with each other, each trying to get the other into a headlock.

This was her family now, too, Sadie realized as she glanced around the room. Angel and her husband, Richie, were at the bar, sharing one glass of wine and smiling over the rim at each other.

Evan sat, glass in hand, a cautious half smile on his face. He looked content, which was nice to see, though she wouldn't go so far as to say he was happy. The happiest she'd seen him was when he'd tucked Lyon into bed after the kid slipped into a sugar coma from eating the contents of his stocking.

Mike leaned on the mantle, his own glass of scotch nearby, watching his brood with a mix of sadness and pride. He missed Kathy, Sadie knew. They all did. Even Sadie, who didn't need to meet the woman to know the world was less special without her in it.

Crickitt was settled on Shane's lap, his wide palm covering her middle. Crickitt lifted her mug in a silent cheers to Sadie. Sadie smiled, knowing just how her best friend felt. They'd both lucked into this family. Into forever. It was almost too much.

Aiden came to Sadie a second later, smoothing his hair and issuing an empty warning at Landon, who uttered the very un-CEO-like retort of, "Whenever you're ready, bro."

"Miss me?" Aiden asked, pulling her attention from his family. He dropped a kiss on her lips as Landon and Shane booed, and Evan insisted they "get a room."

Angel and Crickitt argued they thought it was sweet.

Sadie crooked her finger and Aiden leaned down so she could whisper in his ear. She grasped his face and whispered, "We would make beautiful babies."

He lifted his head so he could look at her, the emotion in his eyes leagues deep, and filled with desire.

Finally, Sadie had let herself want all the things she'd longed for deep in her heart. And, finally, she believed she could have them. With Aiden, she could have anything. She could have everything.

There never should have been any doubt.

Business or pleasure?

Please turn this page for an
excerpt from the first book
in Jessica Lemmon's
Love in the Balance series

Tempting the Billionaire

CHAPTER ONE

$\mathcal{O}$scillating red, green, and blue lights sliced through the smoke-filled club. Men and women cluttered the floor, their arms pumping in time with the throbbing speakers as an unseen fog machine muddied the air.

Shane August resisted the urge to press his fingertips into his eyelids and stave off the headache that'd begun forming there an hour ago.

Tonight marked the end of a grueling six-day work-week, one he would have preferred to end in his home gym, or in the company of a glass of red wine. He frowned at the bottle of light beer in his hand. Six dollars. That was fifty cents an ounce.

The sound of laughter pulled his attention from the overpriced brew, and he found a pair of girls sidling by his table. They offered twin grins and waved in tandem, hips swaying as they strode by.

"Damn," Aiden muttered over his shoulder. "I should have worn a suit."

Shane angled a glance at his cousin's T-shirt and jeans. "Do you even *own* a suit?"

"Shut up."

Shane suppressed a budding smile and tipped his beer bottle to his lips. It was Aiden who'd dragged him here tonight. Shane could give him a hard time, but Aiden was here to forget about his ex-wife, and she'd given him a hard enough time for both of them.

"This is where you're making your foray into the dating world?" Shane asked, glancing around the room at the bevy of flesh peeking out from beneath skintight skirts and shorts.

"Seemed like a good place to pick up chicks," Aiden answered with a roll of one shoulder.

Shane tamped down another smile. Aiden was recently divorced, though *finally* might be a better term. Two years of wedded bliss had been anything but, thanks to Harmony's wandering eye. Shane couldn't blame Aiden for exercising a bit of freedom. God knows, if Shane were in his shoes, he'd have bailed a long time ago. This time when Harmony left, she'd followed her sucker-punch with a TKO: the man she left Aiden for was his—now *former*—best friend. At first Aiden had been withdrawn, then angry. Tonight he appeared to be masking his emotions beneath a cloak of overconfidence.

"Right," Shane muttered. "Chicks."

"Well, excuse me, Mr. Moneybags." Aiden leaned one arm on the high-top table and faced him. "Women may throw themselves at you like live grenades, but the rest of us commoners have to come out to the trenches and hunt."

Shane gave him a dubious look, in part for the sloppily mixed metaphor, but mostly because dodging incoming women didn't exactly describe his lackluster love life. If he'd learned anything from his last girlfriend, it was how to spot a girl who wanted to take a dip in his cash pool.

He only had himself to blame, he supposed. He was accustomed to solving problems with money. Problem-free living just happened to be at the top of his priority list. Unfortunately, relationships didn't file away neatly into manila folders, weren't able to be delegated in afternoon conference meetings. Relationships were complicated, messy. Time-consuming.

No, thanks.

"I can pick up a girl in a club," Shane found himself arguing. It'd been a while, but he never was one to shy away from a challenge. Self-made men didn't shrink in the face of adversity.

Aiden laughed and clapped him on the shoulder. "Don't embarrass yourself."

Shane straightened and pushed the beer bottle aside. "Wanna bet?"

"With you?" Aiden lifted a thick blond eyebrow. "Forget it! You wipe your ass with fifties."

"Hundreds," Shane corrected, earning a hearty chuckle.

"Then again," Aiden said after finishing off his bottle, "I wouldn't mind seeing you in action, learn what not to do now that I'm single again. Find a cute girl and I'll be your wingman." Before Shane could respond, Aiden elbowed him. "Except for her."

Shane followed his cousin's pointing finger to the bar, where a woman dabbed at her eyes with a napkin. She looked so delicate sitting there, folded over in her chair, an array of brown curls concealing part of her face.

"Crying chicks either have too much baggage, or they're wasted."

Says Aiden Downey, dating guru.

"Drunk can be good," he continued, "but by the time you get close enough to find out, it's too late."

Shane frowned. He didn't like being told what to do. Or what not to. He wasn't sure if that's what made him decide to approach her, or if he'd decided the second Aiden pointed her out. He felt his lips pull into a deeper frown. He shouldn't be considering it at all.

A cocktail waitress stopped at their table. Shane waved off the offer of another, his eyes rooted on the crying girl at the bar. She looked as out of place in this crowd as he felt, dressed unassumingly in jeans and a black top, her brown hair a curly crown that stopped at her jawline. In the flashy crowd, she could have been dismissed as plain...but she wasn't plain. She was pretty.

He watched as she brushed a lock from her damp face as her shoulders rose and fell. The pile of crumpled napkins next to her paired with the far-off look in her eyes suggested she was barely keeping it together. Grief radiated off of her in waves Shane swore he could feel from where he sat. Witnessing her pain made his gut clench. Probably because somewhere deep inside, he could relate.

Aiden said something about a girl on the dance floor, and Shane flicked him an irritated glance before his eyes tracked back to the girl at the bar. She sipped her drink and offered the bartender a tight nod of thanks as he placed a stack of fresh napkins in front of her.

Shane felt an inexplicable, almost gravitational pull toward her, his feet urging him forward even as his brain raised one argument after another. Part of him wanted to help, though if she wanted to have a heart-to-heart, she'd be better off talking to Aiden. But if she needed advice or a solution to a tangible problem, well, that he could handle.

He glanced around the room at the predatory males lurking in every corner and wondered again why she was here. If he did approach her, an idea becoming more compelling by the moment, she'd likely shoot him down before he said a single word. So why was he mentally mapping a path to her chair? He pressed his lips together in thought. Because there was a good chance he could erase the despair from her face, a prospect he found more appealing than anything else.

"Okay, her friend is hot, I'll give you that," Aiden piped up.

Shane blinked before snapping his eyes to the brunette's left. Her "hot friend," as Aiden so eloquently put it, showcased her assets in a scandalously short skirt and backless silver top. He'd admit she was hard to miss. Yet Shane hadn't noticed her until Aiden pointed her out. His eyes trailed back to the brunette.

"Okay," Aiden said on a sigh of resignation. "Because I so desperately want to see this, I'm going to take a bullet for you. I'll distract the crier. You hit on the blonde." That said, he stood up and headed toward the bar ... to flirt with the *wrong girl*.

The platitude of only having one chance to make a first impression flitted through Shane's head. He called Aiden's name, but his shout was lost under the music blasting at near-ear-bleeding decibels. Aiden may be younger and less experienced, but he also had an undeniable charm girls didn't often turn down. If the brunette spotted his cousin first, she wouldn't so much as look at Shane. He abandoned his beer, doing a neat jog across the room and reaching Aiden just as he was moving in to tap the brunette's shoulder.

"My cousin thought he recognized you," Shane blurted to the blonde, grabbing Aiden by the arm and spinning him in her direction.

The blonde surveyed Aiden with lazy disinterest. "I don't think so."

Aiden lifted his eyebrows to ask, *What the hell are you doing?*

Rather than explain, Shane clapped both palms on Aiden's shoulders and shoved him closer to the blonde. "His sister's in the art business." It was a terrible segue if the expression on Aiden's face was anything to go by, but it was the first thing that popped into Shane's head.

The music changed abruptly, slowing into a rhythmic techno-pop remix that had dancers slowing down and pairing up. Aiden slipped into an easy, confident smile. "Wanna dance?" he asked the blonde.

The moment the question was out of his mouth, the scratches and hissing of snare drums shifted into the melodic chimes of the tired and all-too-familiar line dance, "The Electric Slide."

Aiden winced.

Shane coughed to cover a laugh. "He's a great dancer," he said to the blonde.

Aiden shot his elbow into Shane's ribs but recovered his smile a second later. Turning to the blonde, he said, "He's right, I am," then offered his hand.

The blonde glanced at his palm, then leaned past Shane to talk to her friend. "You gonna be okay here?" she called over the music.

The brunette flicked a look from her friend to Shane. The moment he locked on to her bright blue eyes, his heart galloped to life, picking up speed as if running for an invisible finish line. Her eyes left his as she addressed her friend. "Fine."

It wasn't the most wholehearted endorsement, but at least she'd agreed to stay.

Aiden and the blonde made their way to the dance floor, and Shane gave his collar a sharp tug and straightened his suit jacket before turning toward the brunette. She examined him, almost warily, her lids heavy over earnest blue eyes. He'd seen that kind of soul-rendering sadness before, a long time ago. Staring back at him from his bathroom mirror.

"That was my cousin, Aiden." He bumbled to fill the dead air between them. "He wanted to meet your friend."

"Figures," the brunette said, barely audible over the music.

He ignored the whistling sound of their conversation plummeting to its imminent death. "She seems nice. Aiden can be kind of an ass around nice girls," he added, leaning in so she could hear him.

She rewarded him with a tentative upward curve of her lips, the top capping a plumper bottom lip that looked good enough to eat. He offered a small smile of his own, perplexed by the direction of his thoughts. When was the last time he'd been thrown this off-kilter by a woman? Let alone one he'd just met? She shifted in her seat to face him, and a warm scent lifted off her skin—vanilla and nutmeg, if he wasn't mistaken. He gripped the back of the chair in front of him and swallowed instinctively. Damn. She *smelled* good enough to eat.

She dipped her head, fiddled with the strap of her handbag, and Shane realized he was staring.

"Shane," he said, offering his hand.

She looked at it a beat before taking it. "Crickitt."

"Like the bug?" He flinched. *Smooth.*

"Thanks for that." She offered a mordant smile.

Evidently he was rustier at this than he'd thought. "Sorry." Best get to the point. "Is there something you need? Something I can get you?"

Her eyes went to the full drink in front of her. "I've had plenty, but thanks. Anyway, I'm about to leave."

"I'm on my way out. Can I drop you somewhere?"

She eyed him cautiously.

Okay. Perhaps offering her a ride was a bit forward and, from her perspective, dangerous.

"No, thank you," she said, turning her body away from his as she reached for her drink.

Great. He was creepy club guy.

He leaned on the bar between the blonde's abandoned chair and Crickitt. Lowering his voice, he said, "I think I'm doing this all wrong. To tell the truth, I saw you crying and I wondered if I could do anything to help. I'd...like to help. If you'll let me."

She turned to him, her eyes softening into what might have been gratitude, before a harder glint returned. Tossing her head, she met his eye. "Help? Sure. Know anyone who'd like to hire a previously self-employed person for a position for which she has little to no experience?"

He had to smile at her pluck...and his good fortune.

Crickitt's problem may be one he could help with after all. "Depends," he answered, watching her eyebrows give the slightest lift. He leaned an elbow on the bar. "In what salary range?"

* * *

Crickitt scanned the well-dressed man in front of her. He wore a streamlined charcoal suit and crisp, white dress shirt. No tie, but she'd bet one had been looped around his neck earlier. She allowed her gaze to trickle to his open collar, lingering over the column of his tanned neck before averting her eyes. What would he say if she blurted out the figure dancing around her head?

Two-hundred fifty thousand a year? Oh, sure, I know lots of people who pay out six figures for a new hire.

Well, he asked.

"Six figures," she said.

He laughed.

That's what she thought. If this Shane guy were in a position to offer that kind of income, would he really be in a club named Lace and hitting on a girl like her? Why hadn't he hit on someone else? Someone without a runny nose and red-rimmed eyes. Someone like Sadie. But he'd rerouted his friend to talk to Sadie. Why had he done that? She smoothed her hair, considering.

Maybe you're an easy target.

He saw her crying and wanted to help? It wasn't the worst pickup line in the world, but it was close.

Crickitt instinctively slid her pinky against her ring finger to straighten her wedding band but only felt the rub of skin on skin. For nine years it had sat at home on her left hand. She used to think of it as a comforting weight, but since Ronald had left, it'd become a reminder of the now-obvious warning signs she'd overlooked. The way he'd pulled away from her both physically and emotionally. The humiliation of scurrying after him, attempting to win his affections even after it was too late. She lifted her shoulders under her ears, wishing she could hide from the recurring memory, the embarrassment. Fresh tears burned the backs of her eyes before she remembered she had a captive audience. She squeezed her eyes closed, willing the helter-skelter emotions to go away.

When she opened them, she saw Shane had backed away some, either to give the semblance of privacy or because he feared she would burst into tears and blow her nose on his expensive jacket. She could choke Sadie for bringing her out tonight.

Come to the club, Sadie had said. *It'll get your mind off of things*, she'd insisted. But it hadn't. Even when faced with a very good-looking, potentially helpful man, she was wallowing in self-doubt and recrimination. She could've done that at home.

"What experience do you have, Crickitt?" Shane asked, interrupting her thoughts.

She tipped her chin up at him. Was he serious? His half smile was either sarcastic or genuinely curious. Hard to tell. The temptation was there to dismiss him as just another jerk in a club, but she couldn't. There was an undeniable warmth in his dark eyes, a certain kindness in the way he leaned toward her when he talked, like he didn't want to intimidate her.

Maybe that's why she told him the truth.

"I'm great with people," she answered.

"And scheduling?"

She considered telling him about the twenty in-home shows she'd held each and every month for the last seven years, but wasn't sure he wouldn't get the wrong idea about exactly what kind of *in-home shows* she'd be referring to. "Absolutely."

"Prioritizing?"

Crickitt almost laughed. Prioritizing was a necessity in her business. She'd been responsible for mentoring and training others, as well as maintaining her personal sales and team. It'd taken her a while to master the art of putting her personal business first, but she'd done it. If she focused too much on others, her numbers soon started circling the drain, and that wasn't good for any of them.

"Definitely," she answered, pausing to consider the fire burning in her belly. How long had it been since she'd talked about her career with confidence? Too long, she realized. By now, her ex-husband would have cut her off midsentence to change the subject.

But Shane's posture was open, receptive, and he faced her, his eyebrows raised as if anticipating what she might say next. So she continued. "I, um, I was responsible for a team of twenty-five salespeople while overseeing ten managers with teams of their own," she finished.

She almost cringed at the calloused description. Those *teams* and *managers* were more like family than coworkers. They'd slap her silly if they ever heard her referring to them with corporate lingo. But if she had to guess, Shane was a corporate man and Crickitt doubted he'd know the first thing about direct sales.

"You sound overqualified," he said.

"That's what I . . . wait, did you just say *over*qualified?"

Crickitt stammered. She blinked up at him, shocked. She'd fully expected him to tell her to peddle her questionable work background elsewhere.

Shane reached into his pocket and offered a business card between two outstretched fingers. "Even so, I'd like to talk to you in more detail. Are you available for an interview on Monday?"

Crickitt stared at the card like it was a trick buzzer.

"I'm serious." He dropped the card on the bar. "This isn't typically how I find employees, but"—he shrugged—"I need a personal assistant. And someone with your background and experience is hard to come by."

She blinked at him again. This had to be some elaborate scheme to get her to bed, right? Isn't that what Sadie told her to expect from the men in these places?

"How about one o'clock, Monday afternoon? I have meetings in the morning, but I should be done by then. If the job's not a good fit, at least you looked into it."

Well. The only interview she'd managed to arrange since her self-inflicted unemployment was for a thirty-thousand-dollar salary and involved her working in a government office. And she'd lost that job to a kid ten years her junior. She'd be stupid to pass up the opportunity for an interview with this man. Even though part of her couldn't imagine working for someone as put together as Shane. But he didn't seem demanding, or overly confident, just...nice.

Which brought about another niggling thought. This was too easy. And if she'd learned a lesson from recent events, wasn't it to be cautious when things were going suspiciously well? And this, she thought, glancing in his direction again, was going a little *too* well.

"What do you say?" he asked.

Then again, as her dwindling savings account constantly reminded her, she needed to find some sort of viable income. And soon. If the interview turned out to be a sham, the experience would still be worthwhile, she thought with knee-jerk optimism.

"One o'clock," she heard herself say.

Shane extended his hand and she shook it, ignoring how seamlessly her palm fit against his and the warmth radiating up her arm even after he'd pulled away. He excused himself and made his way to the door. Crickitt watched his every long-legged step, musing how he was taller than Ronald and walked with infinitely more confidence.

A tall, confident man had approached *her*. And, okay, it may have been because she looked needy, but she couldn't keep from being flattered that Shane had taken it upon himself to talk to her.

Lifting the business card between her thumb and fingers, she studied the front. The top read, AUGUST INDUSTRIES, LEADER IN BUSINESS STRATEGIES. No name on the card, just an address and a phone number. She flipped it over. Blank.

Sadie returned as Crickitt hopped off her barstool.

"Where're you going?" Sadie asked with a breathless smile. Shane's cousin stood at Sadie's side, a matching grin on his tanned face. Crickitt regarded his surfer-dude style skeptically. Cute. A departure from Sadie's usual type, but cute.

Of course, there was a good chance Sadie would never see Aiden again given her first-date-only rule. Crickitt looked down at the business card again, chewing her lip.

Maybe it wasn't a good idea to see Shane again, either. She already felt as if she'd revealed too much about herself in their short conversation. Wasn't it too soon for her to trust a man after the one she'd trusted implicitly had left her behind?

"What's with the card? Did you get a date?" Sadie asked.

"No." She laughed, her temporarily reclaimed confidence ebbing. She considered crumpling the card in her hand, dropping it onto the bar. The message would get back to Shane via his cousin, she was sure. Then she wouldn't have to worry about standing him up or canceling the interview.

Chicken.

Despite the very tempting option to stay in her comfort zone, Crickitt decided maybe it was time to take a risk. Even a small one.

"Better," she told Sadie, snapping up her purse. "A job."

THE DISH

Where Authors Give You the Inside Scoop

♥ ♥ ♥ ♥ ♥ ♥ ♥ ♥ ♥ ♥ ♥ ♥ ♥ ♥ ♥ ♥

From the desk of Vicky Dreiling

Dear Reader,

I had a lot of imaginary boyfriends when I was a kid. My friend Kim and I read *Tiger Beat* magazine and chose our loves. I "dated" David Cassidy, a yesteryear heartthrob from a TV show called *The Partridge Family*. Kim's "boyfriend" was Donny Osmond, although she might have had a brief crush on Barry Williams, better known as Greg from *The Brady Bunch*. I did a quick search online and discovered that *Tiger Beat* magazine still exists, but the stars for today's preteens are Justin Bieber, Taylor Lautner, and members of the boy band One Direction.

The idea of a big family and rock-star boyfriends really appealed to us. We traveled in imaginary tour buses to imaginary concerts. We listened to the music and sang along, pretending we were onstage, too. Of course, we invented drama, such as mean girls trying to steal our famous boyfriends backstage.

Recently, I realized that the seeds of the families I create in my novels were sown in my preteen years as Kim and I pretended to date our celebrity crushes. As I got older, imaginary boyfriends led to real-life boyfriends in high school and college. Eventually, marriage and kids led to an extended family, one that continues to grow.

In WHAT A RECKLESS ROGUE NEEDS, two close families meet once a year at a month-long house party. As in real life, much has changed for Colin and Angeline. While they were born only a week apart, they never really got along very well. An incident at Angeline's come-out ball didn't help matters, either. Many years have elapsed, and now Colin finds he needs Angeline's help to keep from losing a property that holds very deep emotional ties for him. Once they cross the threshold of Sommerall House, their lives are never the same again, but they will always have their families.

May the Magic Romance Fairies be with all of you and your families!

www.VickyDreiling.com
Twitter @VickyDreiling
Facebook.com/VickyDreilingHistoricalAuthor

♥ ♥ ♥ ♥ ♥ ♥ ♥ ♥ ♥ ♥ ♥ ♥ ♥ ♥ ♥

From the desk of Paula Quinn

Dear Reader,

As most of you know, I love dogs. I have six of them. I see your eyes bugging out. Six?? Yes, six precious tiny Chihuahuas and all together they weight approximately twenty-seven pounds. I've had dogs my whole life—big ones, little ones. So it's not surprising that I would want to write dogs into my books. This time I went big: 140 pounds of big.

In THE SEDUCTION OF MISS AMELIA BELL we meet Grendel, an Irish wolfhound mix, who along with our hero, Edmund MacGregor, wins the heart of our heroine, Amelia Bell. Grendel is the son of Aurelius, whom some of you might remember as the puppy Colin MacGregor gave to Edmund, his stepson, in *Conquered by a Highlander*. Since this series is called Highland Heirs, I figured why not include the family dog heirs as well?

I loved writing a dog as a secondary character, and Grendel is an important part of Edmund and Amelia's story. Now, really, what's better than a big, brawny, sexy Highlander? Right: a big, brawny, sexy Highlander with a dog. Or if you live in NYC, you can settle for a hunky guy playing with his dog in the park.

My six babies all have distinct personalities. For instance, Riley loves to bark and be an all-around pain in the neck. He's high-strung and loves it. Layla, my biggest girl, must "mother" all the others. She keeps them in line with a soft growl and a lick to the eyeball. Liam, my tiny three-pound boy, isn't sure if he's Don Juan or Napoleon. He'll drop and show you his package if you call him cute. They are all different and I wanted Grendel to have his own personality, too.

Much like his namesake, Grendel hates music and powdered periwigs. He's faithful and loyal, and he loves to chase smaller things…like people. Even though Edmund is his master and Grendel does, of course, love him best, it doesn't take Amelia long to win his heart, or for Grendel to win hers, and he soon finds himself following at her heels. Some of my favorite scenes involve the subtle interactions between Amelia and Grendel. This big, seemingly vicious dog is always close by when Amelia is sad or afraid. When things are going on all around them, Amelia just has to rest her hand on Grendel's head and it completely calms her. We witness a partial transformation of ownership in the small, telltale ways Grendel remains ever constant at Amelia's side.

Even when Grendel finds Gaza, his own love interest (hey, I'm a romance writer, what can I say?), he is still faithful to his human lady. We won't get into doggy love, but suffice it to say, there will be plenty of furry heirs living in Camlochlin for a long time to come. They might not be the prettiest dogs in Skye, but they are the most loyal.

This was my first foray into writing a dog as a secondary character and I must say I fell in love with a big, slobbering mutt named after a fiend who killed men for singing. I wasn't surprised that Grendel filled his place so well in Edmund and Amelia's story. Each of my dogs does the same in mine and my kids' stories. That's what dogs do. They run headlong into our lives barking, tail wagging, sharing wet, sloppy kisses. They love us with an almost supernatural, unconditional love. And we love them back.

I hope you get a chance to pick up THE SEDUCTION OF MISS AMELIA BELL and meet Edmund and Amelia and, of course, Grendel.

Happy reading!

Paula Quinn

♥ ♥ ♥ ♥ ♥ ♥ ♥ ♥ ♥ ♥ ♥ ♥ ♥ ♥ ♥ ♥

From the desk of Kristen Ashley

Dear Reader,

Years ago, I was walking to the local shops and, as usual, I had my headphones in. As I was walking, Bob Seger & The Silver Bullet Band's "You'll Accomp'ny Me" came on and somehow, even having heard this song dozens and dozens of times before, the lyrics suddenly hit me.

This isn't unusual. I have to be in a certain mood to absorb lyrics. But when I am, sometimes they'll seep into my soul, making me smile, or making me cry.

"You'll Accomp'ny Me" made me smile. It made me feel warm. And it made me feel happy because the lyrics are beautiful, the message of love and devotion is strong, the passion is palpable, and the way it's written states that Bob definitely has Kristen Ashley alpha traits.

I loved it. I've always loved that song, but then I loved it even more. It was like one of my books in song form. How could I not love that?

At the time, however, I didn't consider it for a book, not inspiring one or not to be used in a scene. For a long time, it was just mine, giving me that warm feeling and a smile on my face at the thought that there is musical proof out there that these men exist.

Better, they wield guitars.

Now, from the very moment I introduced Hop in *Motorcycle Man*, he intrigued me. And as we learned more about him in that book, my knowing why he was doing what he was doing, I knew he'd have to be redeemed in my readers' eyes by sharing his whole story. I just didn't know who was going to give him the kind of epic happy ending I felt he deserved.

Therefore, I didn't know that Lanie would be the woman of his dreams. Truth be told, I didn't even expect Lanie to have her own book. But her story as told in *Motorcycle Man* was just too heartbreaking to leave her hanging. I just had no idea what to do with her.

But I didn't think a stylish, professional, accomplished "lady" and a biker would jibe, so I never considered these two together. Or, in fact, Lanie with any of the Chaos brothers at all.

That is, until this song came up on shuffle again and I knew that was how Hop would consider his relationship with Lanie. Even as she pushed him away due to her past, he'd do what he could to convince her that, someday, she'd accompany him.

I mean, just those words—how cool are they? "You'll accompany me." Brilliant.

But Bob, his Silver Bullet Band, and their music did

quadruple duty in FIRE INSIDE. Not only did they give me "You'll Accomp'ny Me," which was the perfect way for Hop to express his feelings to Lanie; they also gave me Hop's nickname for Lanie: "lady". And they gave me "We've Got Tonight," yet another perfect song to fit what was happening between Lanie and Hop. And last, the way Bob sings is also the way I hear Hop in my head.

I interweave music in my books all the time and my selections are always emotional and, to me, perfect.

But I've never had a song, or artist, so beautifully help me tell my tale than when I utilized the extraordinary storytelling abilities of Bob Seger in my novel FIRE INSIDE.

It's a pleasure listening to his music.

It's a gift to be inspired by it.

Kristen Ashley

❤ ❤ ❤ ❤ ❤ ❤ ❤ ❤ ❤ ❤ ❤ ❤ ❤ ❤ ❤ ❤ ❤

From the desk of Mimi Jean Pamfiloff

Dear Reader,

When it came time to decide which god or goddess in my Accidentally Yours series would get their HEA in book four, I sat back and looked at who was most in need of salvation. Hands down, the winner was Ixtab, the Goddess of Suicide. Before you judge the title, however, I'd like to explain why this goddess is not the dreary soul you might imagine. Fact is she's more like the Goddess of Anti-Suicide, with the ability to drain dark feelings from one person and redeploy them to another. Naturally, being a deity, she tends to help those who are down on their luck and punish those who are truly deserving.

However, every now and again, someone bumps into her while she's not looking. The results are fatal. So after thousands of years and thousands of accidental deaths, she's determined to keep everyone away. Who could blame her?

But fate has other plans for this antisocial goddess with a kind streak. His name is Dr. Antonio Acero, and this sexy Spaniard has just become the lynchpin in the gods' plans for saving the planet from destruction. He's also in need of a little therapy, and Ixtab is the only one who can help him.

When these two meet, they quickly realize there are forces greater than them both, trying to pull them apart and push them together. Which force will win?

Mimi

♥ ♥ ♥ ♥ ♥ ♥ ♥ ♥ ♥ ♥ ♥ ♥ ♥ ♥ ♥ ♥ ♥

From the desk of Katie Lane

Dear Reader,

As some of you may already know, the idea for my fictional town of Bramble, Texas, came from the hours I spent watching *The Andy Griffith Show*. When Barney, Aunt Bee, and Opie were on, my mom couldn't peel me away from our console television. The townsfolk's antics held me spellbound. Which is probably why I made my characters a little crazy, too. (Okay, so I made them a lot crazy.) But while the people of Mayberry had levelheaded Sheriff Andy Taylor to keep them in line, the townsfolk of Bramble have been allowed to run wild.

Until now.

I'm pleased as punch to introduce Sheriff Dusty Hicks, the hero of my newest Deep in the Heart of Texas novel, A MATCH MADE IN TEXAS. Like Andy, he's a dedicated lawman who loves his job and the people of his community. Unlike Andy, he carries a gun, has a wee bit of a temper, and is blessed with the kind of looks and hard body that can make a good girl turn bad. And after just one glimpse of Dusty's shiny handcuffs, Brianne Cates wants to turn bad. Real bad.

But it won't be easy for Brianne to seduce a little lawman lovin' out of my hero. Dusty has his hands full trying to regain joint custody of his precocious three-year-old daughter and, at the same time, deal with a con-artist television evangelist and a vengeful cartel drug lord. Not to mention the townsfolk of Bramble, who have suddenly gone wa-a-ay off their rockers.

All I can say is, what started out as a desire to give Bramble its very own Sheriff Taylor quickly turned into a fast-paced joyride that left my hair standing on end and my heart as warm and gooey as a toaster strudel. I hope it will do the same for you. :o)

Much love,

Katie Lane

♥ ♥ ♥ ♥ ♥ ♥ ♥ ♥ ♥ ♥ ♥ ♥ ♥ ♥ ♥ ♥ ♥

From the desk of Jessica Lemmon

Dear Reader,

I love a scruffy-faced, tattooed, motorcycle-riding bad boy as much as the next girl, so when it came time to write HARD TO HANDLE, I knew what qualities I wanted Aiden Downey to possess.

For inspiration, I needed to look no further than Charlie Hunnam from the famed TV show *Sons of Anarchy*. I remember watching Season 1 on Netflix, mouth agape and eyes wide. When Charlie's character, Jax Teller, finished his first scene, I looked over at my husband and said, *"That's Aiden!"*

In HARD TO HANDLE, Aiden may have been crafted with a bad-boy starter kit: He has the scruff, the tattoo, the knee-weakening dimples that make him look like sin on a stick, and yeah, a custom Harley-Davidson to boot. But Aiden also has something extra special that derails his bad-boy image: a heart of near-solid gold.

When we first met Aiden and Sadie in *Tempting the Billionaire* (and again in the e-novella *Can't Let Go*), there wasn't much hope for these two hurting hearts to work out their differences. Aiden had been saddled with devastating news and familial responsibilities, and Sadie (poor Sadie!) had just opened up her heart to Aiden, who stomped on it, broke it into pieces, and set it on fire for good measure. How could they forgive each other after things had gone so horribly, terribly wrong?

Aiden has suffered a lot of loss, but in HARD TO HANDLE, he's on a mission to get his life *back*. A very large piece of that puzzle is winning back the woman he never meant to hurt, the woman he loved. Sadie, with her walled-up heart, smart, sassy mouth, and fiery attitude isn't going to be an easy nut to crack. Especially after she vowed to never, ever get hurt again. That goes *double* for the blond Adonis with the unforgettable mouth and ability to turn her brain into Silly Putty.

The best part about this good "bad" boy? Aiden's determination is as rock-hard as his abs. He's not going to let Sadie walk away, not now that he sees how much she still cares for him. Having been to hell and back, Aiden isn't intimidated by her. Not even a little bit. Sadie is his Achilles' heel, and Aiden accepts that it's going to take time (and plenty of seduction!) to win her over. He also knows that she's worth it.

Think you're up for a ride around the block with a bad-boy-done-good? I have to say, Aiden left a pretty deep mark on my heart and I'm still a little in love with him! He may change your mind about scruffy, motorcycle-riding hotties...He certainly managed to change Sadie's.

Happy reading!

Jessica Lemmon

www.jessicalemmon.com

3 3132 03571 9576